TAMING THE RINGMASTER

HER FREAKS BOOK 2

ERIN O'KANE AND K.A. KNIGHT

Taming The Ringmaster (Her Freaks Book Two).
Copyright © 2019 K.A. Knight & Erin O'Kane, all rights reserved.

Written by K.A. Knight & Erin O'Kane
Edited By Jess from Elemental Editing and Proofreading.
Proofreading by Norma's Nook Proofreading LLC
Formatted by The Nutty Formatter
Cover by Jay Aheer at Simply Defined Art

DON'T MISS OUT...

Make sure to catch up on Rhea and her men's adventures in these short stories (especially if you want all the steam)

https://books2read.com/DTvolumeone

DEDICATION

For all those who have fallen into the darkness and clawed your way back. You are stronger than you ever know.

Chapter One

T he road smooths out under the wagon wheels, signalling the change from the rougher back road to the paved one that leads into the city. The clacking of the horses' hooves against the concrete is a welcome variation from the rattling of the wagons that have seen better days on the dusty, barren land we have been travelling across.

Poking my head out of the window in the side of the wagon, I spot the sign proudly welcoming us to "Last Stop." To my disappointment, there isn't much to see yet, just the same barren land on either side of the paved road, but the sign fills me with hope.

"What have you heard about the city?" I ask curiously.

Bringing my head back in, I sit in my seat and face Alcide, where he watches me from the opposite bench. Rex is riding with the animals, Nixon is to my left, and Blain and Jesse are in the next carriage.

"Not much, other than they have more wealth and food than they know what to do with. It's a mecca of a kind, people always want to journey here, but afterwards you don't hear much. Maybe they find peace, maybe they don't, but I guess we are going to see," he says matter-of-factly.

His words from our last show ring in my head. He mentioned a storm, and even now his eyes are shrouded with doubts and worry. *What's my strong ringmaster so scared of?* The thought sends a shiver down my spine. Whatever it is…it isn't good. I'm about to ask why we are still journeying to the city when it's obvious he has worries about what we'll face here.

"It will be a place of choices," Nixon declares, his voice ringing with knowing. When I look over in question, he gives me an unreadable look. Sometimes, I don't think he even knows where the words and feelings come from, but they are always right. I wonder what choices await us? For a girl who was a slave, with every decision made for her, choice can only be a good thing. Right?

We sit in silence after that, all of us lost in our own thoughts. I'm hoping this will be good for us. More money means more visitors, and that can only help our show, right? Worry worms through me, but I force it away, trying to be positive. It's no good going into the city already judging it. Life always finds a way to give you the unexpected, and it's usually what you need.

"We're here," Nixon announces, and I lean over him to look out of the window again.

My mouth drops open in awe, my eyes widening and my breath nearly stopping. It's...imposing. A giant, rough grey wall rises as far as the eye can see, appearing to touch the sky. As we move closer to the large gate, I start to see the tops of buildings. Guards await us, standing outside of the metal entryway, their eyes harsh and postures rigid. At their sides, I spot the weapons of old...guns, I think they were called—to protect its inhabitants, or to keep people out?

The wagon stops and Alcide forces a smile. "It's show time," he declares, before sliding across the bench and opening the door. He gets out in one smooth move and I follow after him, with Nixon hot on my heels. I see the change happen in Alcide as he puts on his ringmaster facade, stepping confidently towards the guards who are eyeing us with suspicion.

"I am Alcide, of Alcide's Circus. We were invited here to perform." His voice is strong, demanding, as if he belongs here, and none of his previous apprehension is visible. Extending his arm towards the guards, he holds out a cream envelope I have never seen before. The guard takes the letter and scans it before handing it to his colleague. I can't read what it says from here, but I can see the paper is creased and worn, like it has been opened and folded countless times. How long has he had this?

Shock courses through me. When Alcide mentioned coming to the city, he didn't say we were invited. Why would he keep that from us...from me? I throw him a look, but he purposely averts his gaze and I make a mental note to ask him about it later. We are a family and we promised to tell each other the truth, no matter the outcome. I push these thoughts aside, knowing we need to focus on getting into the city right now. I'll deal with Alcide later.

The guards watch us as one of them brings a radio to their mouth and speaks into it. Not two minutes later, I hear the noise of cogs and machines and the gate starts to open.

"You're expected. Your...circus, can head to the grounds we have cleared for you, but you are required to meet the Masters before you perform." With no other words, they back away, watching us carefully as Alcide nods and makes his way to the wagon. I watch the huge gates roll open for a minute before turning and joining him. I've never seen anything like it.

Once back on the wagon, we start to move again, heading inside the city. It's slow going, and when I glance out of the window, I spot the crowd of people littering the sides. People working, living, and everything between, I realise.

"It might be faster for me to walk to see the Masters and then meet you at the grounds," Alcide suggests, avoiding our gazes and looking out of the window.

"You don't go alone," I state, my voice coming out stronger than I intended. I shrink a little bit when his eyes lock on me. He is silent for a moment as he weighs my words before nodding sharply.

"I won't be, you and Nixon are coming with me." He knocks on the carriage door and it comes to a stop. Jumping out onto the paved street, he straightens up and leans back in to offer me his hand. I take it slowly and step out into the bustling street, with Nixon following closely behind.

"Wait here, I will let the others know, *cariño*," Alcide orders, as he kisses my hand before moving to the next carriage, which has been following us.

I wait there with Nixon, fighting the urge to fidget, but no one pays us any mind. It's as if a circus rolling into their town isn't unusual to them. Apart from one—a young boy sitting on the dirty ground. His big, blue eyes are locked on me, and if I wasn't scanning the crowd, I wouldn't have noticed him, he blends in that well. His skin is a dark brown, brushed with pale dust from the street. His hair is black, the dark locks a tangled mess on this head. And his only clothing are shorts made of rags. I see the scars raised on his skin and my heart pangs in pain for this young boy. Scars like that only come from being beaten. If it wasn't for my own abilities, I would be covered in the same scars. Frowning when I spot his ribs sticking out and the cracked quality of his lips, I lean back into the carriage and grab my own rations. I know a starving child when I see one.

Stepping through the crowd, I crouch before him when I reach him. Nixon doesn't try to stop me, just follows silently behind me. The boy doesn't flinch or run away, just stares with eyes that know too much, and are too knowing for such one so young.

"Here," I offer softly, thrusting the water and food at him. He eyes them before looking back at me.

"Why?" One word, one simple question, but it shatters my heart because it holds so much distrust.

"Why not?" I counter.

He slowly reaches out and I spot a black mark on the inside of his wrist. It appears to be a tattoo, a symbol of two swords crossing. I lean closer to get a better look, but he snatches the food from me and moves back before I can.

"Thank you, your kindness will not be forgotten," he replies formally, before rushing away.

Frowning, I stand up and look over my shoulder to see Alcide and Nixon waiting for me, both watching the boy and me.

"Come, we better not keep the Masters waiting," he calls. Nodding, I give the crowd where the boy disappeared one last look before walking back and taking his offered arm.

A guard waits for us, his expression blank but his eyes sharp as he watches us walk towards him. Without a word, he turns on his heel and leads the way through the city. It is nothing like Cinders or even the other villages we have performed in, all of which were much bigger than where I grew up. This city has buildings and more people than I can count. The people openly wear jewels and clean clothes, which look like they haven't seen any wear and tear or wars. Even the shops are open and clear, selling things I can't even begin to name or describe, but if you look closely, under all the brightness and show of wealth, it seems...off.

Children are quiet, often dirty, and I spot the odd beggar here and there before they are quickly ushered away by guards. It's not the fact that there are beggars that disturbs me. In our fucked up world, beggars are the norm, so I would expect to see them, but I only see them because I am looking for them. Everything here is all so...controlled. Beneath the beauty hides a darkness, I know that more than most. Could Last Stop be the same? Or is the richness of this city a true paradise?

The guard leads us through the streets at a breakneck pace, and I find myself having to concentrate on walking rather than on looking around. We make so many twists and turns, that I know we'd get lost trying to find our way back. Maybe that's what they intended.

We follow the guard as he marches through a bustling square, where a water fountain and statue stand proudly in the middle. I've never seen anything like it. It's beautiful and I want to stop to admire the craftsmanship, but we swerve around it, stopping before a towering building, which proudly boasts "City Hall."

"They are waiting inside," the guard states, watching us as we climb the stone steps to the wooden doors. Glass, unbroken and clean, allows us to see through the doors, and I spot more guards waiting inside.

Nixon opens the door and holds it for us as Alcide leads the way. Another set of doors with golden inlays stand open, and we are stopped by two guards who, upon our entrance, immediately step forward to block our path.

"You must be scanned for security," one announces on the left, his eyes hard and cold.

"Scanned?" I echo, but Alcide gives me a tight look and steps forward, blocking the guards' view of me.

"Of course." With a flourish, he bows, pulling off his hat as he dips low. If I didn't know him, I would've thought he's just an eccentric performer, which is probably exactly what he wants them to believe. The distraction works and their attention moves off of me and lands on him as he effortlessly works his charm.

"This way," the guard orders, and we're shuffled to the side where a strange contraption awaits. The technology here is strange.

A guard sits to the side facing a monitor, his eyes focused on it with rapt attention. I reluctantly drag my eyes back as Alcide steps up to the towering silver machine that stands before us. It's tall and rectangular, like a doorway, but it's freestanding and has a blinking green light at the top. The guard gestures Alcide towards the machine and he walks through to the other side, the green light still flashing brightly.

"Next," the guard calls, and the attention is once again on me.

Alcide turns and faces me, giving me a nod as he waits on the other side. I step up to the machine and blow out a breath as I step through. A small alarm sounds and I look up in horror to see the light flashing red. My panicked gaze meets Alcide's, as two guards step up to me. Am I in trouble?

"Please step through," they order, and I do as I am told, my gut clenching in fear of the unknown.

He stops before me and holds his arms to the side. "Please hold your arms like this."

Again, I do as I'm told and he steps closer, pulling a silver wand from his side. He hovers it over me, starting at my head and working down to my neck, chest, and arms, until he waves it around my middle where it bleeps. He continues down to my legs and when no other sound emits from the machine, he hovers it over my waist again.

"Please untuck your shirt," he demands, watching me closely.

My cheeks flame and I hear Nixon move behind me, but I hold up my hand to stop him, knowing he wants to protect my dignity. I pull the hem of the red, gypsy style top out from my tight, black leather trousers, exposing the tanned skin of my waist. The gold chains hanging from my waist sway as the guard waves the wand again. When it hovers over the chains, it beeps.

"That's fine." He waves me away and I pull down my shirt, tucking it in again before joining Alcide. I breathe a sigh of relief before looking at the machine with interest, realizing it must have detected the metal in my clothing.

I turn in time to see Nixon tilt his head down so he can get through the machine. It doesn't bleep, but I doubt they would've scanned him with the wand if it had. As he comes through, the guards actually take a step back. Sometimes I forget how massive he is until other people react. He's just my gentle Nixon, but they only see his hulking size.

"Fourth floor, first door on your left," one of them calls, before going back to watch the entrance.

We all turn, looking for the stairs, when a man in a black shirt and trousers waves us over to a silver door. He presses a button in the wall next to it and we wait in an awkward silence. I start to fidget as unease courses through me, but I freeze when the doors open to reveal a small room. The man steps inside before gesturing for us to join him and I cautiously follow. As we all shuffle around the tight space, I end up squeezed between Alcide and Nixon.

The doors close and then the room suddenly jolts, moving upwards. My eyes widen and I suck in a breath, reaching out to my men as my stomach flips and my legs turn wobbly. The whole world feels as if it's moving around us.

The box slows to a stop and as the doors open, I rush forward with a relieved sigh. Once again on solid ground, I give the moving room a dirty look. Alcide grins, his expression full of amusement, as he and Nixon step out to join me. We watch as the doors shut once more with the man still inside, presumably returning to the floor we just left.

Turning to the hallway, our boots meet soft carpet as we follow the directions the guard had given us. Paintings adorn the walls, all depicting men in suits looking away into the distance. To me, they just look bored, but what do I know about art?

Artificial lights shine down on the dull corridor and the door we arrive at is a deep brown with a golden handle. The amount of technology astounds me again. In Cinders, we mostly used candlelight, since the power was never reliable that far out into the wilds.

"Should we knock?" I whispered, looking around anxiously. It reminds me of Frederick's house to a degree, and that in and of itself makes me want to cringe and abandon my newfound confidence, and retreat back into that meek little slave I used to be.

"No, *they* invited *us*." Alcide sniffs, standing taller as he tugs his jacket straight. He grins down at me, but he can't hide the worry in his eyes.

"Rhea, I know it will be hard, but for our sakes, please try to stay quiet. These men won't be like us, they won't see you as anything else but a slave and a woman, it could put you in danger," he explains and I nod. I know exactly the type of men we are about to see, but Alcide is wrong—whether I speak or not, they will see me.

I point out as much. "Even if I don't speak, they will notice me, and if they want to hurt me badly enough they will, slave or no slave, woman or no woman. They are rich, that makes them powerful and power is heady. It makes them think they are on top of the world. Whether I talk or not, I have no protection from them. But for you, I won't," I offer, and look back at the door.

"Sometimes, I forget how far you have come from being that slave we brought home, Rhea. I fear you're right, but let's not provoke them." He grabs my hand and kisses my knuckles, before letting go and opening the door without bothering to knock.

He steps into the room like he owns it, and I follow after him with Nixon barely a step behind me. I make sure to hide behind Alcide slightly without looking like I'm doing it on purpose. I know how to play invisible, and I hope it will come in useful now. A table is all that fills the room. It's long and the same kind of wood from the doorway —dark and expensive. Six chairs surround the table and only three are filled, all of which by men. More paintings fill the wall, one of the city itself after the wars. Two windows frame that painting, looking down onto the city. A silver chandelier hangs from the ceiling, and I take it all in before focusing back on the men who called us here. The room is opulent and the obvious display of wealth here when the world is suffering fills me with anger, which I have to stifle. These guys are obviously in charge of the city, and I could create a lot of trouble for us if I start causing problems.

A guard stands in the corner, watching us carefully. For their protection or to keep us in line? Maybe both.

"Please, do come in," the man at the head of the table sneers sarcastically.

"You were expecting us, weren't you? We didn't want to be rude and keep you waiting," Alcide answers smoothly, the charm being laid on thick. I notice with amusement that it works, the man's scorn disappearing as he sits back in his chair.

He's old, and his grey hair is neatly styled and combed. His face is clean, with lines around his eyes and mouth. He appears harmless, just an average, older gentleman, but his eyes betray that image. They're icy-blue, cold, and empty.

He's wearing a black suit with a plain white shirt. His perfectly put together appearance and pressed attire screams money. Yet some of the people outside were hungry and dirty. That puts a sour taste in my mouth.

The other two men are just as well dressed, but they don't carry as much power as the other man. It's clear from the way they hold themselves that they defer to him. One is a younger man with blond hair and green eyes—handsome but with a shark-like smile. The other is an older version of the younger man, with greying hair and the start of wrinkles. They look like they have never done a day of hard work in their lives.

"Indeed," the first man replies, his silver eyebrow arching. "Take a seat, won't you?" His words are phrased like a question, but with an undertone of a command that suggests it's more of an order.

Alcide pulls out a chair and looks at me. I smile, sliding into the seat before he moves to sit in the chair beside me, blocking me slightly from the men. Nixon takes the one on my other side, both of them blocking me in and I know it's on purpose.

Alcide leans back in his chair, silent as he keenly watches the men before us. The younger man shuffles nervously before his eyes lock on me, and the blue depths heat as he runs them down the parts of my body that aren't obscured by the table. Alcide must notice, because he leans forward again, blocking the younger man's view, and clears his throat.

"You *requested* to meet?" Alcide inquires calmly, emphasising the word request.

"Yes, we did. News travelled to us of...amazing feats being accomplished by a travelling circus—by you. Naturally, we were intrigued," the man responds.

"Naturally," Alcide repeats dryly, with none of his usual charm present. I can tell from that just how much he hates everything they represent. While the rest of the world starves and begs, they sit in their city with their riches.

"That's why we invited you here. You must have been curious about us to come, no?"

When Alcide doesn't reply, the man waves his hand in the air.

"Where are my manners? I apologise, but your sudden entry took me off guard. I am Mr. Lennon, but please call me Arthur. The gentlemen beside me are Chester Franklin and," he points at the older man and then to the younger man, "Oliver Franklin." They both nod in greeting and Arthur carries on. "We represent some of the ruling parties of this city. We run it just as we did before the bombs, as a government."

Interesting.

"Now, as for your show. We, of course, invite you to perform for our residents. I'm sure they would enjoy your...peculiarities as much as the normal, uneducated masses you are used to. There is, however, a condition," Arthur informs us, leaning back in his chair. His eyes flicker to me with interest before Alcide's stare draws him back.

"And what condition is that? I'm sure you're right. The...people of this city would enjoy our acts as much as everyone else of this world." I can hear the undertone of anger in Alcide's words, and I place a hand on his thigh under the table. I notice him suck in a slight breath before he grabs my hand and holds on, using me for strength in the face of this cruel man.

"We, of course, must see the show on the first night, to ensure our audiences will enjoy it," he explains.

"That is all?" Alcide questions, leaning back in his seat as his brows furrow in confusion.

"Yes." Arthur grins, but the look gives me a bad feeling.

"Then please join us tonight for our first show." Alcide smiles, but there is nothing warm about it.

"That soon?" Arthur's eyebrows go up.

"We move fast, Arthur, and we work harder. I'm sure you will enjoy the show as much as...the uneducated masses," Alcide finishes.

"Tonight then," Arthur agrees.

Alcide stands, and Nixon and I rise with him. "Tonight."

We turn to leave, but Arthur's voice stops us at the door. "Oh, and Alcide, was it? I hope your little...*circus* truly is all it's made out to be. We could use something a little...different."

I look over my shoulder, shivering at the greed in the man's eyes. Nixon opens the door and I rush through it, with Alcide right behind me. Only when the door is shut and there's a barrier between us do we start to relax, but I know I won't be truly calm until we get back to the circus.

"Alcide—" I start, but he holds his finger to his lips so I seal mine again.

"Not here, come on. We need to get back and get ready for tonight's show. It appears we'll have some special guests this evening," he growls.

Chapter Two

Once we leave City Hall, another guard waits to escort us through the city to our family, where they are waiting to see whether or not they should to unpack. The guard cuts through alleys and back roads, but it still takes us twenty minutes to make it through the city and to the cleared patch of dirt where the wagons and my guys are waiting, looking anxious.

When they spot us, they deflate—even Blain, before he puts on his signature asshole look. "'Bout time!" he calls.

"Aww, Blainy, did you miss me?" I wink as we get closer.

He rolls his eyes, but there is a smirk on his lips. "You wish, Harpy," he mocks, but he pulls me into his arms, betraying his words as he turns us and leans on me while he watches Alcide, whose eyes are on the retreating back of the guard.

Alcide waits until he is out of view before turning to us, his shoulders slumping and life coming back into his face. "We are staying, start unpacking. We have a show tonight. I want the set up done in two hours and I want a practice there," he yells out, and the hands rush off, starting to get every unloaded.

Rex whistles. "That's a tight turn around," he comments.

Alcide nods. "Yes, but I don't want to be here any longer than we have to be," he mutters, but I catch it, and so do the others.

"Bad feeling?" Jessie asks, playing with my hair.

"Something like that. Come on then. We have a show to prepare for," he calls, his smile forced and his eyes worried.

Blain lets go of me, spinning me into Rex who catches me. Rex smiles down at me, his eyes sparkling in the sun and his hair messy as always. "Come check on the animals with me?" he requests, brushing a stray lock of my hair behind my ear.

"Yes!" I almost shout, making him laugh.

I have started looking after the animals with Rex and they listen to me now, not as much as him, but definitely more than Blain. They are just as much a part of this family as we are. With being stuck on the road for the last two weeks, it has been hard. We would just set up a tent or two on a night and pack up early the next day to keep moving, which means I haven't got to spend a lot of time with them and I miss them fiercely.

He grabs my hand, twining our fingers as we make our way to the wagons at the back they are riding in. I already spot Sid and Fluffy stretching out on the dirt, sunbathing. When they see us, they bound over—Fluffy knocking me on my ass and into the dirt.

"I know you do that on purpose," I scold playfully, laughing as Fluffy rubs his head against my chest, making me smile and run my fingers through his soft fur.

"I missed you too, baby!" I coo, scratching his head.

"We better see the others," Rex advises with a laugh, reaching down and stroking Fluffy, making the cat's tawny eyes slit in pleasure as he purrs.

I nod and get to my feet. I drop my hand onto Fluffy's back and he walks next to us, with Sid following as we head around the back of the wagon to see the others. Bubbles and Rumple are curled up in the corner, glaring at Tiny as he moves around the wagon before jumping down to greet me.

I step back, already giggling as I warn, "No, Tiny, no!" I laugh as he wraps his trunk around me and picks me up, holding me to his face. I wrap my arms around him as much as I can and rain kisses on his face.

He blinks his eyes, his lashes kissing me, before putting me back on the ground again as he goes to greet Rex. I crouch into the wagon, smiling at Rumple and Bubbles.

"Hey, cuties. What, no hug?" I joke.

They slither closer, but instead of hugging me or anything, they stick their tongues out before moving away.

I hop down and go back to playing with Fluffy, Sid, and Tiny, and before I know it, the camp is up around me.

I pout as I say goodbye, knowing I need to go to practice, but not wanting to leave the animals' tent. Shaking it off, I skip over to the main tent, which they finished putting up around half an hour ago. The red and white reaches into the sky with lights strung off it and a sign on top.

We started a new show a couple of towns ago, and bit by bit we have been practicing new and more dangerous stunts to keep audiences interested, but tonight we are trying to put it all together. If we can impress those men, they might invite us back, and as much as I hate it here, I am betting it is good money.

The front tent flap stands open and I make my way through, stopping with a smile. It's good to be home, even if it is one on wheels. Stands of chairs line the perimeter of the tent with aisles in between. Stairs lead down to the circle of sand in the middle where we perform, a ring of stones surrounding it to separate us and them. Ropes, nets, and platforms are strung up in the rafters, waiting for us, and I spot Nixon and Jessie already warming up in the middle.

Jogging down the steps, I pop my head over their shoulders.

"Boo!"

I laugh when Jessie screams and whirls, only for his eyes to narrow and his lips to tip up in a smile. "Oh, you're going to get it now, Firecracker," he calls.

I scream as he pushes off and races after me. Moving around Nixon, I jump up and start climbing him. He smiles before grabbing me and lifting me in the air, until I am away from Jessie's grasp.

"Nix," Jessie whines, those lush lips pushed together in a pout, and he makes sad, puppy dog eyes.

The big guy arches an eyebrow and Jessie relents. "Fine, let's get warmed up before Alcide kicks our arses." He starts to walk away and Nixon puts me down. As soon as my feet touch the floor, with Nixon's hands on my hips and me smiling up at him, Jessie rushes back. His hand lands on my arse with a resounding smack, making me jump and bump into Nixon as I yelp.

I turn with a glare as he jogs away laughing. Blain stands near us, watching, and he winks at me. "Need it rubbed better, Harpy?" he rumbles, his eyes dark with heat, and when he runs his tongue over his pierced bottom lip, I swallow hard, my pussy starting to pulse.

He is shirtless, his wide, perfectly carved chest on display and his black tattoos standing out against his dark skin. He has a little stubble gracing his jaw and it only makes him look more dangerous, and I'm hoping he never shaves it off. He steps closer, leaning down to whisper, "Maybe if you're a good girl, I'll even make it red again later." He grins as he backs away. Bastard.

"Alright, let's get going, shall we? Only three hours until show time!" Alcide calls, and I look over to see him striding down the stairs towards us, his ringmaster hat firmly in place.

SWEATING, I land hard on the sand. We have mastered the new moves, but they are still hard and we have run through the show three times now, making sure we have it down to a T before we call it good. I head back to my tent to get ready, knowing I need to look amazing tonight.

An outfit is waiting for me on my bed in my tent when I get back, and I smile as I head over and stroke the material—a corset and trousers, and there are even boots. I quickly change out of my clothes and have a wash in the bowl in the corner of my tent. I grab some underwear and a bra and pull them on, then stare at the corset. I am going to need help.

No sooner does the thought form when someone pushes into my tent. I look over my shoulder and smile when I spot Rex. He grins and an adorable blush stains his cheeks when he spots me half naked. You thought he would have gotten over that by now, but he still acts like that shy man I first met.

"Alcide mentioned you might need help getting dressed," he says, moving closer, surprising me.

He comes up behind me and I turn as he pushes his chest to mine. I curl my hands against his solid, still sweaty chest as he looks down at me. "Rhea," he whispers, his hand coming up and tracing my lips.

I open them slowly and draw his finger into my mouth, sucking it as he watches. His eyes fly wide before they turn smouldering, his Adam's apple bobbing as he watches me. I slowly pull his finger from my mouth, and when it breaks free with a pop, he groans and leans down slowly, giving me every chance to stop him. I don't.

His lips meet mine, softly at first, before they become more insistent. Leaning up on my tiptoes, I press myself against him and open my mouth, so he sweeps his tongue in as his hands come up and tangle in my hair. He pulls me closer, his hard body pressed to mine, and I groan into his mouth, loving the taste of him.

"Thirty minutes!" one of the hands shouts from outside.

We break away reluctantly and watch each other with desire filled eyes, our mouths parted. "I better get you dressed," he whispers roughly.

"Then later you can undress me," I tease, my cheeks heating at my boldness, but with how intimate we have all become since Christmas, I should be used to it. He grins naughtily.

"Oh, I plan to, Wildcat." He drops a chaste kiss on my lips before moving away, and I turn back to the clothes, giving my heart a chance to slow down from its racing. He only needs to be near and he sends it into overdrive.

He helps me into the corset and trousers, his knuckles running along my skin lightly, and he drops kisses on the back of my neck, sending heat through me and making me shiver. When he steps back with a nod, I find myself disappointed. He must notice it, because he smiles and steps forward again, tilting his head and whispering against my lips.

"You look beautiful as always. Later," he promises, before stepping back.

He walks backwards out of the tent, his eyes stuck on me like he can't look away, and I giggle as he trips over a rug, going down hard. He jumps to his feet, his face red, but his smile genuine, before he ducks out of my tent.

Blowing out a breath, I wander over to the long golden mirror, wanting to see the outfit in all its glory. I suck in a breath when I do. My hands skate down the corset, which sucks in my already skinny waist, and accentuates my curves.

I turn after spotting a flash of red in the mirror and stop cold, my mouth dropping open. Alcide is standing at the tent flap and he looks delicious. He has a new black top hat on, tilted to the side and showing off his hair. His eyes are dark and his lips pursed. His wide chest is encased in a red and gold jacket, with buttoning up the front and a long tail at the back. His thighs are moulded by black leather trousers with crisscross lacing on the sides, exposing flashes of skin as he steps inside and comes towards me. He looks amazing, and I have to snap my mouth shut, feeling speechless and oh so young in his presence.

"Here, I got you something, *cariño*," he says softly, holding out his hand and slowly peeling open his fingers to expose a beautiful necklace.

A bright red stone sits in a gold clasp with a long, golden chain with moons hanging off it.

"Turn around," he whispers, his voice rough and velvety.

I nod, doing as I am told, and watch in the mirror as he lifts my hair, and I quickly grab the curls and hold them in my hands on top of my head, exposing my pale neck.

He runs the chain over my skin, making me shiver and fastens the clasp at the back. His hands come to rest on my shoulders as the jewel settles between the tops of my breasts exposed in the corset. "Beautiful," he says softly, running his hand along my shoulder and down next to the chain, his knuckles catching my breast and making me suck in a deep breath.

"Do you know why I got a red coat?" he inquires, watching me in the mirror.

I shake my head mutely, afraid to break this moment with my words. He leans closer, his eyes on me in the mirror, as his mouth meets my ear. "It reminds me of the colour of your hair, you're always with me and we match," he whispers, before pulling back, and I let my hair down and look at us both in the mirror—observing for a moment what he sees.

My black corset has gold lace running through it, and my black leather trousers are tucked into knee-high red boots. My hair is bright red on the top, fading to orange and then blonde on the ends like a flame. My eyes sparkle in the light, my mouth is tipped up and my cheeks pink. He stands slightly behind me, looking dark and temping, and he's right. We look good together, we match. He designed these outfits so we would. I gulp, fluttering my lashes before I meet his gaze confidently in the mirror.

"We look good together," I offer, my words husky.

His lips curl up in a smile. "We do, *cariño*."

A noise has us both turning to the tent flap, which is moving, but there is no breeze. Frowning, my eyes catch on something on the floor. Alcide strides over and I follow him as he picks it up. I peek my head out of the flap and freeze. The boy from when I first came to the city, the one I gave my rations to, is stopped half behind a tent, his eyes on me. He nods, touching his wrist before he races away into the night.

"Rhea," Alcide says sharply, and I pull my head back in and look at him.

You shouldn't have come here, this place isn't safe for you.

The message is scrawled on a tattered piece of paper, and it's hard to read, but I can just about manage. "Alcide?" I whisper.

He screws it into a ball and shoves it into his coat. "After, after the show, Rhea. We can't afford to look suspicious now. Act normal, then we are leaving." He shakes his head, his eyes angry. "I don't like this place." He strides out of my tent, leaving me alone.

Wrapping my arms around myself, I look at where the message was. Why did he warn us? What does he mean that we aren't safe?

Either way, we would be stupid to ignore it. Alcide is right, we need to leave. I just need to make it through the show. Turning back to the mirror, I blow out a breath before dropping my hands to my side and tilting my head back defiantly. Forcing a smile, I tell myself I can do this.

I turn and leave the tent, ready to get this show over with. The faster we do, the faster we can come up with a plan and leave. I head to the main tent where I can hear the audience already hollering and stamping, impatient for the show.

I slip in through the back and join the others. Rex sees me and smiles, but it drops when he looks at my face. "Rhea?" he murmurs, concerned, but the lights go down and it's our cue. I smile shakily at him and walk past, his worried gaze boring into my back as I make my way into the middle of the tent. The lights are still off as I hit my mark and still.

Pushing the warning from my mind, I force a big, fake grin on my face as the spotlight hits me where I stand waiting in the sand. The music starts and I hold my arms up, bowing to the audience. A shiver races through me at the thought of the men from earlier with their eyes on me. Maybe coming here wasn't a good idea, but I need to forget that because it's show time.

CIRCUS

Chapter Three

With the bright lights shining down on me, it's difficult to see beyond the circle of sand that is my stage. But by the excitement and anticipation in the air, and the hush of voices filling the tent, I know this show has been a sell out. Glancing up at the lights, my pupils dilate against the brightness, and I feel the telltale tingle that my body has adapted to protect me.

For years I just thought my powers hardened my skin to protect me from harm, and I was lucky never to fall ill from the unclean, dirty water back in Cinders. Since I joined Alcide and the guys, I've learned that my powers are so much more than that. My body is able to adapt as I need it, protecting me from whatever threat or harm comes my way. It isn't always in the most obvious ways, and I never know what it is going to do, but my powers have never let me down so far.

Pulling my eyes from the lights, I realise how my body has changed this time. My eyesight is better, I'm able to look at the bright stage lights without it hurting, and I can also see beyond into the darkened crowd. This audience is different than what we have had before... Where are the regular working people that usually come to our shows? We always put aside a certain amount of free tickets for those who truly can't afford to come, but everyone in this crowd looks well fed, and they are dressed in clothing the looks new.

The sound of footsteps coming towards me reminds me of what I'm supposed to be doing, and I pull my gaze away from the crowd to smile at Blain. He looks dangerous as he stalks closer to me, pulling a black blindfold from his waistband, his dark eyes glittering under the stage lights. Spinning me around, he ties the blindfold over my eyes before walking me over to a large dartboard.

The audience holds their breath as they wait to see what Blain will do when he stalks to his spot on the other side of the ring. The first dagger flies past me before the audience even has a chance to realise what he's done. The next four follow in quick succession, each hitting the dartboard and missing me by millimeters. The crowd starts to politely clap, since they think the act is over, and I can't help the grin that spreads across my face as I anticipate their reactions.

A drumbeat starts in the background and a stagehand runs into the ring, handing me a small, circular target. I can't see any of this as the blindfold is still in place, but we have rehearsed this many times— Blain is obsessed with my safety. He never doubted his power until his act involved me. He may act tough and like he doesn't give a damn, but I know he cares deeply.

I take a step forward, each step in time with a beat of the drum. The faint whistle in the air is the only indication that Blain has thrown a dagger. There is a gasp from the crowd and it is not because the dagger has been imbedded in the target, but because he *created* the dagger— the blade flying from his wrist like magic. I know from watching him practice that the daggers just seem to appear, like an illusion, but they are very real.

I continue to walk confidently towards him, my hips swaying to the drumbeat. Some people might worry or be nervous about walking in the path of a flying dagger, but I know he won't hit me, and I have learned to trust my powers to protect me. I used to worry that they wouldn't be quick enough, but the more I trust them, the greater they seem to grow. But the crowd doesn't know this, which is evident from the tension building in the tent. As I get closer, the force of the knives being thrown into the targets gets more intense, reverberating up my arms.

Expanding my senses, I listen for changes in the air around me. At the last second, I drop the target and bring my hands together to catch the knife between my palms, stopping it just before it pierces my heart. The tent is so quiet you could hear a pin drop, and then the crowd erupts into applause. I feel Blain come up behind me to untie the blindfold, his breath tickling my ear as he whispers to me.

"You were cutting that a bit fucking close, Harpy," he scolds, and as he pulls away the blindfold, I smile at his scowling face. He can't stay mad at me in front of all these people. Turning my attention back to the crowd, I grin and make a show of opening my palms, displaying my uninjured hands. Blain takes the dagger from me and imbeds the knife in a block of wood to show how sharp the blade is, before leading me into a quick bow and dragging me out of the ring into the backstage area.

"What the hell do you think you're playing at?" His voice is harsh as he pins me against one of the posts holding up this part of the tent. "You left it to the last moment to catch the knife. You know the timings, why did you wait?" he demands, his arms bracketing me in on either side, so I have no choice but to look at him. Not that I am complaining. Raising my hand to his cheek, I smile at him, knowing he can't resist it, not that he would ever admit it.

"Blain, we've spoken about this, I trust you not to hurt me. Besides, my powers will protect me." He frowns at my words, but I feel some of the tension in his shoulders relax a little.

"I can't control the dagger once it has left my hand, you know that!"

I take a deep breath. Talking with Blain about my safety always gets him worked up and if he had his way, I wouldn't be involved in his act at all.

"It was a fraction of a second, Blain. Trust me, you can't always be there to protect or save me," I justify, and I know he knows I can protect myself, but his jaw just tightens at my comment. He's shutting down.

"I'm not willing to risk—" Cutting him off, I press a firm kiss to his lips. My core heats up at the masculine groan he makes before returning the kiss, his hands gripping my arms and pulling me closer.

Someone clears their throat, reminding me where we are, but that doesn't stop Blain from finishing what I started. He continues to kiss me for another few seconds before pulling away with a half sigh, half growl.

"This isn't over, Harpy. I'll fucking deal with you later," he mutters, before stalking away and leaving me panting. I know I should probably be upset over our fight, but I can't help the little smile that crosses my lips as I watch him walk away.

I watch the rest of the show from behind the curtains, heading out to assist with acts as I'm needed for. It goes off without a hitch and the crowd loves us, except I can't help but eye the quiet group of official looking people in the front row of the audience. There's something different about them, and it's not until nearly the end of the show that I realise why. It's the officials from the city we met earlier. I had expected they would send someone to make sure we were following their rules, but I hadn't anticipated for *them* to show up, not for something like a circus show. They already made it clear that they believe themselves to be above us.

Alcide has been watching them too, and I know something is worrying him since he has been getting quieter and quieter as the show goes on. Stalking back through the curtains that separates the ring from backstage, he growls quietly as he takes off his hat and throws it to the floor. Silently, I walk towards him and pick it up, brushing off the sawdust before cradling the hat in my arms.

"You okay?" I ask softly, watching as he runs his hands through his hair.

"Yes, it's just that nothing we seem to do is good enough for those entitled idiots." He gestures at the curtain separating us from the crowd.

"But they love us, can't you hear their cheering?" I say with a frown, confused.

"Not them—the Masters. I know you've seen them in the audience." He nods as he sees the understanding dawning on my face. So that is why he is upset? He wants to impress the Masters?

"Yes, I have, but why does it matter? The people that matter are the ones who actually wanted to see the show, the people like you and me.

Why do you care about what the Masters of the city think? As long as they allow us to perform here, that's the only thing that matters, right?" I inquire gently, as I walk to his side, handing him his hat with a smile.

He's silent for a moment as he looks down at me, then frowns at the curtain again, almost as if he can see the Masters through it.

"All my early life I was looked down upon, then I created the circus and we became something else, something people would pay to come and see. And now we are beckoned like stray dogs and expected to heel. They come here, into our home, and continue to deem us unworthy."

As Alcide speaks, I wonder where this is coming from. I've never seen him like this before.

"Everything okay?" Rex questions, making me jump. I didn't even see him walking towards us since I was so focused on Alcide.

"Yes. We're changing the last act, we need something bigger. The act you and Rhea have been working on, we will use that as the finale," Alcide instructs. I gape at him as he straightens his hat on his head firmly before he walks away.

"Wait, you can't be serious, we haven't finished working on that yet. We aren't even sure it's safe," Rex argues, as he takes a step towards Alcide.

Freezing, Alcide turns to face us, every inch the ringmaster. "No questions, we are doing this. Rhea is ready, right?" he asks, and his expression is telling me to trust him. Biting down on my lip, I look between the two of them before nodding.

"Okay, yes, I'm ready," I reply, wishing I felt as confident as I sounded.

I TAKE a deep breath as I stand backstage, imagining that I could blow out the nerves that are racking my body over this act. I trust Rex, and I know this act will be amazing and shock the audience, but the only reason our shows work is because we rehearse and train nonstop.

Rex is already in the ring with the animals, warming up the audience for the finale. A hand firmly grips my arm and shakes me out of my thoughts. Whipping my head around, I see that it's Blain, his face contorted with anger.

"Are you fucking out of your mind?"

"Blain—" I begin, but I'm cut off when he shakes me, not hard enough to hurt, but enough that it makes me dizzy.

"What are you thinking? This act is not ready, it's dangerous!" he shouts.

A movement from the corner catches my eye and I see Nixon walking over to us, his face hard as he sees Blain's hands gripping my arms. I smile hurriedly at him, knowing I need to de-escalate the situation before Nix thinks I'm being hurt and gets triggered.

"Nix, I'm okay. Blain is just worried," I explain, gesturing for him to stay where he is. Realising what's about to happen, Blain quickly lets go of me, looking disgusted at the whole situation.

"What's going on here?" Alcide's voice cuts through the tent, but it doesn't have the effect I was hoping for.

Spinning around, Blain strides up to Alcide and grabs him by the lapels of his red jacket. "What the fuck are you doing, sending her out there with an unfinished act? You could kill her!" His voice is loud, and Alcide acts as if the words have physically injured him before his face hardens and he pushes Blain away.

"I would never put her at risk if I didn't think she was ready." The two of them face off against each other, both furious. My heart thuds in my chest at the thought of them fighting, all because of me. "When have I ever done that?" His voice lowers and he steps closer to Blain, whispering something to him.

Nodding sharply, Blain pulls away, throwing a quick glance at me. "Let's hope you're right," he replies, maintaining his stare with Alcide for a tense moment before storming away.

The moment Blain leaves, Alcide seems to deflate, looking around at those of us gathered nearby before his gaze lands on me.

"If you choose not to do this, that's okay, this is your choice." His words are meant for me alone, but I see the others nod, agreeing with him. I would have done it anyway, but his words warm something inside me. He knows that choice is something I lacked for most of my life, and that he is giving this to me now is a greater gift than he could imagine.

Giving him a beatific smile in answer, I push past the curtains and step out into the circus ring to the applause of the crowd.

REX IS STANDING in the center of the ring, facing Bubbles and Rumple, our double-headed snake. When Bubbles/Rumple rears up, he's taller than Rex, and I'd struggle to put my arms around a snake his size. The snake hisses as Rex places his hand on him, his fangs gleaming as Rex speaks in a low voice. There is a flash in Rex's eyes, and the next moment scales appear on the arm that is touching the snake, spreading across his body. Taking a step back, he looks up and smiles at me as I walk closer to him.

I take his outstretched hand and smile as he spins me exactly as discussed. We have only ever outlined this act, walked it through. We've never put it all together or rehearsed it fully.

As I take Rex's hand, the snake rears away, facing me with an intelligence that you wouldn't see in a normal animal, their fangs glinting as both heads hiss at me.

"Rumple," Rex warns, his voice a gentle scold, but he doesn't seem worried, so I take a step closer to him, only to be wrenched from his grip with a cry as a scaly tail wraps around me.

"Rumple! Put her down!" he demands, his voice firm as his body ripples with scales. I take a couple of deep breaths as I feel the scales tighten against me, unable to fight the flash of fear I feel.

"Rex?" I didn't mean for the word to come out as a question, but I can't help it. Reacting to the note of fear in my voice, Rex takes a step closer, which only angers the snake even more. The snake tightens its grip around my body, raising me slightly in the air with my arms trapped at my sides. I can feel my body protesting the crushing hold, but instead of panicking, I close my eyes and focus, pushing past my discomfort.

Muttering fills the audience as they realise something is going wrong, the tension in the tent increasing as hurried footsteps fill the air. Opening my eyes, I see Alcide, Nixon, and Jesse run into the ring next to Rex, seeing me trapped within Rumple's grasp.

Rumple hisses and starts to move backwards, away from the people now circling us. In a flash, both of the heads turn towards me and sink their fangs into my body. Although I know this is part of the show, I can't stop the scream of agony as their venom is pumped into me, my back arching as the poison works its way through my system. The snake drops my body to the ground and slithers towards the backstage area behind the curtain.

Bodies surround me and the crowd starts shouting, all wanting to know what is going on. They demand to know whether this is part of the show or if they've just witnessed some terrible accident.

Worried faces greet me as I peel open my eyes I hadn't realised I had shut. Jesse puts his hand on my arm, and I can't help but cry out at the touch.

"Shit, I'm sorry." He starts to pull back his hand, but I stop him with a touch of my fingers.

"It's okay, it's passing. I'm ready," I tell him quietly. The others move away, giving us space and calming the crowd while blocking us from their view. Smiling, Jesse takes my hand again before pulling a lighter from his pocket and holding a ball of flame in his hand then spinning around us, blowing into the fire and extending it in a wall of flames between the two of us and the rest of the tent. Standing up with his help, I smile at him. Taking a deep breath, I walk *through* the wall of flames with a grin on my face.

"Rhea the Immortal!" Alcide announces, filling the silence in the tent before loud applause sounds. Everyone is on their feet, exclaiming that they thought I was dead. "Thank you for coming to the show, don't forget to tell your friends about what you have seen!"

"Rhea, you're glowing," Jesse whispers to me, and I look down in surprise. Well, that's new. Usually my skin hardens to protect me, or turns me into flame, but now I see that Jesse is right, my whole body is glowing like I'm an ember.

The show went really well, the whole audience seemed to enjoy it, and I'm sure we will end up doing more shows here. We line up to bow when chills spread down my spine, making me look up directly into the gaze of the four Masters who had been watching. The grins on their faces make me nervous, like we have just played right into their hands. But I'm sure I just have an overactive imagination, they can't mean us any harm, right?

Chapter Four

"So, we aren't leaving?" I ask around a mouthful of breakfast, which Rex had placed in front of me a few moments earlier.

We're spread out around benches in the middle of the camp while the stagehands rush around us, already busy for the next show, even though the sun has barely risen.

"No," Alcide answers, his eyes darting around. His voice seems distracted. And he has yet to look at Blain since their argument yesterday. "Not yet, I thought we could explore the city," he replies calmly, and the others nod, obviously wondering why we would leave when we had just arrived the day before.

I sit back, trying to catch Alcide's eyes, and he finally looks over at me, pressing a finger to his lips. "I thought we would stay a few days, check some things out." He puts on an air of fake excitement, but his eyes are warning me and begging me to trust him at the same time. So I nod and go back to eating, trusting our ringmaster to keep us safe. He knows what he's doing, so if he says we are staying despite the warning, there is a reason. I'll just have to make sure to get him alone to find out what it is.

The rest of breakfast passes in a blur as the half asleep men stuff their faces and finally wake up. Jessie, fully awake now, seems excited about the prospect of exploring the city and orders us all to go get ready before bouncing away.

Blain mutters something under his breath as we all stand and stretch, knowing if we don't get ready to head out, Jesse will only keep coming back to pester us. I wait until Alcide stands and when he walks away, I follow him.

He turns the corner of the tent next to us and when I pass it, I don't spot him. I frown hard before a hand wraps around my mouth and pulls me back into a hard chest. I'm yanked into the dark tent, the flap closing behind us and enclosing us in total darkness. I start to struggle, my powers rising instantly, but when his smell hits me, I relax.

"It's me, *cariño*," he says anyway, reassuring me, his voice soft and velvety as he whispers into my ear. "There are eyes and ears everywhere, we need to act normal. If we try and leave now, I fear they will follow us. We will do our planned shows and then we are gone, understood? Until then, act as you normally would, but be wary," he warns, his voice deadly serious. Worry passes through me even as I'm distracted by his body pressing against mine, his moist breath on my skin, and his lips so close.

"Okay," I reply breathlessly, trying to control my reaction to him, but it's no use. I know he can hear the pounding of my heart, like a trapped animal trying to break free.

He kisses my neck ever so gently and I freeze, the darkness closing around us and sparking with electricity. I bite my lower lip, fighting the noise that wants to escape and the need to press back into his body, too afraid he'll pull away. Something about being completely alone, completely in the dark with him, has me nearly panting into his hand, my need rising with my powers like it always does when he's around.

I dart my tongue out to moisten my lips, but it catches his hand and he groans into my ear, pressing closer, letting me feel his hardness against my ass.

"We relax today, look like we are having fun. It's just another day out for us. Do what you would normally do," he repeats, sealing it with another gentle kiss before letting go as quickly as he grabbed me.

I whirl to search the tent, but he's gone, the flaps on the side moving with his fast exit. My hand moves up slowly, covering the spot of skin he kissed, trying to trap the heat of his lips as I force myself to listen to his warnings. Did he mean that they are watching us, listening to us, even here? One thing is for sure, I need to be careful. This is a twisted game we're playing with the Masters of the city. Their moves are cloaked in shadows, forcing our hands, surrounding us. I just hope we win.

I make myself drop my hand and leave the tent, trying not to look over my shoulders. The space between my shoulder blades itches like I'm being watched, but is that me or my imagination after Alcide's warning?

I head straight to my tent, trying to act normal and determined to enjoy today. There might be something wrong with this city, but I'm going to enjoy my downtime with my men. Far too often we are on the move or going from one bad situation to another, so even if things are unravelling around us, I will enjoy the moment and worry about that later. Life is—for now—for living. I've learned that from my past, and I refuse to let the Masters ruin my present.

I get dressed as fast as I can, knowing Jesse will already be impatiently waiting. I choose some red and gold harem pants that Rex got for me, and a plain top. It ends just under my breasts, exposing some skin between the high waist of the pants and the shirt. The sleeves are capped with holes in the shoulders and down the back. It's extremely comfy, and when I twirl, I nod in appreciation.

I quickly braid my hair, not wanting it down if it's going to be windy, and add some gold, jangling jewels that Jesse got me for Christmas through the plait. I still have Alcide's necklace on from last night and I tuck it under the shirt, close to my skin. Grabbing my bag and money, I quickly leave my tent and head back to where we eat. As I expected, Jesse is already there, almost bouncing up and down in front of an annoyed looking Blain.

Blain's arms are bulging and on display in his tight black t-shirt, his legs encased in his usual leather trousers. His hair is perfectly slicked back, and his lips are thin and annoyed. He watches Jesse as the smaller man stands in front of him with a pout.

"Ready?" I interrupt, not wanting Jesse to push Blain over the edge before we even leave camp.

Blain tips his head to me, his eyes locked on my body as he

watches me come closer. Most people would take that look to mean fuck off, but I see the flare of heat in his eyes and the slight relaxing of his muscles. I kiss Jesse on the cheek and quickly move him away from a ready to swing Blain.

"Why don't you go grab the others?" I suggest, looking in his excited eyes.

"Good idea, Firecracker," he gushes, bending me backwards over his arm and kissing me quickly before pulling me up from the dipped position and racing away.

I shake my head with a smile, watching him go, before looking back at Blain. I arch my eyebrow and cross my arms, copying his movements and pout.

"What's wrong, grumpy pants?" I deepen my voice, mocking him. I love riling him up. We have a love hate relationship, and honestly, I shouldn't enjoy his anger as much as I do.

"Harpy," he warns, his eyes narrowed as he steps closer, pressing his arms into mine.

"Blainy," I mimic.

He drops his arms and I squeal when he picks me up. He turns with me in his arms and presses me into a nearby post. He holds me there as he smirks, his eyes dark and vacillating between anger and desire like they always do when it comes to me.

"Does someone need a reminder of what happens to naughty girls?" he asks, his voice sharp and deadly like the knives he always carries and can produce. He leans closer, looking me dead in the eye.

"Maybe," I tease, my voice already breathless from just being close to him and having all that power and strength aimed my way. He has a sweeter side buried beneath all this angst, but I love this side as well.

He groans, his eyes dropping to my lips and staying there. "I don't think Alcide would be too pleased if I fucked you here and now," he murmurs, his dirty words causing heat to gather low in my stomach.

"Or maybe he would love it," I joke, begging him with my eyes to kiss me.

He feathers his lips across mine, teasing me. "They're coming back, I can hear them. We better get going." With that, he pulls away and drops me to my feet.

What the— "Blainy," I whine, needy as hell.

He grins down at me, his eyes sparkling. "Need something, Harpy?"

I throw my hair over my shoulder, my jewels making a soft tinkling noise as they move. "You," I state confidently, before smiling and stepping around him when I hear the others.

He catches my hand and drags me to his side. "Better watch that mouth, Harpy, it might just get you into trouble."

"That's what I'm hoping," I reply, before shaking off his hold and smiling at the others as they stop before us.

"Ready?" Rex inquires, with an excited Jesse at his side and a silent Nixon behind him.

"Yes, let's go!" I grin, ready to explore.

They turn to leave and Blain slaps my ass lightly. "You are going to pay later."

Fuck, I hope so. I'll take Blain any way I can have him. In fact, I have a reoccurring fantasy of being strapped to his board while he fucks me, not that I will ever tell him that. The asshole would never let me live it down, even as he dragged me into the tent and tied me up and fucked out my brains.

THE CITY IS BUSIER than ever. Luckily, no one seems to pay us any mind as we slip into their bustling depths and follow the roads. It goes from fields straight into skyscrapers, shops, roads, and stalls. It's all so closed in that there's no privacy. There are so many people, I find them blurring together.

I've gained a lot of confidence since Cinders, but even now I find myself stepping closer to Nixon. Last time I was in a city like this, the breeders captured me. I know they won't dare with my silent giant at my side, and even if they did, I now have the powers to protect myself, but it's better to be safe than sorry.

There are so many shops and pubs and even restaurants that we find ourselves just wandering, unsure where to start until a man waves us over to the front of his shop. Exchanging curious glances, we walk over to what appears to be a bakery. Wooden crates stand upside down with bread, cakes, and much more spread over the tops outside the window of the shop. It all smells delicious and I get a waft of warm bread drifting to me from inside. The man is stocky with greying hair, mud brown eyes, and a belly protruding from behind his flour covered white apron.

"Lady and gentlemen, won't you try our freshly baked goods? Made here every day by myself and my wife! The pound cake is to die for!" he gushes, rushing forward and offering me a slice from a tray he's holding.

I take it hesitantly before popping it into my mouth. Flavour explodes straight away and I groan, closing my eyes and savouring the sweet, soft, warm texture of the cake. I open them again to find everyone looking at me. Covering my mouth, I speak as I chew. "It's amazing," I confirm.

That's all the prodding they need, because the poor man finds himself surrounded by hungry carnies, all grabbing samples and throwing them back as quick as they can and reaching for more.

"Boys, manners," I warn, throwing the man an apologetic look as he holds the now empty tray to his chest with a shocked look.

They all stop eating and look at me with various expressions on their faces. After a moment, Nixon slowly hands over the half bitten piece of cake to me as a peace offering. I accept it with a soft smile.

"Thank you," I whisper, popping it into my mouth and chewing before looking at the man.

"We'll take four of the pound cakes and ten loaves of bread." I nod, knowing we need to stock up. Plus, it's rare we have such treats and the stagehands deserve one for all their hard work. I look at the boys staring sadly at the empty tray and laugh. "Better make it eight pound cakes," I correct myself.

"Yes, miss, straight away!" the man gushes, jumping as if forgetting himself while he turns to rush inside. He hesitates, coming back out and placing the tray down before rushing back inside, shouting the order to the his wife.

I smile, looking out over the street as we wait for our order. Jesse slips his hand in mine and I weave our fingers together, just people watching. The way they dress here is so strange, all bright colours and tight clothing. It shows how wealthy this city is compared to others we've been to, where people wore clothes made of random scraps of fabric sewn together.

I hear the man come back outside, packing our order and talking to the guys, but something catches my eye across the street. I squint, letting go of Jesse's hand as I step off the curb and onto the cobbled road to try to get a closer look. The voices of the guys and the baker fade away as I meet a piercing gaze across the road.

There, standing next to a bookstore, is the same child as before. The one who warned me, the one who I gave food to when we first arrived. Two other dirty looking children are behind him, their eyes locked on me. My attention is drawn back to the boy when I notice him mouthing the same word over and over.

Leave.

The sound of spinning wheels and a horse neighing causes me to jerk my eyes from the boy. I jump back right before a wagon speeds over the spot where I was just standing. With a shaky inhale, I look back at the children and see they are gone.

"Rhea?" Nixon asks quietly, placing his hand on my shoulder. I drag my gaze away from the bookstore and glance behind me. Nixon and the others are standing there waiting for me, looking worried.

I shake it off, forcing a smile. "Sorry, was just looking around. We ready to move on?"

"Yeah, the baker told us about a shop up here he thinks we should visit," Jesse says, sounding excited. His enthusiasm dims when he notices the look on my face, so I force myself to get as excited as him as I remember Alcide's words.

"Let's go then!" I grin.

He smiles and turns to lead the way. I look back over to the book-shop one more time, but it remains empty. Holding on to Nixon's arm, I force myself to ignore the child and continue enjoying my day.

Act natural, Rhea.

The shop they want to visit is only down the street on the corner of a junction with steps leading up to the black, three-story building. Gold calligraphy lettering fills the frosted windows, proudly declaring the shop "Gregoria's Tailoring."

I follow them as they head inside, and I feel eyes on me again. Glancing over my shoulder, I see a man completely dressed in black with a whip at his hip watching us from the other side of the road. When I meet his gaze, he smiles slowly, and I shiver from that look and the lack of humanity in his eyes. He wants me to know he's following us...why?

I speed up and shut the door behind me, peeking through the glass and see the man still there. Stepping back, I turn to look into the shop and my mouth drops open.

"Er, I think we are in the wrong shop," I whisper to the others, crowding the entrance.

We stick out like a sore thumb. The walls are all open brick with fancy gold decorations. A clean, white table and glass cabinet lay at the back with an old-school, golden cash register. The rest of the shop is filled with racks and racks of suits, all grey, black, and sophisticated.

There's a curtain next to the desk covering what must be a doorway to the back, and it flutters open as a tall man bustles out, carrying a suit. He steps up to the white table and carefully lays the suit down.

He has a measuring tape in one hand, one wrapped around his neck, and a piece of chalk behind his ear. His hair is shaved at the sides with swirls through it, and what looks like golden glitter carefully encrusted in the swirls. The top is large and fluffy, with big curls, and it's, well, wild. His eyes are hidden behind big, black framed glasses, and his face is thin and long. He looks like a man who laughs a lot and belongs here, if the tailored trousers, shining shoes, and waistcoat are anything to go by. Hell, he even has a bow tie on.

I look down at myself and at the others with a cringe, knowing we are about to get thrown out. You can take us freaks out of the circus, but you can't take the circus out of the freaks. Our clothes are bright and in your face, daring you to question what and who we are. They mark us a different, something we usually like.

The man is muttering to himself before he glances up and spots us, freezing before bursting into action. He slides around the counter and heads our way while I step back, expecting to be thrown out. His eyes are open wide and a smile splits his face, lighting up his brown eyes. I frown in confusion, not expecting him to react to our presence this way.

"Welcome, welcome, pleased to meet you! I'm Gregor of Gregoria's Tailoring, obviously. What can I seam you?" He laughs at his joke and I raise my eyebrows, looking at the others to see them with the same unsure expression.

"Er, hi?" I offer, when no one else speaks.

His smile swings my way and he checks out my outfit and gasps. "Oh my, those colours are marvellous!" He grabs me and the others quickly move to stop him, but all he does is spin me around, humming and harring.

"I love it. The gold, the black. Oh my, your hair is marvellous!" he gushes, touching the ends, his eyes bright. I side-eye the guys for help, but they just grin. Traitors.

"You would look amazing in that dress. Yes, you would, yes. It was made for you. I knew it was, I saw it. Come, come!" he shouts, grabbing my hand and pulling me after him. I look over my shoulder with a pleading look and the others follow us with a laugh as Gregor leads us through the curtain to the back. I thought there'd be storage back here, but I'm surprised when it opens up into a windowless room. Bright lights hang from the ceiling, somehow not making it feel closed in, and there's a dressing room tucked in the corner. Along the opposite wall is a mannequin and a workbench, and in the middle of the room is a white, circular pedestal. If a person were to stand on the platform, they'd be able to see themselves from all angles in the mirrors placed around the room.

He lets go of my hands and rushes over to his work bench, which is piled so high I'm not sure how he finds anything, but he seems to know exactly where to go. When he runs his hands above the garments, he tilts his head in concentration before his hand stops above a pile.

"Yes, yes, for you. It was you, I knew it!" he shouts, digging through the pile.

I look over at the guys and my eyes are drawn to Nixon. He always seems to have some sort of sixth sense about things, and I trust his intuition. So when he nods and gives me a reassuring smile, some of my nerves settle. We watch the man rush around the room as things pile up in his arms, before he comes to a stop in front of me. His arms are full of various material and he has a wide grin on his face.

"Yes, come on then!" he says impatiently, reaching out to grab my hand and nearly dropping everything he's holding. "Corner." He nods at the dressing room and when I don't move, he sighs. "You're from Cinders, I've seen you. You're different, like me. These are for you, please," he adds, and I stiffen.

"You've seen me? How do you know where I am from?" I ask, stepping back, but I hit a hard chest. I crane my neck and look back to see Nixon staring hard at the man. After a moment, he glances down at me, his face softening.

"Trust him." He nods once again.

Okay then. I slowly walk over to the dressing room and slip behind the curtain, spotting a sofa and some more mirrors with bright lights. He follows me in, shutting the curtain behind him before dropping the armful onto the sofa with a grunt.

With a small smile, he steps back. "You will need them, I've *seen* it. You can't tell anyone I have seen it though," he states seriously.

I nod before walking over and picking up what looks like a silver bracelet. "I won't. You are like us? A freak?" I whisper.

"Eh, freak, wonder, miracle, whatever you want to call it. They don't know, but sometimes I see things. I saw you, Rhea from Cinders, and I knew you would come here on this day. I knew you would need these things, but I don't know what for. I'm sorry, all I know is that if you don't have these, you will suffer." He shrugs, his smile turning into a frown as his eyes go distant. "Yes, suffer. You must take them, you are our future. Save us," he whispers, before turning and leaving, pulling the curtain shut behind him.

I blow out a breath and run my fingers over the silver bracelet. It's heavy, and while I play around with the clasp, trying to figure out what's so special about it, I press down on some form of button. It does nothing, so I set it down for now, reminding myself to ask Gregor about it.

On top of the pile are what appears to be leather braces for my arms. I set them aside after brushing my fingers over the smooth leather. Under that is a matching scabbard for what looks like a sword or a knife. I put that to the side as well, revealing a pile of black material underneath.

I grab it and hold it up to the light. The material floats down and I realise it's a dress. It's not too long, it'll probably hang down just past my knees. The bodice has a sweetheart neckline and tucks in at the waist before flaring out. But the most amazing thing about it are the feathers. They're black, like the darkest night. They're sewn on to the dress from bust to end, getting larger the lower you go and giving it an almost fluid look. I stroke my hand across the soft feathers and gasp when one lifts up, revealing bright yellow fabric underneath.

Laying the dress down gently, I trail my hand upwards and watch as red, orange, and yellow are all revealed underneath like a fire burning through the feathers.

"For the fire that burns in you," Gregor interrupts from behind me, and I whirl around.

He nods at the dress. "One of my best pieces. Sometimes, the most beautiful things hide in plain sight."

"It's amazing," I say in awe.

"Did you try on the bracelet?" he inquires, blinking hard before rushing in and grabbing it.

I hold out my hand and he slips it on, locking it in place, and I watch in amazement as it tightens to my wrist. I try to get it off, but it won't budge.

"Intention is everything. I can create wonders and you can do so much more. When you no longer need it, just think those words, but be careful because once off, it won't work again," he explains.

"What does it do?" I ask.

"It helps magnify and control what you naturally have," he whispers, and then his eyes gloss over.

"You should go now, it's almost time," he says, before disappearing behind the curtain. I grab everything else and walk outside the changing room, finding Gregor waiting. He takes the items and places them into a bag before handing it to me and meeting my eyes.

"Everything happens for a reason. We are made because we are needed. Remember your strength, Rhea from Cinders, I fear you will need it," he warns softly, before hustling us all out.

I blink when we get outside onto the stone steps, feeling like I just broke a spell. It was a crazy whirlwind in there, but his words stick with me even as we head back to camp.

MY FEELINGS ARE all mixed up after exploring the city this morning. There is so much beauty there, but it feels like if you look too hard, something is waiting to jump out. I just can't quite see it yet, so when the tents of home come into view, I sigh, relieved, and cuddle closer to Jesse, finally relaxing.

Alcide is waiting for us at the entrance to the camp.

"Have a good time?" he asks, looking at the bags we have.

"I liked the shops," I offer with a smile. I want to tell him about seeing the boy again, but I feel now isn't the time.

"Are we rehearsing today?" I inquire.

"No," Alcide answers, looking around. "We aren't leaving either, not yet. Stay close to each other though. You can have the afternoon off, I have some digging to do," he replies before striding away, moving through the camp with his head held high and his shoulders tight. He seems to be pulling away, apart from our moment this morning, ever since his fight with Blain yesterday.

I head to my tent silently, and for some reason I feel the need not to unpack, so I place the bag the tailor gave me at the foot of my bed. I leave everything he gave me in the bag except for the bracelet, which is still clasped firmly around my wrist.

"What do you want to do for the rest of the day?" Jesse asks behind me, and when I look over my shoulder, I see him wiggling his eyebrows, which makes me laugh.

I narrow my eyes as he comes towards me and I squeal when he grabs me and tosses me on the bed, covering my body with his while he tickles me.

"Harpy, did you—" Blain's words cut off, and Jesse and I freeze on the bed, glancing over at him.

"May we help you?" Jesse asks formally, as if he isn't pressing me down on the bed.

"I was going to spank and fuck that mouth out of Harpy." Blain shrugs, making me draw in a breath. My pussy pulses as heat races through me at his dirty words.

"Sounds like a plan." Jesse grins as they share a smug look before they both turn to me.

"You-I—" I sputter, even as I try to clench my thighs around Jesse, not denying how much I love the idea. I discovered my love for having more than one man during our Christmas break, and I have been dying to repeat it again, but we have been so busy...

I can't help but crave the picture they are painting, and I swallow hard, grinning back. "Well, you going to put your dick where your words are?" I joke.

Jesse turns back to me, his hands skimming up the side of my waist, teasing a path along my belly and up between my breasts before he cups my chin and brings my face to his, kissing me softly. I gasp and he sweeps his tongue into my mouth, tangling with mine as his hands cup my breasts through my clothing, squeezing hard enough to have me arching up into his touch.

Another hand weaves into my hair, yanking my mouth from Jesse and craning my neck back until I see a grinning Blain smirking down at me. He kneels down and kisses me hard, creating that special blend of pleasure and pain he doles out, as his tongue lashes me, and his grip hardens on my hair even as his lips are soft and sure.

Jesse doesn't seem to mind. He kisses down my neck, across my collarbone, and pulls down my shirt, groaning when he discovers I haven't been wearing a bra all day.

"Fuck, Firecracker."

His big hands cup my breasts as Blain and I fight for control, my neck straining. I groan into his mouth when Jesse flicks and twists my nipples before laving them with his tongue. Reaching down blindly, I grab his springy hair and pull him to me. He grins against my skin, peppering soft kisses against me, creating a contrast so opposite to Blain's rough treatment that I mewl, wrapping my legs around Jesse's waist. He gives into my tugging and pulls my nipple into his mouth, sucking hard and making me moan into Blain's mouth. He pulls away, his dark eyes watching me with desire as he smiles lazily, running his sharp nails down my throat.

"Don't move, Harpy, unless you want blood on your sheets," he teases, and I freeze, narrowing my eyes as I feel a blade drag against my skin softly, making me shiver. He smirks down at me. "Seems Harpy likes my blades along her skin," he tells Jesse, who hums with my nipple still in his mouth before popping it out with a wet sound and moving to the other.

I glance down, watching Blain slice through my top in one smooth move, and yanking it away from my body, leaving me bare apart from my trousers. "Blain," I grumble, and he traces the knife slowly across my neck, up over my cheek, and stops with the cold metal against my lips.

"Yes, Harpy? Problem?" he asks.

He keeps the blade there, both of us just staring at each other as Jesse moves down my body, pushing my trousers down as he goes. He quickly strips them off my feet and my panties go next until I'm a flushed, needy mess spread out between them.

"How about a little competition, Harpy?" Blain grins.

"What's that?" I mumble, trying not to cut myself on the blade.

"Jesse is going to play with your pretty little pussy and you are going to suck my fat cock. Whoever comes first doesn't get to come again for the rest of the night," he suggests.

"Deal." I narrow my eyes on him. Our play always goes dark, but I love pushing Blain and I love the way he pushes me. He doesn't flinch at having the other man here, though we have done it before. Blain demands my attention, pushing me to unravel with their touches. He takes control and I crave that with him, because I trust him implicitly.

He runs the knife back down to my throat, grazing my skin and leaving pink lines behind that have me panting. I lock my eyes on him and lean up for a kiss, showing my trust. He snatches the blade away quickly and growls as I kiss him gently. "Oh, it's on, Blainy," I purr.

"On your knees then, Harpy," he orders.

Jesse grabs my hips and flips me before yanking me back, so I am on all fours, my pussy on display for him. He strokes down my already wet lips, humming again. "Oh, I reckon you might win here, Blain, she is already wet," Jesse jokes. He rubs my clit, making me jerk back and push against his fingers, but he pulls them away with a laugh and kisses my ass. "Not yet, Firecracker, I want you to win," he whispers against my skin and I grin, staring up at Blain.

Jesse was my first. We learned together and he knows my body better than anyone. He knows exactly where to touch, where to kiss, and he worships me. Both of us lost ourselves in just exploring and learning each other, so I have no doubt if he wanted Blain to win, he would.

He rubs my ass softly, massaging as I watch Blain flick open the button of his trousers and yank down the zipper, the sound loud in my quiet tent. He widens his legs, pulling out his already hard cock, the tip wet, making me lick my lips and him groan.

He watches me as he casually pumps himself before pressing the tip to my lips. "Open up, Harpy. I told you I would fuck that mouth," he orders, and I dart my tongue out, licking away the salty drop on the tip and he growls.

He grips my hair and tugs me closer until his cock presses against my lips. "Open the fuck up," he demands.

Teasing him is fun, so I gently blow my breath over the head of his cock and he shivers, his hand tightening in my hair just as Jesse runs his fingers down my pussy again, making me gasp. Blain takes that opportunity to push into my mouth, forcing me to swallow his hard length.

Humming, I scrape my teeth over his cock and he groans, thrusting all the way in. I have to breathe deeply through my nose and try not to gag when he hits the back of my throat. Pulling out of my mouth slowly, he pushes back in, finding his rhythm as I hold on to his hips.

Jesse lightly runs his finger along my pussy, circling my clit before dipping inside and doing it all again. Whimpering in frustration, I push back onto his hands, needing more.

I feel his hot breath on my pussy a moment before he licks a long line across me, making me cry out around Blain's cock. He laps around my clit, slowly pushing two fingers inside of me and leaving them there as he licks me. Heat races through my body as I push back against his face, riding it as I suck Blain desperately. I know it won't be long before Jesse has me coming on his talented tongue.

He pulls his fingers out and thrusts them back in, curling them inside me and hitting a spot that makes me groan around Blain's length, and dig my nails into Blain's hips.

Jessie keeps up his brutal pace, pushing me steadily higher and higher. His fingers and tongue give me just enough to have me rocking back and craving more, even as Blain fucks my mouth harder with each thrust, until he is pushing me back onto Jesse's fingers and tongue. Jesse grabs my hips to stop my movements, holding on until I'm trapped between them, unable to even scream as I feel my orgasm just out of reach.

I know I need to win this bet, so I draw on my powers. I have been practicing more and more, but I've never tried it during sex. There's no better time than now. I concentrate on my mouth, making it heat up so it's warmer around Blain's cock.

His thrusts stutter and he cries out, his hands tangling in my hair. "Fuck, Harpy, what the hell is that?"

Trying something else, I focus on mimicking Fluffy's purr. My voice box changes and now I'm purring around his cock.

"Oh fuck, fuck, fuck," Blain grunts, his hips jerking with his desperate thrusts.

"Struggling there?" Jessie jokes and I purr harder, the vibrations moving through my body. "Oh, good one, Firecracker!" He laughs, obviously feeling it.

Releasing one hand from Blain's hip, I reach down and cup his balls, squeezing gently and he yells, his cock exploding in my mouth and forcing me to swallow him. I swallow him down, using my hand to pull him out of my mouth, and slowly licking it clean before I grin up at him.

He falls to his knees, his eyes dazed and his breathing laboured as he grips the bed next to my head. "I win," I tease, kissing him gently.

He mumbles something, shaking his head before he glares at me. "Not fair." He pouts and I laugh.

"You used yours first." I wink and then gasp when Jesse flips me over and drags my ass along the bed until it meets his hips. My legs wrap around his waist again as he leans over me with a satisfied grin.

"Guess that means you're all mine, Firecracker." He kisses me, no doubt tasting Blain in my mouth, but he doesn't seem to mind.

Feeling mean, I grip his hips and flip us, so I am hovering on top of him, keeping my pussy away from his hard cock. I didn't even see him strip, but he's naked beneath me, his cock hard and reaching towards me. He's leaner than the others, but no less impressive and oh so fucking sexy as he grins up at me. His eyes sparkle and his longer hair is spread across my bed as he reaches up and grips my hips, always letting me do whatever I want to him.

I look up at Blain and wink as I reach down and circle Jesse's cock, jerking him a few times and making him cry out and push into my touch. I rub it along my wet pussy before pausing at my entrance.

He's panting now, staring up at me with crazed eyes, his jaw tight as he watches me, never forcing me, just letting me set the pace. Keeping my eyes on his, I slowly seat myself on him, working myself down his thick, hard length. Biting down on my lip, I hold in my groan until he's fully inside me, filling me up and stretching me. Gasping, I throw my head back, my hands landing on his stomach as I struggle not to move. My orgasm rushes back through my body and is heading towards me like a freight train.

Starting to move, I dig my nails into his stomach as he rolls his hips under me, matching my rhythm. I lift myself up and down, riding him hard and fast, chasing my release. He reaches up and grips my swaying breasts, flicking my nipples before he traces down my clenching stomach and rubs my clit, sending me careening over the edge.

I scream, my pussy clamping down on his cock as I shake above him, coming so hard I see stars. Breathing heavily, I open my eyes and look down at him to see him grinning.

"My turn." He winks and I yelp as he flips us so I am on the bottom again, his cock still buried deep inside me, and then he starts to move.

I grip onto the edge of the bed above my head as he thrusts deep and hard, his pace speeding up until he's hammering into me, forcing me back up over that edge until I am chasing another release. I watch the way his body moves, loving it, reminding me of when he dances or performs—it's so silky and sexy as hell. His hips roll with each move-ment, his chest muscles clenching and his arms not even straining as he holds himself above me.

Hands cover mine, turning them over and weaving our fingers together, keeping them pressed to the mattress. I look up into a grin-ning Blain's face as he watches Jesse fuck me. I don't even realise little noises are leaving my throat until he silences them with a hard kiss.

"So fucking sexy, Harpy. Is he buried in you deep? Is your sweet little pussy clamping down on him?" he asks, pulling away and stroking my bottom lip with his thumb.

Jesse's even thrusts stutter and he starts to fuck me for real. No finesse or timely thrusts, just pure and utter need as he rams into me again and again, moving me up the bed with the power of his thrusts.

"Fuck, she's so tight," Jesse cries out, his hand gripping my hip, no doubt leaving bruises. The pain mixes with pleasure as Blain kisses down my neck to my breasts, teasing my nipples. They both play my body like they are performing.

"You should feel her ass, man, it's like a vice. I came so hard I couldn't walk for hours," Blain admits, licking my nipple as I arch into him and lift my hips to meet Jesse's thrusts.

Jesse cries out again, his hand moving between us and flicking my clit and, before I know it, I'm coming again, screaming into the night as he fills me once more before stilling. He groans above me, holding me still as he fills me with his come before collapsing onto my chest. He kisses over my heart softly before moving to the side slightly, both of us groaning as he pulls out. Blain lets go of my hands before climbing up on the bed next to me.

My eyes are starting to close, with a sleepy, satisfied smile on my face as I turn and bury my face in Jesse's arm. Blain curls around my back, keeping me warm. "Fucking perfect, Harpy," he whispers, and my heart constricts at his soft words.

I open my eyes, blinking away sudden tears, and stare into Jesse's face from inches away, his expression full of love as he watches me.

"I love you, Firecracker," Jesse whispers, brushing my hair back from my face. His face is serious, but there's a hint of worry, of nervousness, in his eyes.

"I love you too," I whisper back, kissing his fingers as his smile returns and his eyes light up. He snuggles closer to me, pulling my leg over his.

Blain grumbles and kisses my shoulder. He wraps his arm around my waist and yanks me back into his body, pressing his cock against my ass. "Love you too, Harpy," he murmurs sleepily, kissing my shoulder again before burying his face in my hair.

I FALL asleep in their arms, their bodies wrapped around me like a giant puppy pile. A feeling of safety blooms in my chest, but I can't ignore the darkness gathering around us. I know Alcide is out there… watching, waiting for something to happen. The thought sends a nervous flutter through my chest, even as sleep claims me.

Chapter Five

I wake up long before the others and try not to disturb them as I climb out of the puppy pile, smiling as I look down on my guys. Pulling on my loose training clothing, I quietly leave the tent, heading towards the animal tent, knowing I need to do this sooner rather than later. I push through the flap and smile as Sid runs up to me, winding between my legs, almost tripping me up as I try to get farther into the tent.

Laughing, I lean down and run my fingers through his short fur. "Morning, buddy, I missed you too."

A choked sounding growl has me raising an eyebrow and looking for the sound. I find Fluffy glaring at the cat winding through my legs for attention. I have to stifle the giggle that threatens to leave my lips, knowing Fluffy would sulk if I laughed at him.

"It's okay, big guy! I missed you too!" I coo as I walk towards him. "Oof—" I exclaim, getting the air knocked out of me as he butts my stomach with his large head, pushing at me until I stroke him. I grin as I rub his head, his purr rumbling through my whole body. A trumpeting noise, followed by loud, stomping footsteps lets me know Tiny is on his way over to see me, along with various other animals.

I eventually manage to untangle myself from the onslaught of animal greetings with the promise I would return later to play with them. Dusting myself off, I look around for the reason I came here, a slight smile on my face as I notice two faces peeking at me from behind a hay bale.

"Rumples, Bubbles, come on, come see me," I call, walking closer to where they are hiding. "Come on, guys, you did exactly as planned, it was brilliant! If I didn't know you, I would have thought you *were* attacking me. Great acting!" I exclaim, sitting down on the other side of the bale of hay, smiling as Rumple sticks he head out to look at me. "I'm sorry I didn't come and see you yesterday, it was a bit crazy."

Some might think I'm mad for the way I talk to the animals, but our animals are way more than *just* animals. They have all been altered, just like we have been, to the point where they understand me. Rumple and Bubbles slither out from behind the hay bales, his heads drooping in shame as they make their way over to me.

"Oh, come now, don't look so sad!" I hold out my hand, showing them I'm not afraid of them. Rex and I had worked really closely with the snake and it had taken a lot of training to make him understand that the biting was necessary for the show, but we had never practiced that part. There was always a risk that my body wouldn't be immune to Rumple's venom, but my powers hadn't failed me so far, so there was no reason to think that they might now.

Slithering closer, Rumple pushes his head into my hand, enjoying the attention and forgiveness, but his other head, Bubbles, avoids my gaze.

"Bubbles," I call softly, waiting for him to meet my eyes. Bubbles was the more difficult of the snake's personalities to win over, but really he is a big softy. "You did exactly as you were supposed to, we couldn't have done it without you." He blinks once, as if considering what I'm saying. "You're the star of the show really," I conclude, smiling as he pushes his head into my waiting hand, their body wiggling in happiness as I stroke them.

I spend a little longer in the animal tent, making sure to cuddle each of them before I exit with a smile, always feeling better after spending time with them. The early morning chill has burned off now, the sun high in the sky as I walk through the camp. The hustle and bustle of circus life sounds around me as people get started for the day.

Smiling at some of the crew as they walk past me, I think back over the last year with the circus and how much my life has changed since joining them. Rounding one of the communal tents, my smile widens as I see the reasons behind the change.

Rex is standing by the cooking pot, helping the cook get breakfast ready, while Jessie is juggling the bowls with a scowling Blain telling him to knock it off. Nixon is standing to the side of the cooking area, watching with his arms crossed, our ever-present protector, as Alcide sits on a bench, nursing a mug of coffee.

Nixon sees me first, a rare smile pulling at his handsome face. "Rhea." His call causes a chain reaction. Everyone looks at him then over to me, smiles lighting their faces. Nixon doesn't speak often, but when he does, we have learned to pay attention since he seems to *know* things. Walking over, I wrap my arms around his waist, my head coming to rest on his chest as he hums in happiness, his large arms cradling me against him.

"Morning." Glancing up, I see Nixon's eyes shining with unspoken words as he leans down and presses a small kiss to my nose. I laugh and untangle myself from my gentle giant before walking over to greet the rest of the guys. Everyone seems to be in a jovial mood this morning after last night's show. Smiling and joking as they prepare breakfast. Even Blain has a smirk in place as he scolds Jessie. Helping myself to a bowl of porridge, I make my way over to the bench where Alcide sits, his gaze on me as I move closer and I rethink my earlier thought—*almost* everyone seems happy today.

"You okay?" I ask quietly, as I sit at the table next to him, facing out across the cooking area. "The show went really well the other day," I comment, when he doesn't answer my first question, trying to fill the silence. I feel Alcide's attention back on me and glance across to see his frown.

"Yes, that's what I'm worried about." His voice is quiet, meant only for my ears.

Frowning, I tilt my head, not understanding his concern. "What do you mean?" Leaning closer, I place my hand on his, resting it on the table.

"Why did they invite us here? Our circus has travelled past here before, but they have never shown any interest. Now, you join us and they are suddenly 'inviting' us to come perform." His words are frustrated, and he pulls his hand from mine, before running it through his hair as he lets out a pent-up breath. "And what was with all of the shared looks between them and making us jump through hoops before we could perform? I feel like they are testing us."

"Testing us for what?" I question, trying to understand his frustrations.

"I don't know." His voice is quiet, lost.

We sit in silence, picking at our breakfasts, but I don't think either of us have much of an appetite. Alcide's words run through my head, turning me off from my food.

Once everyone is done, we head into the big top to rehearse and train. Walking into the big tent, I look up at the towering peaks, the red and white of the fabric bright and familiar, but I can't shake the feeling of unease that seems to follow me like a shadow. This place has always felt safe to me, even though we do dangerous acts, it's been my home, so why do I feel this way? Perhaps it's being so close to this city with its scheming Masters.

Shaking off the feeling, I begin to warm up with the others, working through a series of stretches and exercises until my muscles are aching and a fine layer of sweat covers my skin.

"Something big is coming." Nixon's words cut through the tent, making all of us freeze. The words are sent with such conviction that I have no doubt this is Nixon's gift warning us. We all share a look before turning to Alcide, our ringmaster, since he calls the shots. I see that flash of uncertainty in his eyes for a second before he straightens his posture, standing tall as he looks directly at me.

"Let's not panic. This could be something good?" Alcide inquires, glancing over at Nixon to see if he has any more words of wisdom for us, but the big guy just shrugs, back to his silent self. Alcide nods as he paces the tent, turning his attention to the rest of us as he walks. "Either way, we need to be prepared. I need everyone to focus on their gifts today, you need to be able to protect yourselves if necessary.

Those are our strongest weapons in case we are attacked, so we need to make the most of it, make sure we are at our strongest." There is a chorus of agreement from the guys as we break up and start to train. We need to be alert, we have gotten too comfortable over the last couple of months. If there is anything I have learned since I joined the circus, it is that I will do anything to protect my new family, I just hope it doesn't come to that.

Jessie smiles as he jaunts over to me, his usual happy-go-lucky self. Anyone who doesn't know him would think what we learned hasn't bothered him at all, but I can tell from the tightness of his smile that he's worried.

"Ready to train?" he asks as he throws his arm around my shoulders, pulling me into his chest for a hug, extracting a giggle from me, which I'm sure is what he was after in the first place. Jessie is the kind of guy who will do almost anything to make others happy, including playing the fool.

Extracting myself from his arms with a smile, I walk over to our training mats. "What did you want to work on today?" When Jessie and I train together we usually work on our acrobatics and gymnastic acts. While I may have the power to adapt and protect myself, it does not make me any more flexible or improve my balance, no, these acts take hours and hours of practice and working out to keep our bodies in shape, especially as we keep making our routines more and more difficult. A thought comes to me and I feel the grin spread across my lips.

"Why don't we try your ice?" I suggest, and watch in confusion as his hand comes up to rub the back of his neck sheepishly.

During the last winter months, we learned about a celebration they did pre-war called Christmas from an old magazine we found during our exploration of a derelict building. While we were creating our own traditions as a family, Jessie discovered a new aspect of his powers—ice. Since we moved on from that town and headed farther south, he hasn't tried to use his ice powers again, preferring to use his flames for our shows.

"Or we could try something else?" I reply, unsure where his reluctance to use these powers has come from. He has never said as much, but I think it frightens him to have this power that he knows nothing about.

"Just...I nearly hurt you with it before..." He hesitates with a flash of fear in his eyes, and I realise what has been holding him back. I had been practicing a new act where I was submerged in a tank of water, which Jessie had accidentally frozen with me still inside. I can still remember the terror that ran through me as I felt the water freeze and lock me in place.

"Jessie..." My voice is soft as I take a step towards him, gently putting a hand on his arm until he meets my eyes. "It was an accident, I'm okay, I'm still here. If you learned to control it, nothing like that will happen again, I promise."

I can see he isn't sure, but eventually he nods, and I pull him farther onto the mats. We spend the next couple of hours with him focusing on creating ice. It takes some work and encouragement, the others taking it in turns to help out, but when Jessie feels more in control of his ice powers, I call everyone over.

"Show them what you can do." I feel like a little girl again. Pride and excitement runs through me from what he has achieved in a few short hours. Taking on a wider stance, he clicks his left hand and flames appear in his palm, harmlessly licking against his fingers, before he turns his focus on his right. Frowning in concentration, he takes a deep breath as he silently stares at his hand.

"What are we waiting for?" Blaine sneers, acting like we are wasting his time, but I can see the glint of interest in his eyes.

"You will see." Whispering, I keep my eyes locked on Jessie, and my patience is rewarded as his palm suddenly freezes over, seeming not only to produce the ice, but to *become* it. Looking up at me in excitement, his smile is huge as he manages to maintain both fire *and* ice at the same time. He still has a long way to go, nowhere near mastering his new gift, but he has made a huge step in learning to control his gift rather than let it control him.

For the rest of the session, we go through our acts, pushing our gifts as far as they go until we are panting, and my muscles feel like they are going to give way.

"Rhea, do that flip again, focus on your skin as you do it," Alcide calls out. I want to protest, but when I glance across, I see that worried look in his eyes again and decide not to push it. I'm in my heavier stone form and moving is much harder, so performing flips is tricky. My concentration often wavers and my skin flickers back to normal. This would be fine, but during this act Blaine is throwing knives at me, so I can't risk that happening. Taking up my position, I draw in a deep breath, allowing my body to change, feeling the heaviness of the stone weighing down my limbs as Blaine lines up, a knife appearing in his hand like magic. I get no warning before he throws it, trusting my instincts to keep me safe as the blade blurs through the air, moving too fast for my eyes to track.

The knife misses me by less than an inch, but trying to move this fast in my stone form causes me to misjudge my landing, and I fall to the ground, the sound much louder thanks to my stone body.

"Rhea! Are you okay?" the guys call out as Rex jogs towards me.

Winded, I lay on my back and my body releases the stone form, my breath panting from my chest as I let out a little chuckle. "I guess I need to work on my landing."

Crouching down by my side, Rex runs his eyes over my body, checking for any signs of injury. "You okay, Wild Cat?" Holding out his hand, I reach forward to accept his offer to help me up, but the sun glints against something and catches my eye. Frowning, I look for what caught my attention. I use Rex's hand to stand up before walking towards the corner of the tent, tilting my head in different directions. I can hear the guys behind me, wondering what I'm doing, but I pay them no attention. Something in my gut telling me this is important.

There. Right on the top of one of the struts holding up tent is something glinting, like glass.

"Guys, what's that?" A hush follows my words before they come and join me, looking up at where I'm pointing. I've never seen anything like it, something like a circle of glass contained in some metal container, but I know for certain that it's not part of the tent. I've helped put it up enough times to know. The silence continues and I pull my gaze away to look at the guys, but my attention gets stuck on Alcide. His face is grave as he looks at the object.

"It's a camera, they have been watching us." The temperature in the tent seems to drop about five degrees at his words, all of us sharing looks at this statement. I don't know what a camera is, we didn't have them in Cinders, but I can tell from everyone's reactions that this is bad. "No more practice, no one is to use their powers. We keep our heads down, and in the morning, we get out of here," he commands, before storming out and leaving the rest of us to stand awkwardly in the practice tent. What do we do now?

"Come on, Wild Cat, it's time for dinner anyway." Rex tries to keep his tone light, but I can tell he's worried, we all are, and as I am led away, I can't help but keep looking up at the camera and wonder why such a small object could cause us so much trouble. There is no way that this could hurt us, right?

Chapter Six

Light pierces my eyes as I try to peel them open, they feel heavy and uncooperative, like that time Lil convinced me to drink too much. Raising my hand, I attempt to protect them as I wake up, fighting against the sleep that claimed me. I don't even remember coming back to my tent last night, my last memories are of the dinner we shared together. Why is it so bright in my tent? Did I leave the entrance flaps open? My head is pounding and as I sit up, the world seems to spin around me. A groan slips from my lips as I try to balance myself. I've never felt so weak or disoriented before.

Why do I feel so rough? Am I coming down with something? I've never been sick before, thanks to my power, is this what it feels like? I finally manage to open my eyes against the onslaught of bright light and frown at what I see, not understanding. The hard dirt ground under me bites into my skin, causing me to wince as I move and gravel and stones cut me. Shit, that hurts, why isn't my body protecting me? Even from small pains like this, it should. Why am I on the floor, did I fall from bed in my sleep? Looking around again, a gasp escapes my cracked, sore lips.

This is not my tent. Dread fills me as I push up onto shaking legs as I take in the scene before me, unable to believe what I am seeing. We appear to be in a large, circular cage, roughly the same size as our circus ring that we perform in. Sand and dirt fills the hard packed ground and I flinch when I spot dried blood splattered about, wondering what poor soul it has come from. I seem to be against the edge of the cage, feeling cold, metal bars at my back as I stare into the circle.

Bodies litter the cage and it takes me a moment to realise that they are the bodies of my guys. A strangled cry leaves my lips as I hurry to the nearest person who happens to be Rex. He's lying on his back, his face slack and pale, with none of his usual colouring or cheer evident. That's what scares me the most.

Dropping to my knees, I grab his shoulders and shake him, desperate to wake him. He can't be dead, he just can't. "Rex! Wake up! Please!" I cry, sobbing with relief as he groans, bringing a hand to his eyes, and I finally notice the rise and fall of his chest, but it's faint.

"Rhea? What's wrong? What's going on?" His voice is rough and confused as he tries to sit up, but his body doesn't seem to want to.

"Oh, gods. I thought you were dead." My words end on a sob. *Come on, Rhea, get it together*. Taking a deep breath, I look around again, seeing the others beginning to stir from where they have been placed around the cage. *Placed.*

Now that the initial shock has worn off, I gaze around us again with a frown, seeing where each of us lies. Each member of my family has been positioned around the cage in equal distance from the other, like playing pieces on a board. It reminds me of the game of chess Alcide played with Rex while we were travelling. Everything is in perfect position, players ready to be moved like puppets. Is that what we are...is that what we are doing here?

My eyes catch on Alcide's to see him staring out of the cage, a narrow-eyed look on his face, but it's the fear that makes me shiver. Alcide fears nothing. Following his gaze, I stop when I notice the men watching from outside the cage, waiting for us.

"Rhea," a voice calls, a familiar voice. I get to my feet slowly, shielding a still struggling Rex with my body. Alcide wobbles over and joins me, his body straightening and none of the weakness I know he must be feeling showing. Together, we walk to the bars of the cage, and I realise that they have been watching us this whole time. The Masters, the three men I met before, plus another two I have never seen. They are sitting just behind the bars in gilded seats with trays of food next to goblets full of wine next to them. Anger lines my stomach as we reach the bars, but I try to keep my face blank.

"So nice of you to join us," Mr. Lennon jokes, sitting forward while watching us with barely disguised glee as the rest of my family circles around us.

"Glad we could make it. The invite must've come very late," I growl back, but then frown as I realise something, anger is coursing through me...why aren't my powers?

"Alcide," I hiss, as he glares at the men. "Alcide," I say louder, before turning to the others. "Something is wrong, can anyone reach their powers?" I ask, truly scared as I reach deep inside and find the place where my adaptability usually comes from...it's empty, like a part of me has been taken away.

"No," Blain gasps, recoiling, his face horrified as he looks down at his hands.

"Me either," Jessie whispers.

"Ah, sorry to interrupt, but I'm afraid we couldn't let you use those pesky little powers of yours to hurt us. We have to take precautions of course. You will notice your new jewellery, we took the liberty of placing it on you while you were asleep," he sneers.

Looking down, I spot the two, brown metal shackles covering both wrists...how did I not notice them before? The plain metal bands are about two inches wide and completely encompass my wrists. I pull at the bands, trying to see if there are any weak points in the metal, but stop when pain zips through my wrist, as if I've been stung. I can't even see any seam in the metal, I have no idea how they got them on us. If I concentrate hard enough, I can almost feel the sucking edge to them, like they are draining my powers away. Feeling sick, I look back up at the Masters.

"You drugged us, took us from our home, and took away our powers. Why? You invited us here!" I spit, enraged that they would trick us like this. Why did we ignore Alcide's bad feelings about coming to the city? We should have left the moment Nixon said something big was coming, we should know better than to ignore his *feeling*.

"Yes we did, my dear. You see, the tales of the traveling freaks had spread even to our small corner of the world. I had to see if it was true. We here in The Last Stop don't hurt freaks, no, we do much better. We let them flourish, we use their unique capabilities for the entertainment and betterment of our society. Out there, you are nothing, not even wanted by the world, shunned and hunted. Here, you have a chance at life, you have meals and a bed to sleep in." He nods, his speech sounding rehearsed, but the scary thing is he actually believes this, I can hear the sincerity in his words and the light shining in his eyes tells me that he believes he is doing a good thing. He truly believes he is helping us, all the while sneering the word freak.

"If you help people by drugging them and throwing them in a cell, then I hate to see what you do to your enemies," Blain drawls, rubbing at his wrists where his daggers usually appear from, and I know he is envisioning what he would do with them if his powers weren't being held back by the shackles.

"Yes, well, let's hope you never find out," one of the new men comments, his haughty attitude telling me all I need to know about him. He believes we are beneath him, nothing more than trash, and that we should be grateful for this *opportunity* they are offering us.

"You still haven't answered the question. Why are we here?" Alcide demands, his voice hard, but I notice that without his powers, he sounds different. His voice is somehow weaker, nothing like the confident Alcide that I have come to know and love.

"Isn't it obvious?" Blain retorts, as he pushes past us to the bars, gripping them as he stares at the Masters. "They mean for us to fight for their entertainment. Using our powers against each other. I've heard the rumours, but I thought they were just that, rumours." He spits the last word, his face contorted in fury and I gasp, stepping up next to him.

"We will never fight for you, we are a family, we would never hurt each other," I yell.

"We'll see, everyone says that at first. It takes a little...persuading...but everyone has a price, Rhea, what's yours? The life of your men, your family, how about the life of the animals you love so dearly. Or maybe it's simpler...your life?"

The first man that spoke, Master Lennon, who he truly believes he is helping us, is looking flustered as if the threatening talk is upsetting him.

"Of course, you won't...fight against your family to start with, you will build up to that. You might never even fight against them. It all depends on the draw on the day! Besides, we don't like to call it that, no, you are doing a service. You will be doing your job, you will have a job at least once a week," he explains with a smile.

"Right... our *job*." Jessie catches on, walking closer to the bars, his tone light as he questions the Masters. "And how exactly do these *jobs* work? How do we leave here?"

The Masters share an amused glance, a couple of them even laughing. "Oh, I always find it funny when they ask that," one of them comments to the other. "You won't. This is your life now, so you better get used to it. We have some who think they can escape, who reject their place in this society and fight against us, but they quickly learn their place. Do your job properly, follow the rules, and things will be better for you. You could even be rewarded. Those who think they are better than us, who reject our... *kindness,* always suffer for it in the long run." The cold eyes of the Masters bore into me and I don't bother to hide the shudder that runs through me at their words. Their minds are warped. They have actually convinced themselves we are nothing but...but slaves or toys to them. They believe they are helping us. "Don't be like them." I feel like this last part is being aimed at me and I take a small step back, only to walk into a wall of muscle. Looking up sharply, I see that Nixon is standing protectively behind me, his arms wrapping around me, claiming me as his. However, his narrowed gaze stays on the Masters, almost daring them to try and take me from him.

I can feel the tension rising and know I need to try and diffuse the situation before Nixon triggers and they step in. I know they aren't afraid to hurt us, they don't see us as human. They see us as *theirs*, theirs to do what they please with, and they won't hesitate to teach us that.

"What happens now?" I ask, interrupting the strain I can feel building between my family and them.

"Well, we test your powers first, then we group you. From there you will begin training," he explains with a shrug, like it is simple.

"Wait. We won't be kept together?" I gasp, unable to hide my horror, which only grows as the Masters grin, one even chuckles a little, the sound distinctly evil.

"No, of course not. We wouldn't want you ganging up on us. Until we know you can be trusted, this is the last time you will all be together in the same place." Horror races through my body, I can't remember the last time I wasn't with my men. We spend every day together and most nights...without them, what am I?

No powers.

No family.

Just me.

Fear seeps through me. Will I go back to being nothing but a slave? Afraid to speak, afraid of doing something wrong, willingly bowing to their every demand...No. No. That's not me, not anymore. I'm stronger than that, just because they won't be by my side doesn't mean I will be alone. We will get out of this, we always do.

We have to...right?

Until then, I will play the game, but I won't remain silent. I refuse to let them break me like before. I am adaptable, I am strong, and they picked the wrong fucking circus to mess with.

Before I know it, men are streaming into the cage, pulling us away from each other. I kick and scream, but when they hold a gun to Jessie's head, I stop and let them drag me over to the edge of the enclosure. They line us up, their weapons held on Jessie.

"Release his shackles, let's see what he can do," one of the Masters orders.

A man steps forward and unlocks his shackles. Jessie rounds his shoulders, stretching out, and they follow every movement, ready at a moment's notice to strike if he tries anything.

"Go on, show us. Do you really want to risk your family?" one of the masters taunts.

Frowning, Jesse reluctantly hold out his hands, calling his fire, igniting a small flame in his palm, extending it along the skin of his arm before extinguishing it by closing his fist. The Masters all murmur excitedly and gesture for Jessie's shackles to be put back on. I glance at Alcide and see him shake his head slightly. We all know that Jessie can do more than he just showed, but the Masters don't know that, happy at Jesse's apparent compliance.

One by one they lead us forward and unlock our shackles, testing our powers before they place the metal bands back on our wrists. Alcide charms them, but doesn't show too much. Rex shows off his strength and speed, but doesn't explain where it comes from. Nixon simply picks up a man and throws him at the Masters. They laugh, calling off the guards when they try to shoot him. Blain produces his knives, but Alcide warns him with a look not to try throwing them. Then it's my turn.

I step forward, and once I stand in the middle, they unleash my shackles. I watch closely, trying to figure out how they close. They used a blunt looking key and press it to the back of the shackles before they crack open with a hiss. No joints, just the key. I watch the guard drape it around his neck, where it hangs from a string.

"Rhea, if you would be so kind," the Master calls. "I heard they call you the immortal, will you show us why?"

Heeding Alcide's looks, I make sure not to show them my true strength or abilities, but I also want them to know I'm not weak. They might have us right now, but I won't sit meekly. I will fight them and I will get free.

I have no masters anymore because I am not a slave any longer, I am Rhea the Immortal. Alcide and my men made it so, and I won't disappoint them now.

I let my skin harden, visibly turning to stone under their inspection. Tilting my chin up at them, I smile. "Whip me," I order.

They make no moves, the guards shifting, clearly unsure. "Whip me!" I scream. "Unless your words were just that, words," I dare them.

"Rhea," Nixon hisses, but I don't draw my eyes away from the Masters. I am drawing a line in the sand and daring them to cross it. I want to know how far they will take this. How far they will go to control us.

"Whip her," he orders, and I hear the guard step forward, his whip curling through the sand with a hiss before it whistles through the air. When it hits my skin, it bangs before falling back uselessly.

Sarcastically, I bow with a flourish. "Thank you, you have been an incredible crowd." I hold my hands out, and the guards come back and place my shackles on, then lead me back over to the others.

Blain is grinning, Nixon is glaring, Jessie looks worried, but Alcide is calculating. "Good, but don't push them too far," he whispers and I nod.

We stand silently, waiting for the verdict between the whispering Masters. I grab Nixon's hand and weave our fingers together, before grabbing Blain's on my other side and doing the same thing. I'm sending a message—you can split us up, but you will never break us apart.

"All separate!" they eventually call, and Alcide swears as they start to separate us, I lose my grip on Blain's and Nixon's hands.

When they start to lead me away from Nixon, he goes apeshit. With a roar, he begins throwing men like they are weightless, fighting and ignoring their weapons.

A whip slashes through the air with a crack, winding around his neck as he snarls, fighting it with men hanging from his body, trying to get to me, his face turning red as he takes step after step towards me. This is with his powers blocked, and I marvel at his strength once again.

Kicking the man holding me, I pull from his grip and race over before pulling at the men clinging on to him, trying to stop them from hurting him.

"Nix, Nix, look at me!" I yell, and he stops struggling, his eyes staring into mine.

A Master's voice cuts through the air. "Keep those two together, it could be useful. Now, get them inside, I've grown bored with them. I want them checked out, branded, and ready to train before tomorrow!" the man shouts, and I watch as the Masters disappear, leaving us with the guards who seem all too happy to follow their orders as they point their weapons at us.

Chapter Seven

We are led from the cage one by one.

Guards shackle our hands before chaining us to another guard who starts to lead us away. He tugs me, making me stumble over my feet, but I refuse to fall. I'm not used to being without my powers, and it has made me weaker, off kilter. Walking without them filling my body is strange. I can hear Blain growling at the guards, Alcide charming them, and Jessie playing nice. Only Rex, Nixon, and I remain silent.

The passageway we are led to has a fence all the way around it, even arching over the top. It's as if they think we would try to climb the sides and escape. Maybe it has happened in the past and they are trying to learn from their mistakes.

People line the side of the caged passageway, their fingers gripping the fence as they watch us. Their eyes are seeking our weaknesses, the way a predator observes its prey. It reminds me of when Frederick bought me from the slave markets. But these people don't want to keep us. No, they want to see us suffer and die, it's clear to see in their eyes —the need for blood, the hope that we will bring excitement to their otherwise dull and meaningless lives.

Refusing to look at them, I face forward and eye the towering building we are being led to. A big, brown, wooden gate stands open at the end of the winding passage, but the room beyond it is dark, leaving me unable to make anything out. The building itself is made of grey stone, stretching high into the sky, and from what I can see, it's round like our stage.

Chanting can be heard, even from here. A large crowd is begging for blood, begging for more. The sound of thousands of stomping feet, shaking the ground like thunder, has me hunching into myself. I can almost taste the blood and death in the air.

When we reach the gate, I'm shoved inside from behind, and I'm glad to be away from prying eyes. It takes a moment for my eyes to adjust, but the guards don't wait, they carry on shoving me and I tumble forward—my feet catching on steps I didn't know were there.

I bite my lip to stop from crying out and blink rapidly until I can see in front of me. A wide staircase with dirty, wet, sand-coloured walls leads downwards, with torches hanging every few steps to provide minimal lighting. Each step is steep, much more suited for Nixon's large stride, and I struggle to keep up as I'm yanked down them quickly.

The heat hits me the farther we go down, like when you're in a crowded room with too many people. I crinkle my nose at the smell of unwashed bodies and copper, like it has sunken into the walls and ground, never to be free of this place.

When I reach the bottom of the staircase, I gawk at the place around me. It's like being thrown into a completely new world. It looks like something out of a story…or a nightmare.

Sand and dirt cover the hard floor beneath my feet, and I wrinkle my nose at the blood and various stains dotted here and there, but my blood runs cold as I take in the rest of the space. Directly across from the stairs are a row of cells. Dirty, concrete walls line the back of each cell with only bars separating them, and there's only a simple mat on the ground in each one, presumably to sleep on. Water is dripping from the ceiling and as the crowd cheers and stomps above, sand and dust rain down, covering my hair.

In the middle of the room, set lower into the floor with no steps down, is what looks like a food area. Rough, wooden tables with weapon marks and blood stains are lined by odd stools, chairs, and benches. Silver trays of forgotten food are scattered around the tables as men watch us from their seats. I purposely don't make eye contact, shivering when I realise there are no other women. Just big, hard, sweaty, scarred up men, all looking at me like I am their next meal.

Past the eating area is a long rectangular room I can't see clearly from here, but I spot a man or two walking in there completely naked. A blush steals over my face and I quickly avert my eyes. I'm no prude, how can I be with all my guys, but when faced with this bunch of naked, hard men, I shrink back slightly.

The guard pushes me forward once again and I stumble, hitting my knees on the floor hard. I hear Nixon roar, so I quickly get to my feet and he stops fighting as I throw him a soft smile over my shoulder. As I move farther into the room, I spot another row of cells on the opposite wall than the first. In the left corner, just past them, are racks and racks of weapons—swords, maces, axes, chains, and pretty much anything you could ever imagine. They're not in good shape. Some are covered in gore and most of them are blunt, but they could still do some damage. In front of them is another brown gate with a guard in front of it, and my hopes of grabbing one and trying to escape decreases.

I crane my neck around, trying to take in the rest of the underground area, but I'm pushed again and dragged along the side of the cages. We're paraded in front of the current fighters and they all track us as we go by. I catch one man's eyes. He looks older than the rest, his hair receding and grey, and wrinkles line his tan face, but his eyes are bright and locked on us, and in them I see...sympathy. He's a big man, not bigger than Nixon, but huge in his own right. He nods at me and the others at his table do the same before I am pulled away.

More torches line the walls, locked into place with chains as if someone tried to steal them before, and I cough as more dust rains down on us from above. The crowd roars and we all look over, even the guards, freezing as the gate near the racks of weapons opens and a man covered in blood stumbles through.

His legs give way and he catches himself on the weapons rack. One of the guards pats his back, congratulating him as they strip him of his weapons and armour. He nods, his eyes cold and dead, but I catch a flame of anger there buried under all that fury. He forces himself to stand.

"Shower off, Xavier, you fight again tonight!" a guard shouts, and the room goes silent as all the other fighters lower their heads in respect as the man makes his way across the room.

A fighter holds out a tarnished silver goblet to him and he grabs it, throwing back the drink before tossing it back to the man. He's dragging one of his legs slightly and I gasp when I spot the massive gash on the back of his leg, almost down to the bone. How is he still walking?

I can't make out much under the blood, apart from that he's a tall, muscular man, his chest almost as wide as Rex's. It's obvious his body is a weapon. He heads past us and I suck in a breath when I spot all the scars that run across his body, unable to be covered by the blood and gore coating him.

One of the guards grunts. "Shame we missed that fight, knew that fucker would take that thief down," he whispers to the guard that led us in here, who laughs as he tugs on my chains.

"Maybe he will get rewarded with the new pussy slave." He throws me forward and I try to catch myself, but I slam into the fighter. He stops, looking down at me as I pull away. His hair is covered in blood, the sides shaved, but the top bit is long and held back in a low ponytail. I'm betting when it's down, it is almost as long as mine.

His eyes flicker to the guards and his lips set in a grim, hard line. "Watch their hands girly," he warns, steadying me before heading to the room I now assume to be the bathroom, not bothering to look back.

I shiver again at the absolute lost look in his eyes...the pain and knowing. He has accepted he is nothing but a slave to them, something to fight and fuck and kill for them. And that's when it clicks. If a man this strong, this imposing, can be broken, then I can be too. We are to be the same.

My horrific thoughts are washed away as we are dragged past the room he disappeared into, and I spot showers, toilets, and sinks inside, which confirms my assumptions. Xavier has his hands braced against the wall of the shower cubicle, water racing down his thick body, washing away blood and sweat. I wince when I spot the horrible wound on his leg, wondering if he will even survive that.

He glances up, our eyes catching, and my heart stops in my chest at the loneliness and longing in those bright blue orbs. I'm dragged away, my eyes staying on his until the last minute, and just before I turn, I see him look away, his head hanging down again. Only then does my heart start to beat, racing in my chest like he controlled it for a second. I was lost in his eyes, my body his to control…to kill. I shiver, not knowing where that thought came from, and concentrate on not falling over as I'm dragged away.

I start to struggle when I notice the small hallway we are being dragged down. Closed doors with locks line one side and the guard holding our chains opens the first one before throwing me inside.

I stumble forward, my eyes landing on a bed made up with clean sheets and pillows. Straightening, I glance around and notice they even put down a rug and there are some chairs and a small bar in one corner.

What did they use this room for?

"What—" I start, but the guard who followed me in turns and back-hands me, sending me sprawling across the bed as my cheek flares hot. Usually my powers would have reacted, changed my skin, but they can't because of the stupid shackles.

The other guards must've brought the guys in the room too, because I hear them shouting and fighting. Sitting up quickly, ignoring the pain in my cheek, I mutter, "I'm fine." They calm down slightly, though I notice their glares locked on the guard who hit me, no doubt thinking of the ways to kill him. But we all know we are out of options right now. There's no other choice but to comply until we figure a way out of here.

"No fucking speaking unless you want a mark on the other cheek, freak," he spits out, kicking my feet so I curl up into myself and go quiet. I know pissing him off will only send my men into a fit as they try to kill them all to get to me.

We sit in silence, all wondering what is happening, until eventually the door opens and a man enters with a flourish, a cart being pushed in behind him by another guard. The man doesn't even spare us a look, just heads over to one of the chairs and starts setting up a gun on his cart. Finally, he turns to the guard holding me.

"Let's begin," he announces.

I'm pulled up from the bed and dragged over to his chair, my eyes sticking on the gun-like machine he's holding in his gloved hands. The guard pushes me down with a hand on my head and I quickly glance back, catching Blain's eyes. He doesn't look concerned, just pissed. That in itself gives me some peace, so I blow out a breath and force myself to sit still.

"Hand," the man calls lazily.

When I just blink at him stupidly, he looks at the guard next to me who grabs my left hand, almost crushing my fingers in his grip, as he turns it over so my palm is facing up. I wince at the crushing hold, my eyes wide as I watch the man dip the tip of the gun into what looks like a pot of black ink before turning back to me. Is it a tattoo gun? Are they marking us? Like cattle and slaves?

My internal questions are answered when the machine fires to life, the buzzing cutting through my body when, without warning, the needle end is pressed against my skin. It doesn't hurt as much as I thought it would, it just feels violating since I don't have a choice but to stand there and let it happen. And I hate that I'm now wearing their mark. Even if I escape here, this reminder will *always* be with me. At least it's not massive, just a small black design on the inside of my wrist. Squinting, I eye it more closely. The design almost seems familiar… like I've seen it before. I gasp, realising where I've seen it.

It's the same mark I saw on the boy. He was a slave? He was one of them? The others take my sound of surprise as one of pain and start shouting again, the guards rushing to restrain them. Still focused on the mark, questions piling up in my mind, I wave a hand at my men to assure them I'm fine… I'm just more confused than ever.

The tattoo doesn't take more than thirty minutes, and once mine is done, I'm shoved back as, one by one, my men are dragged forward to receive their marks. They struggle to find room on Blain's already full arms, and he winks at me as they grunt and groan about it.

My wrist feels heavy and sore as I cradle it to my chest, wishing I could reach out and take comfort from one of my men. But I'm betting that would get us both punished, so instead I resign myself to watching them, tracing their faces and meeting their eyes. Trying to tell them I'm okay and how much I love them.

Once we are all marked, we're lined up outside the room, the guards talking amongst themselves. I reach out on either side, not wanting to take their hands, but I have to touch them, so I settle with brushing my pinkies against Jesse's and Rex's.

"Alright, those two that way, the others this way," a guard orders, and I throw Alcide a panicked look as Nixon and I are shoved down the first row of cells we walked past. The others are dragged along the back of the bathroom wall and out of view to the other cells.

I swallow hard, keeping my eyes on Nixon's back when we are stopped next to two cells. The guards unlock them before shoving us inside. The clank of the lock clicking into place has me wanting to wrap my arms around myself, but I stand tall, noticing all the eyes on me. All looking for weaknesses that I can't afford to show.

"Feeding time's over, you fucking animals! Back to your cages!" a guard screams, and all the men get to their feet, hustling back to their cells with the weapons from the guards trained on their backs.

"Fight between Xavier and Vince in two hours!" another yells, as all the locks click into place on the cells, the sound final and resounding. I head over to the mat and lie down on my side, pressing against the bars closest to Nixon. He drags his mat over and copies me so we're touching through the bars, his warmth offering me some comfort.

Looking around, my eyes catch on the sleeping form of Xavier in the cell to my right. He's lying on his back, his knee bent up, and his arm over his eyes as he snores. I blink in confusion as I stare at the back of his knee, knowing I saw it brutally injured earlier, but all that's there now is a faint, pink line.

Is everyone here freaks like us?

I wonder how they tracked us all down, how long people have been here, but I daren't ask. Instead, I spend my time people watching and learning the layout of the place and the guards' routines until they announce fight time with a bell.

Xavier gets to his feet, stretching out and waiting in the middle of his cell as they unlock his door. I watch as he's led over to the weapons rack where another man is testing out an axe, swinging it through the air.

The guard there automatically hands over armour and two swords to Xavier, and I watch with interest as he slips into it easily, obviously used to it. A gong sounds, the crowd above surging with excitement and raining dust down on us again. I hear the muffled voices of an announcement as the two fighters stand in front of the gate side by side, not talking.

The gate starts to crank open and I watch the other man loosen up, nervously throwing glances at a stoic Xavier.

"Our immortal!" I hear announced, as the crowd goes wild and Xavier steps forward through the gate and disappears into the black beyond. Not two minutes later, the crowd stomps and cheers, obviously catching a glimpse of him.

"Against our reigning champ…Wolfman!" the announcer screams, and the nervous guys steps through after Xavier, the gate closing behind them and cutting off the voices of the announcer and the crowd.

I sit there, counting down the minutes. The crowd is going crazy and not five minutes later, the gate opens again—admitting only Xavier.

He's bloody and sweaty as he hands over his weapons and armour before heading to the showers once again. My eyes follow him, entranced, before I drag them back to the gate, waiting for the other man. But he never shows. The gate shuts and I wince, my heart racing. Did Xavier kill him?

What if he kills one of my men or me?

What if we are asked to kill each other?

Xavier heads back to his cell next to mine after a quick shower and instantly goes back to sleep. I watch him carefully, assessing the killer disguised as a man—a broken one at that.

Nixon's hand slips through the bars and curls around mine and I close my eyes, pressing my cheek to his shoulder.

"I'm scared, Nix," I whisper.

"I know, but don't let them see that. You are our greatest gift and their worst threat. They will realise that soon. Until then, we need to be strong. We have survived worse, and we will survive this," he growls softly, but his words only send more fear through my system. I don't fear for my life as much as I should, I fear for theirs, my men, and I also fear for my soul.

What if I become nothing of the Rhea I know? What if they make me into a killer like Xavier? What if I become cold and withdrawn and they fully break me...turning me into their pet freak?

I don't fear death, no...I fear this life.

Chapter Eight

Aloud, metallic banging wakes me from my fitful sleep, and with my heart in my throat, I jolt upright, my eyes wide as I try to work out what is happening. My stomach drops as I look around at the cell I'm in. It wasn't a nightmare, this is really happening. Panic claws at my insides, working its way up my throat as it tries to consume me, my hands shaking as my vision starts to narrow on the metal bars in front of me. We are trapped, separated, and the only thing that makes me special, that protects me, has been taken away. My chest becomes tight, so I focus on my breathing. In and out. In and out. We *can* survive this.

Something touches my shoulder and I flinch, shuffling back until I'm pressed against the wall, scanning for threats.

"Rhea?" The voice is rough, but I would recognize it anywhere. Blinking past the haze of adrenaline, I glance over to the other side of the cell. Nixon's concerned face stares back at me, his hands wrapped around the bars. I rush over and reach through, desperate to touch as much of him as I can.

"Sorry, Nix. I'm okay," I whisper, pressing my forehead against the bars, smiling softly as he does the same, taking my hand in his. At least they have put us in cells next to each other, I'm not quite sure how either of us would have coped otherwise.

The loud metallic banging comes again, this time from the other side of the room, followed by groans and shuffling feet as people move around in their cells.

"Wake up, you filthy maggots," someone shouts, presumably one of the guards. I follow suit of those in the cages around me and scramble to my feet, Nixon following my lead. The sound of heavy footsteps approaches my cage, but my view is obscured but the showers and feeding area. A moment later, a guard rounds the corner, his eyes lighting up when they land on me.

"Well, well, the rumours are true. We have a new *female* slave. Never had one of those before. Don't suppose you'll last long in the arena," he drawls, as he stalks towards me, coming to a stop in front of my cage, and running his eyes up and down my body before meeting my gaze, smirking. I recognise that look, I've seen it from men back in Cinders, it's the look of men who enjoy hurting women. It makes me feel dirty, like an object for him to use. I decide here and now that I need to make sure I'm never alone with this guy.

"That would be a shame," he continues, licking his lips as his eyes drop to my chest. A shudder of revulsion runs through me. "Perhaps we can come to some sort of agreement? You help me out, and I'll make sure you get the easier fights." His voice drops as he takes a step closer to my cell, and for the first time, I'm thankful for the bars in front of me. I fight down the sick feeling that his words induce in me, knowing exactly what he means by 'helping him out.'

A low growl comes from the cage next to me, causing me to pull my gaze from the guard. Nixon seems to double in size as he snarls, his anger filling the underground room, and he takes a threatening step towards the guard who instinctively moves back. A small smile of satisfaction spreads across my face as I realise he is like any other bully. He is nothing but a scared little boy hiding behind his position. If the bars weren't there protecting him, and we had our powers, he wouldn't dare treat us this way.

The guard's face twists into an angry scowl as he realises he looks weak, his hand dropping to a baton strapped to his waist I hadn't noticed before. Thankfully, he's distracted when more guards swarm into the underground room.

"Come on, Trent, don't play with them. We have work to do," a senior looking guard scolds the man currently glaring at Nixon. The younger guard looks like he may disobey his orders, but he steps back, clenching his jaw.

"This isn't over, freaks," he growls under his breath, before stomping off towards the others. Releasing a breath I hadn't realised I was holding, I reach through the bars once again and squeeze Nixon's hand. He returns the gesture after a tense moment, but his eyes are still locked on the guard, Trent, and I know that his days are numbered. Nixon, as a rule, isn't violent, but he will be to protect his family, even if it puts him in danger.

"Nix, I'm okay," I repeat, and I feel his attention shift to me, the violence leaving his body as he runs his eyes over me, but in a completely different way than the guard. Nixon's never made me feel objectified, and right now his gaze is full of concern and love as he checks that I am unharmed.

The next thirty minutes or so involves us being shepherded into the feeding area in the middle of the room. I was surprised when they let all of us out at the same time, but all of the other slaves have the same bands around their wrists as us, so they're just as powerless as we are —not to mention, the thirty or so weapons pointed at us from the guards stationed around the room. Those are enough to keep us all in line.

It's the first time I've seen my other guys since last night, but a warning look and slight shake of Alcide's head stops me from running to them or saying anything. I long to wrap my arms around them. This is the longest I've been separated from any of them since we thought we lost Nixon, and it's bringing back horrific memories. But I have to resist those worries, those terrifying thoughts. I can see them. I can see that they are unharmed. It's important for us to appear strong, because they will only take our affection for each other as a weakness. They already know Nixon is very protective of me, there is no reversing that, but there is no need to let them know how close I am with the others.

When I'm standing in line for my breakfast, the others brush their hands against me as they walk past. Anyone that was watching would be forgiving, thinking it was accidental, but I can tell from the look in their eyes that they did it on purpose. When Alcide approaches me, he stumbles, surprising me and nearly knocking me over. Alcide isn't a clumsy person. My gaze locks on him as he is hauled up by a guard, and I catch his quiet words before he's shoved down the line.

"Stay close to Nixon. Trust no one."

Nixon helps steady me, baring his teeth at anyone that comes too close to us, his hand staying protectively on my shoulder as we continue to queue. Eventually, we get our breakfast and take a seat at one of the tables. Jessie sits at the opposite end, flashing me a small smile as we sit, before turning his attention back to his bowl. My stomach sours when I spot his swollen eye and various bruises. We'll get through this. We'll be okay.

Our breakfast consists of a bowl of lukewarm gruel, but none of us complain, not knowing when our next meal will be. They lock us in cells and call us slaves, so I doubt they are going to feed us regularly.

As we eat, I try to look around surreptitiously. There seems to be around twenty-five of us. All of my guys are here, spread out around the room, but I can feel their eyes on me. Unfortunately, theirs are not the only ones.

Several slaves are eyeing me up, some bloodthirsty, analysing me as if I'll be their next opponent, while others obviously have more lascivious activities on their mind. I will need to keep my eye on them.

Fighting a shudder, I continue to peruse the room, and my eyes land on the guy I stumbled into the yesterday. Xavier, I think his name was. He's sitting as far away from everyone as he can, keeping his head down as he eats his food. I don't know why my gaze keeps being drawn to him. He's handsome, in a scarred, don't mess with me kinda way, but it's not that that catches my eye. I think it's the air of acceptance and desolation that comes from him.

"I'd avoid that one if you can." A deep voice snaps me from my musings, and I quickly look up, realising it's the older man who had nodded to me yesterday when we arrived. "He's never looked out for anyone here, only himself. You will need allies if you're going to survive this," he finishes quietly, his two companions nodding their head in agreement. I raise an eyebrow, tilting my head to the side.

"Is that what you are, an ally?"

He lets out a short laugh of surprise, as if he wasn't expecting my response. "We shall see. I'm Jacob," he replies, before he backs away as the guards start moving towards him, their weapons pointed at his chest.

"No talking!" one of them barks, jabbing his spear towards Jacob's chest.

The commotion captured the attention of the room, everyone's stares falling on me. I return their gazes with a glare, wishing I felt as confident as my actions as I scan the room, my eyes catching once again on Xavier. His eyes bore into mine, and an expression of interest flashes across his face for a second before it disappears back to the blank mask it was before.

The rest of breakfast passes uneventfully until seemingly as one, the slaves stand and start shuffling towards the large set of doors I'd seen Xavier stumble through yesterday. Nixon and I join the queue, trepidation filling me as we wait. What's waiting for us on the other side of those doors?

"What's happening?" I whisper quietly to the guy in front of me.

He turns suddenly, like I've bitten him, his eyes wide until he sees me behind him. Raising an eyebrow sharply, he responds, "It's training, they'll want to see what you can do. This always happens when we get new slaves." He turns away, and I doubt he'll answer me again if I was to ask another question.

I stay silent after that, and soon we're shepherded through the doorway. It's dark in here, but there are a set of stairs leading up to a bright light ahead. Closing my eyes against the light, I wince as I'm shoved from behind. I stumble forward, prying my eyes open, as I look around us. My jaw drops. There are cages lining the large, circular space, filled with more slaves. Above us in tiers are what seem to be seats. Rows and rows of them all face down into the sandy pit, which we are being shoved towards. The space in the center is lower than we are, and it is surrounded by a wall with large gates providing the only way in and out.

"We are in a fucking amphitheatre." Alcide's voice causes me to jump, and I turn, seeing all my guys standing around me. My heart fills with joy that we are all together again, but seeing the expressions on their faces makes me nervous.

"What's an amphitheatre?" I ask, eyeing the other slaves wearily, most of whom are watching with expectant looks on their faces, like they are waiting for something to happen.

"It's a place where they used to make people fight pre-war, usually to the death, while people bet on who would win," Rex explains quietly, but stops as a guard marches up to us. I can tell he is in charge by the way others react to him, bowing their heads in respect as he walks past, as well as the way he carries himself with confidence.

"Slaves, listen up, because I will only say it once. You will be put in the ring and you will train. You *will not* hold back on your powers, if you do, it could lead to your death. Following today's training, you will be ranked for future fights. Once you have warmed up, the others will be sent in to join you. There will be *no* fighting unless you are directed to by myself or one of the Masters. Once you step foot in the ring, your powers will be returned to you. Don't die. If you fight well, you will be rewarded," the guard concludes, before gesturing towards the staircase. When we hesitate, his face hardens. "You would find it in your best interest to follow my orders. I can make this unpleasant for you, but I would rather avoid that."

We all look to Alcide who is watching the guard with narrowed eyes. When he subtly nods, we start to walk towards the staircase that leads down to the fighting pit. One by one the metal bands that mute our powers are removed, just before we step into the fighting ring.

I immediately feel my powers return, and I hold out my hands to examine them. I've never felt my powers like this before, they've always just been there, ready to protect me when I need them. It wasn't until they were taken away that I realised how lost I felt without them. Looking around, I see the guys are doing something similar, except Jesse, who's standing next to one of the walls, peering at it with a quizzical look on his face. Raising both palms, he presses them against the wall before quickly pulling them away with a grimace.

"Whatever they use in the metal bands is in the walls too, we won't be able to escape using our powers." He keeps his voice low, but I can read the fear in his eyes loud and clear.

The atmosphere in the arena is overwhelming and oppressive. Our every move is watched. From here, I can just about see the area we have just been lead from, the cells just visible, but I realise that those sitting in the seating above wouldn't see them, the area is completely hidden from their view. Looking around the empty arena, I wonder what will happen next. What are we waiting for? Anticipation rises within me, and as I examine my family around me, I see the same in them. I wonder if the guards have made us wait on purpose?

"Should we be warming up or something?" I ask Alcide quietly, the uncertainty of our situation making my anxiety climb to new levels.

"I don't know. I don't want to play their games." Indecision underlines his words and that worries me more than anything else, more than them locking us up and taking away our powers. Alcide is our leader, he always knows what to do, and we look to him for guidance. The fact he doesn't know scares me.

I DON'T KNOW how much time has passed, but I'm starting to feel woozy under the heat of the midday sun. Based on the others' drooping postures, it's affecting them too. A banging catches my attention and we all shuffle closer together as the gates open. Nixon pulls me close as more slaves pile in.

A flash of colour draws my attention to the rows of seats above us. A covered area takes up about a quarter of the space, it is difficult to see from down here, but it looks different than the other seats, more spacious. Squinting, trying to focus, I finally realise what the flash of colour is. Two of the Masters have come to watch us, and a couple of other people I don't recognise are with them. I don't think they are Masters, they don't hold themselves in the same way.

Someone clearing their throat brings us all to attention. The same guard from before, the one who is in charge, is standing up by the cages, frowning down at us.

"Today you will be paired up and your abilities tested further against an opponent. Do not kill or seriously hurt the slave you are partnered with, today is not about fighting." There is a pause before he continues. "You will get plenty of opportunities to hurt one another."

Glancing around, I see five slaves gather together, eyeing us up like we're their next meal. I fight the shudder when their eyes heat up as they land on me, and my guys surround me, protecting me from their sick gazes.

I guess it's inevitable to have so much attention on me, I *am* the only female freak after all. Straightening my back, I stand tall and meet the stares of the other slaves in the arena. The older man who had nodded at me the other day stands to the side with two huge guys, stretching, obviously used to whatever is about to happen. His eyes are on me again, and when I meet his gaze, he smiles slightly, dipping his head in what looks like a show of respect. Perhaps we might have an ally in him?

Most of the other slaves are standing apart from everyone else, eyeing us with distrust. I spin around as a crawling feeling runs down my spine. Standing behind me is...Xavier. He's huge, even more so now that he is so close to me, and I have to arch my neck to look up at him. His skin is covered in old, silver scars, but I can't see any fresh wounds on him like I was expecting. I saw the deep wound on his leg yesterday in the showers, but now there's nothing there. How?

Shaking my head, I look up and freeze when I see his face. It's completely unmarked, unlike the rest of his body. He would probably be considered handsome if it wasn't for the scowl he was aiming at me. Keeping completely still, I wait for him to make the first move, feeling like a mouse being stalked by a lion. Disgust flickers across his features when he registers my fear, before he turns and stalks away.

THE REST of the day seems to go by in a blur of heat, sweat, and fighting. My body is shaking as my sore muscles try to keep up against the onslaught of punches that are aimed at me. Ducking another swing aimed at my head, I jump back and end up pressed against someone's chest. A deep grumbling lets me know it's Nixon, as well as the wide-eyed guy in front of me who holds his hands up in surrender and takes a few steps back. Turning to Nixon, I look up and see his eyes filled with murder, locked on the retreating slave.

"Nix. Look at me," I call to him, waiting until his gaze moves to mine. I nearly wince at the violence I see there, but I know Nixon would never hurt me. "I'm fine, we were training, I'm okay," I say in a cajoling tone, repeating it until the anger fades, and the Nixon I know and love returns. Fighting the urge to wrap my arms around him, I settle with putting my hand on his arm, aware that our every move is being watched.

After everyone's had a chance to warm up, we're split into groups and ordered to spar against each other. Everyone I have sparred with today has taken it easy on me, not really trying to hurt me. No one really seems to want to hurt each other. Well, that's not true. The group of five guys that have been watching me since I arrived exude violence, and all of their opponents have come away sporting bruises and wounds.

The guards have been keeping an eye on them, but other than a few barked commands to take it easy, they haven't stepped in to stop the violent men. The leader of the group, O'Connor, truly scares me. I watched him train as he was paired up with some of the other slaves. His power seems to be pain, all he has to do is touch the person and they double over, crying out. The pain appears to continue long after he lets go of them, their bodies convulsing and facial expressions strained.

When I haven't been fighting, I've watched the others, trying to work out what their powers are. The older slave, Jacob as I learned his name is, seems to have the gift of speed, his body moving so fast my eyes can't keep up with him.

So far, I have managed to come away without having to use my powers. All of my sparring partners have barely touched me, purely going through the motions. However, I'm under no illusion that if we are paired up to fight for real that they would not hurt me to win, it's human nature.

I still get a few lingering stares, but it seems the shock has worn off. Blain and Alcide only had to knock some sense into a couple of guys whose eyes lingered on me for a little too long. The guys all seem to be holding up okay, not having to use too much energy to show off their powers. All except Nixon. So far, he has refused to fight, just following me around like a silent bodyguard, growling at everyone that comes near us, including guards.

"Last pairing of the day," a guard announces. "Girl, you're up with O'Connor."

Whispers and shouts fill the arena. The guys surround me as I stand frozen, my stomach churning with fear. I have seen the look in O'Connor's eyes as he trains, he *enjoys* causing pain. Alcide is shouting at the guards, ordering them to change who I fight, but they're just watching from above with smirks on their faces as if this was exactly what they wanted. They think I'm weak, a pitiful woman that can't protect herself. It's time to show them what this woman can do.

"It's okay," I proclaim, as I start to walk forward, only to come to as stop as Blain stands in front of me, crossing his arms across his muscled chest.

"Harpy, if you think I am letting you get anywhere near that sadistic maniac, then you are fucking crazy."

"You don't get a choice, neither do I. This could go two ways. You stop me and I'm dragged into the ring looking like a scared little girl, or I walk in there with my head held high and I show them what happens when you mess with the freaks." Something changes in his eyes as I speak, and I know he understands. Clenching his jaw, he steps to the side without saying anything. I don't thank him, I know if I do he'll stop me from going again. I don't look at the others. It'll feel like too much of a goodbye if I do.

I step forward to the chalk drawn circle in the center of the arena, covered in sweat and dirt from a day of sparring under the scalding sun. O'Connor is watching me with the grin of a predator about to make a kill, pacing the circle like a caged animal, which is exactly what we are to these people.

I reach the border of the training ring and take a deep breath. The arena has gone silent, since everyone is focusing on the scene about to unfold in front of them. The hairs on my arms suddenly stand to attention and I follow my intuition. Glancing over my shoulder, I see Xavier watching me with the same intense expression from before. I shiver as I pull my gaze away, taking a step over the chalk line and entering the circle.

Facing O'Connor, I mirror his actions. When he stalks around the circle, I do the same. I need to keep as much distance between myself and him as I can. My powers are defensive, I have very little offensive ability, and if he touches me, I don't know if my powers will adapt. They seem to affect the brain since the pain would stop once contact was broken, otherwise, I have not come across abilities like this before to know if I can overcome them.

"Ready, little girl?" he taunts, jumping towards me, reaching out his hand to grab me. At the last moment I leap to the side. He may think I'm just a little girl, but I've worked for the circus—I'm flexible and fast. He will have to work harder than that to catch me. I don't bother replying to him, I need to focus on how I can fight against him without touching him.

This carries on for what feels like hours, but could only be minutes as I dodge O'Connor. He's going to catch me sooner or later, and I'm getting tired. O'Connor gets closer, the narrowing of his eyes telling me he is fed up with my games. He jumps towards me, and I dart to the right, only to find his hand gripped around my upper arm. My eyes widen in horror, but before I have time to register what will happen next, pain like I've never felt before runs through my body.

Collapsing to the ground, I convulse as lightning hot pain shoots along my nerve endings, and my body feels like it's on fire. All sound disappears except for the loudness of my ragged breathing. Forcing open my eyes that I hadn't realised I'd shut, I look up at a smug O'Connor who let go when I dropped to the ground. Trying to focus on my powers, I start to feel my skin shifting to protect me, constantly moving and changing, but nothing eases the pain that ravages my body. A scream tears from my lips, my body feeling like it's on fire.

Fire.

Using all the energy I have left, I lurch forward, gripping onto O'Connor's ankle. Ignoring his laugh as he tries to kick off my hand, I close my eyes, focusing on my power. I need to *become* fire. I know I'm successful when he shouts and starts scrabbling away from me, even more so when the pain stops coursing through my body. I take a deep breath of relief and push myself up to stand on shaky legs. Glancing down, I see that my whole body is glimmering like embers, the air around me sizzling as I take unsteady steps towards O'Connor. He looks nervous now and a smug feeling goes through me.

Oh, how the tables have turned.

"That's enough. You have proved your point, girl," a guard calls out, signalling the end of our fight.

Dropping my fire form, I feel the gravity of what just happened. My body shakes as I walk towards the guys who are waiting for me. Alcide and Jesse have smiles on their faces, while Nixon looks like he is about to go and pummel O'Connor into the ground.

"Nixon, it's okay, I'm okay—" I begin, before a whistling sound has me turning at the last second.

"Rhea!"

"Stop him!"

The arena is full of shouts as O'Connor throws a dagger towards me. Hatred consumes his eyes as the blade flies towards me with deadly accuracy. No one is close enough to help me and time seems to slow as I watch it come towards me. Can my body stop something flying this fast? When I'm caught off guard and not prepared for it like I am with Blain? Before I can even try to shift, a shadow appears in front of me and I close my eyes, bracing for impact.

Nothing happens.

Slowly opening my eyes, I see Xavier in front of me, close enough to touch, and holding the dagger in his palm as if he plucked it out of thin air. Xavier's hard stare bores into me, like he is looking past all of my walls and seeing the real me underneath. His expression is intense, but I can't make out what he's feeling. I want to ask, the words on the tip of my tongue. Why? Why save me when he hates me?

His hand holding the dagger doesn't waver. It must have hurt, the blade looks sharp, deadly. For any normal person, it would have cut their hand to pieces. But then none of us here are normal, are we?

His mouth opens, like he's going to say something, but he closes it and shakes his head. Dropping the blade to the ground, he starts to turn away, but I dart forward and grab his hand to stop him. Freezing, he slowly turns his head to stare at me, but I catch the look in his eyes before he can hide it—a look of astonishment. Glancing down at my hand in his, he frowns at me again.

"Thank you," I blurt out, feeling uncomfortable under his stare, quickly letting go of his hand. I have seen this guy in action, he's a killing machine, and I should be scared of him, we all should, yet I can't fight this feeling in my chest that he is just as afraid as the rest of us.

He holds my gaze for another couple of seconds, and I think I see his lip twitch, but he simply nods and turns away. I still don't know what his power is, but I try to catch a glimpse of his palm again as he walks away. After a moment, I get my opportunity and my suspicions are confirmed. His palm, the one he'd caught the knife in, is completely unmarked.

Chapter Nine

The rest of the day passes in a blur. When we are returned to our underground prison, we are shown to the showers, but as all the men start to strip, I cringe and choose to eat first instead. I sit with Nixon again, feeling Alcide's, Jesse's, and Rex's eyes boring into me. I nod to let them know I'm okay, and I see them give me relieved smiles.

My gaze catches on Xavier's, he's watching me again. His eyes narrow and dart to my other men with a knowing look, but all he does is stare back at me, his lips tilting up slightly.

After we finish eating, we're thrown back into our cells and left alone for the rest of the night. There must be no other fights today—maybe it was a down day or for training, I'm not sure. But even though I'm surrounded by people, Nixon on one side and Xavier on the other, I feel so alone. I wrap my arms around myself, wishing more than anything I was back at camp, enveloped in my men's arms in my tent.

"Come here, baby," Nixon murmurs softly.

I realise I've just been standing, staring at the bars of my cell, when his voice breaks through. I shake off my melancholy and force my legs to move. I shuffle over and slump on the bed roll, leaning my side against the bars again. He moves until he's pressing against me, the cold metal between us. I slip my hand through the bars and he grabs it, weaving our fingers together and offering me comfort. I felt like I had to be so strong today, never showing weakness, not letting anyone catch on to my fear because if they did, they'll use that against me. For now, in the darkness of our cells, I allow myself to be vulnerable, to need Nixon and his warmth. I need to be weak for a moment so I can be strong again tomorrow.

Resting my head against the bars, I stare into his face and he does the same, until we are inches away. His eyes tell me everything that he doesn't say out loud, promises and love shining in those depths. It makes a smile kick up at my lips, even as I hold him tighter. I feel like my family is slipping away from me with every moment. I hate the distance between us, although I know it's for the best.

This isn't just a fight, no, this is a game, and *we* are the game pieces. They are looking for every hint of weakness to use against us and destroy us, defeat us. I can't let that happen. We need to play them at their own game, use it against them and flip the rules. This is more than physical strength, they want our minds as well. And they're going to get it, just not in the way they were thinking.

I have always faded into the background, always been good at being invisible, like every slave is, and I am going to use their own egos against them. I'm going to beat them at their own game and free my family, and then we will rock this city to the core. I won't let the freaks here suffer anymore. It's time for a change in the status quo. It's time for the freaks to have a voice...maybe even rule.

The bracelet Gregor gave me glints, catching my eyes. He said I would need it, is this what he saw? Will it help me in the fights or was it meant for something else? Either way, I am glad I have it.

"You did good today," Nixon murmurs.

I nod, grinning slightly. "They won't let you not fight for long," I warn softly, my voice filled with worry.

He grunts, but offers nothing else. He is my silent giant, a man of few words. We pass the time watching the comings and goings of the guards and slaves. I need to know the schedules, the layouts, and the weak links. Here, information is power. It's hard to tell how much time has passed with no windows, but it must be late when the lights and torches are finally extinguished, plunging us all into complete darkness. Nixon's grip on my hand keeps me centered, locked into the present. The only sounds are the whispers of slaves moving or tossing on their sleeping mats.

My mouth feels glued shut, unwilling to break the silence. I'm wound tight, too stressed to relax and sleep, even though I need to so I can keep up my strength. The food isn't great, it would be easy to lose muscle mass, and in a place like this that would be deadly. I find my eyes drifting to where I know Xavier is in the next cell, my thoughts turning back to him saving me.

Why did he do it? Why do I care?

Something in his eyes stops me every time—a suffering, a pain that echoes within me. I can't seem to stop myself from being drawn to him, even though I know it could cost me my life. A man like that only looks out for himself, and he didn't become champion and survive so long down here by making friends and looking after other people. No, his wins come from blood and suffering. Each scar was earned and paid forward, his body honed into a weapon. He has become what they wanted, nothing but a killing machine with his eyes only set on protecting himself...so why help me?

It shatters the illusion and facade he has tirelessly fought for and makes me re-evaluate him. Maybe he isn't as ruthless and heartless as I first thought. Footsteps heading downstairs, mixed with voices which seem to get closer, have me darting to my feet, reluctantly letting go of my hold on Nixon's hand.

Guards.

Torches flare at the edge of our row of cells, the light bright and almost blinding after being in the dark for so long. I squint, stepping back, until I'm pressed against the wall. I have a bad feeling in my stomach, which is only confirmed when the guards stop outside my cell.

I spot Trent and another guard, both staring in and smirking at me. One holds the torch, the other keys and his baton. Trent's eyes dare me to misbehave and I know he's hoping I will fight them so they have an excuse to hurt me. Swallowing hard, I hold my head high in defiance.

"Lucky you, slut, you have a fan," Trent taunts, laughing, and the other man joins in until their mocking laughter wraps around me and makes me shiver, dread filling me.

I hear Nixon moving closer as if to protect me. "What do you mean?" I force myself to ask, even though in the back of my head, I already know. There's only one reason they would come to my cell at night.

"Every slave down here is for sale for the right price, bitch. Well, for sale for the night or the hour." He laughs again, his eyes dancing with glee. "You seem to have caught someone's attention, and they bought you for the night, so be a good little girl and come here." He unlocks my cell and beckons me over with his finger, but whatever his friend says is drowned out by a roar from Nixon that almost seems to shake the cells.

The guards falter for a second before their bravado bleeds back in, and Trent bangs his baton against the cell bars. "Shut the fuck up, slave, or we will make you watch."

Nixon snarls then and smashes into the bars. All eyes swing his way as the metal actually bends slightly under the pressure from his fists. For a moment, the guards look worried, but when he pushes harder, straining and yelling, and the bars don't break, they laugh.

"Come here, slave bitch. You won't like it if we have to come in and get you," Trent calls, banging on the bars again and making me jump.

Horror is rushing through me, freezing me to the spot. All this time, I survived all this time, and here I will lose the only thing they never took from me...my dignity.

My heart is beating so fast it feels like it might break free from my chest. I wish I could go with it. My body is cold, and shivers rack through me at the thought of someone other than my men touching me. Maybe before I met them, I could have handled it, I was prepared. I'd been told women were nothing more than a hole for men, but then they came along—my men.

They showed me that love and compassion are not lost, they gave me a family and pleasure. I don't think I can come back from that, but I have no choice. If I fight these guards, they will only hurt me, maybe even hurt my men to get to me. I would do anything to protect them, even this.

My shoulders slump and Nixon glances over, obviously seeing my defeated look. That only enrages him further, and now I can hear my other men calling out to us, asking what is happening. I can't answer them, my voice stuck in my throat. They can't know, it will kill them. They will blame themselves, especially my ringmaster.

"Nix," I finally whisper, and it's as if I struck him.

"You touch her, and I will kill you all. Do. You. Hear. Me?" he roars.

The guards stare at him, and I don't like the glint in their eyes. They hadn't been able to get him to fight today, not even lift a finger, and now they're getting a reaction. There is nothing I can do about that, but when they step towards his cage to obviously punish him, I know what I have to do.

Squaring my shoulders and tilting my head back, I step towards the open cell door. I don't look at Nixon as he screams for me, and I ignore the guards' laughter and lewd remarks as they watch me approach them. Nixon's fingers graze my back as he reaches through the bars, but I can't spare him a glance, or I will lose myself. I'll sob, beg them, and fight them, do anything to make this stop, but sometimes you have to grow up and make decisions to protect the ones you love, even at the expense of your own happiness...and life.

I will not let them break me, they will not stop me now.

I chant it in my head as I step closer to that open cell door. They can have my body, they can do what they want to it, but I will lose myself in my mind and when I come back, I will fight harder than ever to free my family. They can have my body, but they can never have my heart or spirit, that belongs to my men. Those are some big, powerful words… let's just hope I'm strong enough to live by them.

"I'll do anything!" Nixon screams. "I'll fight, throw me in the fucking arena!" His voice is desperate as he struggles to reach me, trying to bend the bars. Turning slightly, I grab his hand and squeeze once before forcing myself to let go.

"Shh, it's okay, big guy," I whisper softly, just for him, before taking that final step from my cell. Trent grabs me and throws me into the other guard's chest who wraps his arms around me. He grinds against me, digging his hard cock into my arse as his foul-smelling breath brushes over my face.

"I wonder, little slave… what do you taste like?" he growls, thrusting against me harder.

Trent swings my cell door shut before glancing over. "You know the rules, no touching them unless you pay."

"Aww, come on, just for a second, they won't even know," the guard holding me replies, but Trent grabs my arm, his fingers digging into my skin as he pulls me from the man's grip and yanks me to his side. I collide into him with a gasp. After that, I lock my lips together, knowing each sound I make is only enraging Nixon further, who's pacing and growling in his cage like a trapped animal, looking for his shot. A chance to get to me, to protect me. I know this will hurt him most of all, but I can't let that stop me. Either way, this is happening, and at least this way it's on my terms. At least he didn't see this coming, that would have hurt him more.

I can hear our names being called desperately from my other men, their shouts getting louder and more panicked when we don't reply, but I force them to fade away as well before I do something stupid like try to fight. Trent's grip tightens on me like he knows what I'm thinking, and he leans closer, his evil eyes daring me to try something.

"Do it, then I'll have an excuse to beat that fucking animal and fuck you against his cell like the slut slave you are," he sneers, before pushing me away. I stumble on the uneven ground and slam into Xavier's cell, the bars cutting into my cheek and making me gasp in pain.

Xavier emerges from the darkness, wrapping his hands around the bars on either side of me as he leans in, those intense eyes locked on mine. He lets me see the anger and hatred there, even as his features contort into harsh lines.

"Don't fight them, it will only make it worse," he whispers, clearly speaking from experience. He holds the bars in a white-knuckled grip, before he lets go with a nod and steps back into the awaiting darkness, the shadows wrapping around him.

I'm grabbed again and pulled away from the bars, my cheek sore. Trent tugs me down the hallway, nearly dragging me with his harsh grip and speed. The other guard follows behind us with the torch and I have to listen as Nixon's screams fade with each step. The sound will haunt me forever, I know that, filled with so much pain and grief that it cuts me to my core.

I'm pulled past the other cells and I see more than a few peering eyes watching us as we pass. I spot the bathroom as I am dragged behind it to the rooms on the back row. We don't go into the first room where we were branded, but into the second one. Trent knocks respectfully, and I don't hear a response, but he opens it anyway. He flings me inside, and I stumble and fall to my knees, jarring them hard on the packed earth. They might have covered it in carpet like the other room, but it still hurts.

"As you requested," Trent says, sounding formal and respectful.

My hair has fallen into my face, shielding my view, and I have a horrible moment of not wanting to move, as if that might make them notice me. So instead, I peer through the red locks and see the shining shoes, black trousers, and crossed legs of a man in a chair just in my peripheral.

"Good, leave us," the mystery man orders. A frown tugs at my lips. He sounds familiar...why?

I rack my brain for it, but the conversation distracts me. "Sir, I don't think that's a good idea, we should stay in case she becomes...volatile," Trent argues, almost cringing.

"No. Leave," the man demands, harsher this time, and there are no more words as the guards flee the room, slamming the door behind them in their haste.

"You may get up." His voice has softened, taking on a guilty tone, but it doesn't fool me. I debate my options, but I don't want to remain kneeling. Despite the shackles and brand they placed on me, I'm no longer a slave.

I'm just about to get up when a hand appears in front of my face.

Sitting back, I blow my hair out of my face. I stare at the hand and then glance up to the white, shirt covered arm, and up over broad shoulders before my gaze clashes with the man waiting before me, his face patient and open as he watches me. Now I know why he sounds familiar.

He's a Master. One from the meeting, the older one… Ches-Chest something.

"Rhea, wasn't it?" he asks formally, his hand still outstretched like a symbol of peace, but I push it away and climb to my feet, dusting off my knees. Standing up straight, I meet his eyes head-on. If he wants me crying or begging, he should have let the guards stay and hurt me. He might violate me, but I will keep my eyes on him every inch of the way so he can see what he's is wrecking, so he can see the human he is hurting.

"Yes," I snap.

He sighs before gesturing over to the two seats set up opposite each other in front of a fire, with a small table set between them.

"Please, sit." He gestures again and I finally head that way, watching him the entire time as I sit stiffly on the edge of the seat. Only then does he sit, leaning back in his chair and crossing his legs as his eyes drop to the table.

This wasn't what I was expecting at all, but maybe he's working his way up to it or maybe he wants to talk or taunt me first just because. So far, he's been polite, but that doesn't mean he won't flip in an instant. Men like him crave power, and he clearly has that in droves. I bet he lords it over people, watching their misery and pain as they die trying to reach freedom that he squanders.

He sighs loudly, rubbing at his head, and I frown, tracking his movements. Every time he shifts in his chair, I jump, thinking he's going to lunge across and grab me and force himself on me, but he seems content to just… sit?

"I'm not going to hurt you or touch you," he tells me tiredly, like he was reading my mind, or he simply must know what this looks like, especially with the bed in the corner of the room.

"Why not?" I find myself asking, relaxing slightly into the chair.

His eyes dart up and meet mine with a confused look, wrinkles pulling at the edge of his eyes.

"Excuse me?"

I shrug. "Why not? You had me brought here, you clearly want something. I'm guessing you don't give two fucks about freaks, seeing how you keep them as slaves. So why don't you cross that line?"

I don't know where this boldness is coming from, maybe it's the adrenaline from what I'd thought was going to happen, but I find myself almost demanding answers, watching him intently. He goes slightly pale and flinches at the venom in my words, but nods and sighs.

"That's fair, I deserve that." He drops his hand to his chest and watches me, but not coldly, more like he's seeing me for the first time and actually wants to convey something to me. "I am not a good man, you are correct. I have made mistakes, and I have done deeds most would find horrendous, but everything I do or have done is for my family. I assume you can understand that?"

He watches me knowingly, and I tighten my lips but incline my head, and he carries on, "I thought so. So no, I won't touch you, rest assured you are safe with me."

"So why bring me here?" I ask, relaxing with each second he doesn't spring up and attack. Maybe he *is* being truthful? I just can't get a read on this man.

He looks away for a moment before bringing his eyes back to me. "You remind me of someone. I saw it in the way you fight for your family. Your loyalty and bravery... I just..." He shakes his head, and in that moment, I know why he brought me here. The pain and utter regret in his voice, coupled with his words...

"You're lonely," I surmise.

His jaw grinds before he nods. He's the silent one now. I can work with that. I lean further back, finally relaxing.

"That is one way of looking at things," he murmurs.

"You lead, you collect slaves with the other Masters. You're rich and have everything, but I'm betting no one sees behind the facades you all wear." He blinks in astonishment and I know I have hit the nail on the head.

"Someone used to," he whispers, almost too low for me to hear.

"Who?" I find myself asking.

"Do you play chess?" he inquires randomly, instead of answering my question.

"No," I admit, before looking around the room now that I know he isn't going to attack me. "I was a slave, we weren't allowed to and, well, my family aren't the chess type, but I saw my first master play it a lot."

"Would you like to play?" he asks, sounding excited. "I will teach you."

I look back at him, surprised. "Sure."

He gets to his feet and moves over to the bar in the corner of the room, rooting around behind it as I continue my perusal of the room. It's pretty much the same as the other room, just a bit bigger and posher.

I drag my gaze back to him as he returns with a chess set and places it softly on the table, setting it up as I watch. I take that time to observe him. He doesn't have his suit jacket on, and somehow it makes him less imposing. Up close, he looks younger than I first thought, but his hair is still greying and soft wrinkles line his face, so I would guess he's around forty. He holds himself like only rich, important men do, but some of that...tension has dropped away. I tilt my head, scrutinizing him, considering what his game is here. Either way, I will go with it and see what I can glean from him.

He sits back once the pieces are all set up and I run my eyes over the board. It has been well looked after, and it's similar to the one I saw Frederick play, but I haven't got the first clue on where to start. I scoot to the edge of the seat, leaning closer to the board. I will go along with this and use it against him. He wants company and I want information. Maybe he's the key to figuring a way out of here.

"This is how you set up the board," he explains, showing me each piece on the checkerboard before sitting back. "White always goes first, then the other player goes, we alternate. You...take pieces when you encounter them."

I nod, following so far.

"Okay, pawns," he holds up the piece, "can only move forward. They can move diagonally, for example, but only forward. On their first move, they can move one or two spaces, but only one space after that." He runs through the rest of the rules, showing me each piece and how they move before giving me examples. I follow and watch him intently, knowing if I play well and show enthusiasm, he might invite me back, giving me more of a chance to gain his trust and therefore learn the information that I need. Maybe...he'll even be an ally.

"Okay, shall we give it a go? Just a friendly game and I will give you pointers?" he suggests, sounding excited, even his eyes are alight, and he doesn't look tired anymore.

He makes the first move and I analyse the board before moving my first piece. It goes on like for a while, us just playing the game as I sneak looks at him, deciding how to prod for information without being completely obvious.

"Do you play often?" There, that seems like a safe starting point.

"I used to. This is the first time in a while," he admits, moving a piece and taking my pawn from the board, and placing it to the side.

Frowning at his move, I debate the board. "Why did you stop?" I ask almost distractedly, as I grab my next piece and move it. He grins at me and nods appreciatively at the move.

"You're a natural," he tells me then, in a more somber tone, adds, "I lost my game partner." He stills before shaking it off quickly, though his shoulders slump like they are too heavy to hold up.

"I'm sorry," I offer, and I am. Loss is hard no matter if I think he's a monster or not.

He doesn't reply, but does an impressive move and sits back as I look at the board, trying to plan my next move.

"This game is all about strategy, Rhea. You do not need to be the smartest, simply the most adaptable."

I freeze, does he mean...? No, he couldn't have. I shake off my suspicions. It must be coincidence, even if it doesn't feel like it was.

I move and then sit back, mimicking him. "If I may ask something?" He nods, smiling slightly, no doubt at my manners. "Why do you hate us freaks, so much?"

He winces but doesn't try to deny it. "I don't, this is just business. I didn't invite you to the city, Rhea. Like you, I am just a pawn in a much bigger game, the sooner you make peace with your place in the world, the easier it will be."

"I won't make peace with being oppressed and abused for something I was born with. This is who I am. Those people out there deserve a life, and until that happens, I won't stop fighting. I will never give up. I will never settle for a place that isn't free."

"Then I am afraid you are going to have a hard and painful life," he responds sadly.

"Life is filled with pain, no matter what. How you react to it is what makes us human," I counter, as he leans forward and makes his next move.

"I wish I could believe that as you do, but I have had my share of pain and heartache. Not feeling, simply being led, is sometimes better than that not knowing and the eventual fall," he replies sadly, and his face seems to cloud. "It's late, you should get back."

He goes to stand and I panic, jumping to my feet. "We didn't finish."

He smiles. "Maybe we can finish it another time, would that be okay?"

"Yes, I would like that." I nod, forcing the words out when all I want to do is grab him and demand he lets us free, but I know the guards are waiting outside.

"Very well then, and please, while we are in here, feel free to call me Chester, but out there, it is Master, or I will have to have you punished, understand?"

I nod again, gritting my teeth before forcing a fake smile he ignores, because he goes to the door and opens it. "We are done here. See her back to her cell and make sure no one touches her."

I turn in shock at his words before he glides out of the room. The fire-warmed room suddenly goes cold as Trent and the other guard steps in with lewd grins. "You must have pussy made from gold, or maybe you are just good at sucking cock, eh, slave? Maybe I should test it out." Trent grins, walking over and grabbing me. I don't fight his hold as he drags me from the room and back down to the cells, the other guard hurrying after us. I'm thrown back into my cell and I catch Xavier watching me, but I turn to Nixon who's deadly quiet. That scares me the most.

He's standing in the middle of his cell, his hands clenched into fists. I gasp when I spot the blood covering both of them. He doesn't even look at me, just stares at the darkness beyond. His bed roll is ripped up and hanging out of his cage. Each bar has dents and I spot blood on nearly all of them. I even see a dent in the wall. It looks like he's been trying to break free the whole time. Guilt eats me up, but I know I didn't have a choice.

"Big guy?" I call softly, pressing against the bars.

He slowly turns his head to face me, his eyes murderous and face so cold, I almost flinch, but I know he would never hurt me. This isn't my Nix I'm looking at.

"Nix?" I prompt.

"Did anyone touch you?" he grinds out, his voice filled with loathing.

I can almost feel him holding his breath. Despite it hurting, I slide my arm between the bars, reaching for him as the metal cuts into my shoulder.

"Did they?" he demands.

"No, Nix, look at me. I swear to you, they didn't touch me. I'm fine, I'm okay. It's okay." I just keep repeating the words over and over, soothing him the best I can.

He steps forward and slowly takes my hand, that murderous rage still in his eye. I lean in closer, whispering, "It was one of the Masters. He was lonely and we played chess, that's all. I can use this, Nix. I can use his own emotions to help us. I will get us free."

"Not at a cost to you," he snaps, his hand squeezing mine before his touch gentles and he seems to relax. "I can't, *you* can't. I lost my mind, Rhea. If I lost you or someone hurt you, and I couldn't protect you, no one would be safe."

I swallow, rubbing away the blood on his knuckles, showing him how unafraid of him I am. "I know, I'm okay."

He lets out a shaky breath and all the fight seems to leave him. Stepping closer, he tries to wrap his arms around me ,but the bars get in the way. Kneeling, he presses his forehead to the bars, his head near my chest. Threading my fingers through his hair, I hold him to me.

"Shh, I'm okay. We are okay, we are going to get free. I will get us out of here and we will show them what freaks can do. They will regret everything they have done to these people and us, but I need your support. I need you by my side," I whisper.

"Always," he murmurs, leaning further into me like he can't help himself.

I hold him for a while before a yawn splits my face and he demands I rest. I curl on the bed roll, my hand through the bars, holding his as he sits up and keeps watch, refusing to sleep even when I beg.

"They will break that spirit, they always do," comes a whisper, and I turn my head to the side to meet Xavier's eyes. He's on his side, watching me through the bars.

"They've never met me." I grin.

Maybe it was a trick of the lights, or I imagined it, but I could have sworn a smile tilts his lips up before he turns over, giving me his back again.

"I like him," Nix whispers to me.

"Do you?" I query. Nix likes very few people, so for him to like Xavier, the man must have done something to earn his respect while I was gone.

"He's like us," Nix whispers so softly, I almost don't catch it. I look at him in confusion. Does he mean powers? Everyone here has those. Or did he mean Xavier's like our family? I will never know, because he doesn't elaborate and eventually, I have to close my eyes.

I wonder what tomorrow will hold, because after one day here, I can already feel the outside world slipping away...which is exactly what they want.

Chapter Ten

The atmosphere in the air feels electric today. The guards have a skip in their step and the other slaves are quiet, somber. Something is going to happen, and I can't help feeling that it won't be good for any of us.

I had looked for clues at breakfast, scanning the area for my other guys, all of whom were staring at me with relief lining their faces as I came into their view. They must have been terrified something awful had happened to me. My gentle, silent giant only goes into a rage when someone he loves is hurt or threatened. Once reassured I was still in one piece, we ate our breakfasts silently, while Nixon remained pressed close to my side, glaring at anyone who came near us. His fists were swollen and bloody, but if it's bothering him, he doesn't let it show.

A loud clanging of metal on metal fills the room, bringing my attention back to the present, and I look around the line we have been filed into. Nixon is behind me, of course, and I can see the other guys spread out in the line. Some of the slaves have huddled together, whispering, with a grim excitement lighting their eyes as they eye up the other slaves. The feeling of so many eyes on me makes me shudder, which only makes them grin more.

"I wonder who'll be up today," someone whispers behind us, and I realise what's about to happen. There is going to be a fight today. Dread fills me. We haven't practiced, I don't know how to fight against people like this!

"The new slaves," another voice answers the first, and I have to fight the urge to turn around. "They always try them out early, break 'em in." His voice is quiet, but he might as well have shouted it. The impact of his words hits me like a hammer. I knew they were going to make us fight, but being faced with the reality of it is completely different, and I don't think we're ready, that *I'm* ready.

"You think they'll make the bitch fight today?" the first voice eagerly asks, the bloodlust easy to hear in his whispered tone.

The shuffling of feet sounds, and I realise we are slowly moving forward, one person at a time. My focus shifts back to those behind me as someone starts whispering again. "Nah, they'll parade her around, show her off first."

"That's a shame," the first voice retorts, and I can feel his eyes boring into my back. "I wouldn't mind going head-to-head with her, if you know what I mean."

Anger and disgust roll through me at the thought of any of them touching me. Well, they have another thing coming if they think I'm just going to roll over and let them treat me this way. I have some tricks up my sleeve, they're not going to know what hit them. A grim smile spreads across my face at the thought. They want me to fight? Then that's exactly what I'll do.

Nixon stiffens next to me and I can hear his knuckles crack as he clenches them together, and when I glance up, his jaw is tight, his eyes dark with fury.

"Nix, ignore them," I say quietly, placing my hand on his arm to try and calm him down. I don't envy whoever he's pitted against today.

We continue walking forward, one at a time, being led out of a large door. Every time the door opens, the dull roar of people cheering and hundreds of stamping feet can be heard. Alcide and Rex have already been taken through, and with each step forward, my dread grows.

As Blain reaches the front of the line, the guards step forward to lead him through the doors. Stepping forward, he begins to walk through but stops at the last moment, turning and pinning his piercing eyes on me. He doesn't say anything, but he doesn't need to.

Don't die, his gaze says, firm and unmoving as he waits for my response, the guards manhandling him don't seem to faze him. I nod once, hoping my equally steady gaze portrays the same message back. I don't know what I'll do if one of them is hurt or killed. Blain finally moves as more guards step forward to pull him through the door, he simply glares at them and stalks through the entrance, the guards hurrying behind him.

Movement out of the corner of my eye pulls my gaze away from the door to the two guards marching towards me. One of their meaty hands lands on my arm and pulls me a step towards them. Stumbling, I feel Nixon reach for my other arm, steadying me, but also making the guards pause.

The guard whose hand is tightly wrapped around my arm finally meets my gaze. "You're coming with me." His voice is gruff and firm, but I can see a glint of something that looks like sympathy in his eyes. That can't be right, though, these guards help imprison freaks like me, he can't feel any sympathy for us, otherwise he wouldn't work here. Looking up at him again, I get the feeling I can trust him, maybe not the way I trust my guys, but that he might be nicer than the other guards.

"Rhea." Nixon's voice pulls my attention back to him, and I see his eyes are locked on the guard's hand on my arm. There is a shuffling around us and I'm aware of the other guards all watching our exchange, and if we don't start moving soon, they are going to step in.

Keeping my voice low, I look down at our joined hands and give his a squeeze. "Nixon, I'll be okay," I assure him, hoping that my voice sounds surer than I feel. His hold on my hand loosens, and I start to move with the guard when someone else steps up to us, his stench reaching me first.

"You need a hand with the slut?" Trent sneers, as he steps closer to me, moving between Nixon and me.

The other guard straightens and shakes his head. "No, I can handle one little girl." He drags me away from the queue of slaves and towards the meeting room I was taken to meet Chester the other day.

Although he didn't say as much, I get the distinct impression he dislikes Trent as much as I do.

"Stay away from Trent." His voice is almost too low for me to make out, but his message is clear—Trent is dangerous. Dipping my head in acknowledgement of his warning, I think over this development. Is this someone who could be an ally? Will he help us escape? I want to examine him, but I know that will make the others suspicious.

Behind us, the sounds of a scuffle reaches us as Jessie's voice calls out, "Rhea!" I start to slow my steps, but the hand around my arm tightens.

"Keep walking, don't look back, it will only make his punishment worse." The guard's words make my heart constrict painfully, but I keep my pace steady as my eyes begin stinging when I hear Jessie call out again. I don't let the tears fall.

Reaching the door, the guard pushes it open and gestures me inside, pointing to a pile of cloth resting on one of the benches.

"They want you to get changed into that. I'm coming in, but I'll face away for you to change." He eyes me before he starts speaking again. "Don't make me regret that decision, otherwise this won't be so pleasant next time."

Nodding, I step inside and head towards the bundle of fabric, turning as the door clicks closed behind us. "Thank you," I say, knowing he is showing me a kindness none of the guards outside would.

Picking up the bundle of clothing, I look at them in dismay. There must be pieces missing. Raising the skimpy top up to eye level, I search around in case I dropped something, and then shake my head as I realise this is it. They can't expect me to fight in this.

The top consists of a bright red crop top, with matching red bands that circle the tops of my arms, the loose red harem bottoms have slits up the sides so my legs show as I walk. The cloth is unadorned and plain, but the fabric is high quality, far better than anything I had when I lived in Cinders. Shaking my head, I pull the clothes on, drop my old clothing on the bench, then turn around and call out to the guard.

"They expect me to fight in this?" I probably shouldn't be talking to him like this, but I get the feeling he will answer my questions where others wouldn't.

Turning his head slightly, the guard's eyes flick up to me, and once assured I'm dressed, he turns fully, shaking his head. "You're not fighting today."

Frowning, I pluck at the loose fabric around my legs. "Then what's with the costume? None of the other fighters dress up."

"You're different." For a moment, I think this is all the answer I'm going to get, but he continues as he walks over to a hook on the back of the door, which I hadn't noticed before. "We've never had a woman before. Every slave is for sale, you know that. They are simply… showing off their new merchandise," he explains, but I catch the hint of disgust that enters his voice. Taking a red cloak from the hook on the back of the door, he hands it to me. "Wear this, and these."

The cloak is made from a beautiful light, sheer red fabric attached to a thick golden band, which I clip into place at my neck. The other items he hands me are two matching golden bands which he slides onto my wrists. I frown down at them in confusion before he picks up a chain and steps towards me. I take a hasty step back and he frowns at me.

"Don't make this worse than it is." His words are the conformation I need that he isn't happy with what is happening. Swallowing hard, I nod and stay still as he attaches the chain from one wrist, to the collar at my neck, and then through to the band on my other wrist.

Once I'm dressed, the guard runs a critical gaze over me before nodding and taking my arm to lead me out of the room.

"Wait!" I call and he pauses, glancing back at me for a moment before facing the door again, but I caught his look of guilt before he looked away, his shoulders drooping for a moment...

"I have to take you out there. Please don't ask me not to."

His comment makes me pause, but I ask the question I had wanted to know since he brought me in here. "What's your name?" I ask, staring at his back.

A pause fills the space between us, and for a moment I think he's not going to answer me. "Tobias." His answer is quiet and surprised, like the fact he responded was a shock to him.

Nodding, I straighten my shoulders and hold my head up high. "Okay. I'm ready."

THE ROAR of the crowd hits me almost like a physical force and I feel my mouth drop open in astonishment. I've never seen so many people all in one place. Shielding my eyes as we exit the tunnel-like entrance way into the amphitheatre, I try to look around at the crowd.

They've not seen me yet, their attention on a figure in the center of the sandy pit. The crowd seems to be filled with all men, their cries all mixed together into an almighty roar. Looking around again, I see that I was wrong, there are a few women up there, but they are quietly standing next to their masters, glancing down at their hands, and that's when I realise that they may be dressed in finery, and their manacles might not be visible, but they are just as much a prisoner as I am.

Slaves, so many slaves.

A hand on my shoulder stops me, and I realise Tobias is looking over at one of the other guards, as if waiting for a signal. Using the pause as an excuse to look around, I realise that cages surround pit in the center, facing down into it. In each cage is a slave, their gazes on the figure in the center of the pit. Looking closer, I recognise that it's Xavier currently being paraded around, and something in my gut clenches as I see his blank expression. He's preparing himself to kill, emotionally detaching himself from the situation before he's forced to fight.

"I'd stay away from him too. He's brutal," Tobias warns under his breath and I nod, accepting his warning. He's right, Xavier is brutal, but I suspect that is the person they have made him become and I can't help but wonder what kind of person he was before this.

Xavier finishes his final lap of the pit and turns, starting to prowl back towards the rows of cages, his walk that of a predator. His steely gaze meets the eyes of all his potential opponents, until he sees me. His steps falter, but he covers it up, and before I know it, he's standing in front of me.

Bristling, Tobias puts a hand on his chest to keep him back from me. "Step away, slave," he orders with a bark. Xavier's eyes slide from me to the guard currently touching him, and even I would flinch back from the ice in his expression. At the sound of hurried footsteps crunching on the sandy floor, Xavier takes a step back, his eyes falling once again to me, his gaze intense, and I get the feeling he's trying to tell me something. I just wish I knew what.

Tobias grabs my upper arm again and walks me out to the edge of the pit, the crowd's shouts only getting louder as they see a new slave being shown off, and not only that, but a female slave.

"Walk around the edge of the arena, they want to see you, then come back here and I'll put you in one of the cages," Tobias explains, and I nod sharply at his words, taking the few steps out from the alcove and fully into the fighting pit.

Head held high, I start walking around the edge of the sand, keeping my shoulders back and my steps steady. If I show them any sign of weakness, they are going to eat me alive. The burning midday sun shines down on me, making the golden bands glisten, my red silken 'cape' blowing out behind me as I walk, the chains clinking with each step. The feel of hundreds of eyes on me makes my skin crawl, but knowing that my guys are watching makes me feel stronger.

"Our newest fighter is the lovely Rhea, and we've been told she has the nickname Rhea the Immortal. We will be putting those claims to the test, make sure you place your bets before the big fight." The loud, amplified voice fills the amphitheatre, and almost makes me stumble, but I catch myself at the last moment. A cheer rises up and I realise they don't care that our lives are at risk here. I knew this was a game, but I thought they would want us alive...they don't. They simply don't care.

As I walk back towards Tobias, a rising feeling of defiance runs through me and before I can stop myself, I stop and glare up at the box the Masters are lounging in. I meet their eyes, and I hope they realise that my look holds a promise. I will burn this whole place to the ground if one of my guys gets hurt. Just as the crowd starts to shift restlessly, I break eye contact with the Masters and walk back to Tobias, who leads me to my cage.

Hearing the scrape of the metal lock slide into place, I eye the small space before turning around to face the pit, glancing at the cells on either side of me. I don't recognise the person in the cell to my left, but to my right is Xavier, who is gripping the bar of his cell like it's his lifeline. I look around to see if my guys are nearby, but they seem to have spread out us across the arena.

A curse comes from Xavier, and I see him shaking his head, his face grave as he nods out towards the pit. "He's one of yours, right?"

Confusion makes me slow, but when I turn my head to see what he's talking about, terror freezes the blood in my veins.

"No." With a gasp, I leap forward, grabbing at the cold bars and shaking them in vain as I watch Nixon, my gentle giant, be led into the pit.

"Don't let them see it's getting to you, they will use it against you." Xavier's voice brings me back into the present, and I spin on him, my fear and anger bubbling over until I'm snarling at him.

"That's easy for you to say, someone you love isn't being forced to go out there and fight to the death!" My whisper shout is starting to gather attention, the slaves on either side of us watching and guards striding over with their batons out.

"You know nothing about me," Xavier replies, before stepping away as the guard smashes his baton into the cage door, the loud metal sound making me take a step back. The guards say something, but my full attention is on Nixon, my heart in my throat for each step he takes.

His fight can't last long, ten minutes max, but every second he's out there feels like an eternity, and my hands are burning in pain from where I'm gripping the bars. Nixon's opponent, a thin, weaselly man I've not seen before, didn't stand a chance. Even with his powers of invisibility, Nixon was able to find him and pin him to the ground. At one point, I thought he was going to kill the man, but his eyes shot up and met mine, and he simply pushed the guy into the ground and held him down until the Masters called an end to the fight. They didn't look pleased, and the crowd booed at the lack of bloodshed, until Xavier is sent in to fight against the same guy. The weaselly man was no match, and just before Xavier slits his throat, he raises his eyes to meet mine in a mimicry of Nixon, then he cuts deep and the man's blood turns the sand in the pit red.

Dropping the now dead body to the floor, Xavier stands, his eyes not leaving mine, until he is led out of the arena completely, through the tunnel doors, and back into the room we had all been staying in.

Looking over at the corpse as the crowd starts chanting for the next fight, I can't help but feel responsible for the stranger's death.

Chapter Eleven

"Wake up, you fucking freaks! It's time for a show! You have thirty minutes to eat, shit, and wash before I expect you all at the gate! Get moving!" one of the guards yells, running his baton down the front of the cells, the metal clanking loudly in the early morning. I can't be sure what time it is, due to the lack of windows down here, but it is definitely early. Clambering from my sleeping mat, I hold back a wince at my sore muscles from sleeping on the floor. Twisting in the middle of the cell, I pop my back and quickly re-plait my hair, winding it at the back of my neck to keep it off my face.

I glance over at Nixon to see him waiting in the middle of his cell, watching everything outside. I hope today isn't like yesterday. I can't watch any of my men fight again. Keys jingle as guards unlock the cells. Men burst free and head straight for the showers. I crinkle my nose, looking down at myself. I could really use a shower, but I can't protect myself. I would be vulnerable, naked, and that would be tempting fate down here, especially with all the slaves heading that way. Hey, if I smell, it might even put some of the slaves and Masters off. So I don't shower, leaving that problem for another day, and head for the feeding area.

Nixon follows on my heels and I hear a second pair of footsteps. I glance over my shoulder to see Xavier whispering to Nixon before he throws me a look and breaks away, grabbing his food and sitting at his table away from everyone like usual. I grab a tray of food with Nix and we sit silently at our table. A couple of minutes later, the rest of my men file in. Jessie's hair is wet and shaggy around his face, there are bags under his eyes, and when he spots me, even his smile is weak. This place is grinding us down already. Rex is a little more put together, but he's pale and his usually tanned skin looks dull and life-less. Alcide appears normal, his hair is slicked back and styled even though it's wet, and he is smiling and watching everything like he doesn't have a care in the world. I frown at that before looking away. Alcide is good at pretending, I guess it's part of his charm, but can he really be that unworried? He didn't even look over at us. I shake off the thought and glance down at the gruel on my plate.

It makes the time Nixon tried to cook look like a five-course meal in comparison. It's lumpy and a weird, creamy liquid is forming in the middle. It doesn't look appealing, but I need to keep up my strength, so I grab my spoon, and without even tasting it, I swallow it down, fighting back my grimace at each mouthful.

Nixon just glares down at it before grabbing the tray and holding it to his mouth. He tips it back and swallows it before dropping the tray to the table with a grimace. Guess he isn't a fan of the food either. I manage half of the slop before I drop my spoon and sit back, my stomach too tense to eat much else anyway. I do, however, force myself to drink the cloudy water they provided us with in little silver cups. I can survive without food for a while, but my body needs water, and I know I haven't gotten enough recently. It's evident by the headache lingering in the back of my head and the parched feeling in my mouth. Once I'm done, I look at Nixon and lower my voice to not be overheard.

"I'm heading to the bathroom, will you watch the door for me?" He nods and stands instantly, both of us not wanting to be too careful, it's not just the other slaves I am worried about, but the guards too. I have noticed the way their eyes linger on me, I'm not stupid, I know I'm the only female here. A freak, a slave, and soon they will try something simply because they can. I won't make it easy for them. I head to the bathroom, noticing most of the slaves have made their way to the eating area now. We can't have long left, so I hurry down the hallway to the open doorway of the bathroom. I spot a few naked men still showering in the open cubicles, but I avert my eyes and rush to the empty bathroom stall on the end. I shut the door slowly, watching as Nixon takes stands before it, with his arms crossed and his face daring someone to try and get past him.

There is no lock on the other side, so I keep one hand pressed to the scarred, off green wood as I shimmy my pants and underwear down before squatting over the hole in the floor. I pee as quickly as I can, looking around for the roll, and I groan when I realize there isn't any. Dropping my head back, I blow out a breath before standing and pulling up my underwear and trousers, then I drop my hand from the wood. Pushing it open, I run into Nixon's back, so I tap it and he moves aside. I see both men watching him from the shower stalls, and their eyes instantly dance to me, filled with a recognisable look.

I give them my best 'don't fuck with me face' that I learned from Blain before tilting my head back and prowling from the room, giving them my back to show them I don't fear them ,even though worry snakes through my body. It's easy to feel brave with Nixon at my back though.

As soon as we leave the bathroom, I notice people starting to move to the gate, so we fall in with them and Nixon makes sure to stay so close he's touching me from behind as we line up in front of the closed door. No one is handed weapons today, so I guess we aren't fighting...then what are we doing?

Two lines of slaves, all waiting impatiently, all wondering what is happening. People start to shift and murmurs run through the gathered slaves before we hear the unmistakable grind of the gears as the gate starts to lift, letting in light from outside. It hits the top with a boom, and we are herded into the arena up top, the stone under our feet turning to packed sand as each line is led to the left and right of the gate, until we stand in a semi-circle facing the Masters' box.

"Greetings fighters!" Arthur calls, sounding way too pleased with himself.

My eyes flicker to Chester, who is sitting beside him, but he stares straight ahead, his face blank.

"Today you will understand our entertainment, the pleasure and joy you bring us. Today you are watchers as well!"

I shift my eyes, noting the guards lingering here. The other slaves must be thinking the same, since all of them are looking around in confusion. If we aren't fighting...who is? Just then, the main doors to the theatre are thrown open and my mouth opens in horror as I watch a giant, silver cage be rolled in by guards...with Fluffy inside.

He is roaring, throwing himself at the bars and swiping at the guards he can reach. My eyes fill with tears as I spot Sid in a cage behind him, then Tiny, and Rumples and Bubbles. Not my babies, please, anything but them.

My eyes swerve to the Masters' box and I see all of them looking at us...looking at me. Hardening my gaze, I glare at them, letting them see my hate. With that look, I let them know that I won't take this lying down.

They fucked with the wrong freaks.

Arthur looks away, but Trent stares right back, his lips kicking up in a smirk. "Guards, escort our slaves to their seats," he calls.

A hand grips my upper arm and yanks, I stumble and turn to glare at the guard as we're pulled across the arena and pointed into the first row of seats in the theatre. We all file in. Nixon sits on one side and Xavier sits on my other. I glance back to see Alcide, Jessie, and Rex behind me...all as angry as I am. Alcide's eyes flash dangerously, but he quickly masks it. Rex's hands are fisted, tightly clenched on his knees, his whole body vibrating with hate. Jessie is scowling and sitting straight in his seat.

I turn back to the front when Fluffy howls. Leaning forward, my hands grip the crumbling stone barrier. *Look at me*, I beg him silently. He turns in his cage, puffing up to twice his size, but his amber eyes catch on me and he freezes. They dart behind me and he whines, staring at us so sadly that it breaks my heart.

Tears fill my eyes again, but I blink them away, staying strong for them. I connect my eyes with each animal, each member of my family, and with that I tell them that I will protect them if I can. That I love them. They settle slightly until a guard gets too close, then Fluffy paws at them, Tiny smacks them, Sid hisses, and Rumple and Bubbles curl up, their fangs flashing in warning.

"Let them out, I want to see them fight. The one left alive at the end will become a new fighter," one of the Masters calls, and I watch as the guards unlock the cage doors, swing them open, then hurry away. Four guards, covered head to toe in protective gear, weapons, and shields step into the arena, their gazes locked on the animals.

Panic claws at me and I turn in my seat, facing Alcide, my eyes begging. "Do something," I hiss.

I feel Xavier looking at me, and Nixon's hand lands on my thigh, but I concentrate on our ringmaster. He stares at me, his eyes calculating, and I can see him discarding idea after idea, until his face settles into a blank mask.

"Stay here, *cariño*, and whatever happens, trust your family. Trust me," he whispers, before standing. Even though he's in rags like the rest of us, he straightens out his clothes—wrinkles dare not exist with him—and he holds his head high. If I didn't know him, and without his ringmaster costume, I would mistake him for another rich man in this city. But a fire, a fire they can't put out, burns in his eyes as he steps to the end of the aisle and faces the guards.

"Take me to the Masters' box," he calls, his voice ringing around the arena. I watch the animals respond to that, slowly stepping from their cages.

"Sit down, slave," one of the guards spits, stroking the baton at his waist.

"They will want to hear what I have to say, take me now," Alcide replies. I don't know if it's the confidence or the words, but the guard looks at the Masters' box before grabbing his arm and pulling him along to it. Alcide throws me one last look, searching my eyes—for what, I don't know—before he disappears from view.

Turning to face the front, I grab Nixon's hand and squeeze tightly, my body almost shaking with the need to reach for my powers and protect what is mine. Our animals circle each other in the middle, protecting each other like always as the armed guards close in. Herding them, taunting them.

I hope whatever Alcide does, he does it fast. My heart skips a beat when one of the guards throws a spear straight at Fluffy, but he dodges it and swipes out at the guard. No, no, no. They are taunting them, trying to provoke them into fighting before they kill them.

Another guard unravels a whip from his side and starts smacking the ground as he walks. Fluffy growls as Tiny stomps.

I gasp, my eyes unwilling to look away as they lunge towards him. Only when I feel a hand squeeze mine do I look down in confusion. I have my hand in Xavier's, squeezing hard, and he is holding it back, his fingers twined with mine, letting me take out my frustration and worry. I want to snatch it back, but my eyes slowly rise to his to find him watching me. Something passes from him to me then, our gazes locked together...an understanding?

The sound of a whip has me spinning in my seat, Xavier forgotten, and focusing back on the arena. The guard's whip flies in the air towards Tiny, but Sid throws himself in front of it, taking the lash himself.

Fury like never before rises within me. My body shakes, my ears fill with white noise, and I don't even realise I am on my feet.

"Slave, sit down before I make you!" I hear the yell as if from far away.

"Now, slave!" he yells again. My head slowly turns, my eyes locking on his.

"Rhea, sit down," Nixon hisses, yanking on me. I let him and I fall into my seat, my powers so close I can almost touch them, but held at bay by the bracelets on my arms.

My eyes drop the bracelets, but I freeze when I spot something green at my feet. Leaning down closer, I cover my movement as if I am sucking in air. There, between my legs, touching one of my feet, is a small green bud on a vine, poking through the concrete...how did that get there? My powers seem to dissolve then, and I watch in wide-eyed shock as the bud does also. Did...did I do that?

I glance at the bracelets in confusion...if I got mad enough...if I pushed enough...could I break them? It was only for a moment, a small crack of power leaking out and into the ground, but could it be enough to free us?

I shake my head, reminding myself to worry about that and my obviously new power later. I glance back up at the arena to see the animals curling into a circle together, no longer fighting back, just watching the guards warily.

The armed guards try to provoke them, but the animals are having none of it. In fact, Fluffy goes as far as to yawn in their face, both showing of his impressive teeth and dismissing them. The guards stop and look at the Masters.

Obviously enraged about the lack of results, a Master stands up. "Take the animals away! Maybe not feeding them will work! Slaves, back to your cells!" he screams.

We are pushed towards the guards in two single lines again. I stumble and glare at the guard, but he snaps the baton across my back again and I start moving, my eyes still searching for Alcide. When I find him, I blink, confused at what I am seeing and unwilling to believe it.

His eyes meet mine and they are cold, so cold I shake. He is sitting next to Arthur and Chester, sipping from a chalice and laughing with them as they watch us be herded like animals. He watches us go, with no familiarity, no love or kindness in his eyes.

Is he playing them? Charming them...or has our ringmaster decided to throw his support to the Masters? Has he seen a lost cause? Everyone always told me he knows how to survive, that he can weather anything...has he abandoned us to this storm and found shelter in riches?

We are thrown back into our cells and left alone for hours. I get bored and pace the edge of the bars. I can feel Nixon and Xavier watching me, but I pay them no mind. My mind keeps flicking back to the cold look of our ringmaster and the thought of them starving our animals. I feel like I'm going crazy. We are left locked up, and while most slaves seem to just go to sleep, including Xavier, I am left with nothing to occupy my time.

I sit, I lie, I pace, before doing it all again. Nixon watches me silently the whole time.

"No food tonight! Lights out!" comes a shout a couple of hours later. Some of the other slaves groan or complain, but no one fights back against the guard. Everyone settles in for the night, but I'm still restless, so when over an hour later, two unfamiliar guards head my way with a torch and keys, I am waiting.

I step back into the middle of the cell as they silently unlock the door and gesture for me to come out. I have a feeling this is to meet Chester, so I throw Nixon a reassuring smile. He's on his feet at the bars again, but calmer this time, so I am guessing he had one of his feelings. That more than anything reassures me, and I step out into the hallway as they slam the cell shut and lock it.

The guard holding the keys pushes me along, dragging me past the bathroom and to the private room again. Once there, he throws me inside and slams the door in my face. Blowing out a breath, I turn to see Chester already staring at the setup chess board. When I step closer, I realise he has started a new game and is waiting for me.

I slip into the seat and make my move, staying quiet, letting him simmer in silence. I have to coax him, use him, and manipulate him. Easy, right?

We play silently for a while before he sits back with a sigh, rubbing at his eyes. "You look tired," I say softly.

I feel him staring, so I duck my head and concentrate on the game, making my move before I sit back and face him, giving myself some time to school my expression. Anger is still running through me and I have to hide it.

"I don't sleep well," he replies, and I sense there is more to it than that. Does he want to share? Maybe if he opens up, I can use that weakness against him. Get him to see me as a person.

"Why not?" I ask.

He remains silent, his eyes begging me not to drag up his pain, but

I need it, I need his pain and his trust. As much as I hate him, I need him and his help.

"Who did you lose? You told me I reminded you of someone, someone who saw under your mask, who you would have done anything for. Family...a wife?" He clenches his jaw then. "No...a daughter," I finish, and he looks away. I know I'm right. "What was her name?"

"Marie, her name was Marie." Every word is harsh, like it has been pulled from deep inside, his pain too great to keep locked away when faced with my questions. He needs to talk, he wants to talk, maybe that's why he brought me here without even realising it. He needs someone who can understand, someone who can't use it against him. He needs a place of vulnerability, and whether he or even I like it, this is it, and I can use that against him...if I am cut-throat enough. But all it takes is the thought of my animals, my family locked up and wasting away, and I realise I am. I would do anything, be anything for them. They taught me how to love, how live again, and I won't dishonour that now by being weak when they need me.

I think of Blain and his knives. I will be sharp like them, brutal and unforgiving. Of Rex, and his speed and strength. I will hit strong and true like that. Of Jessie and his fun-loving nature. I will hide behind it...of Nixon and his unwavering loyalty, and Alcide and his charm. I have learned it all, and though they might not be my powers, I will gladly use them now.

"What happened to her?" I inquire softly. I truly do feel sorry for him and I let that show.

He sucks in a shaky breath, his eyes falling to the board like he's unable to bear looking at me as he speaks, pain and guilt lacing each word.

"She was killed, simply for being her," he admits, and even from here I see the tears swimming in his eyes, wetting his lashes.

"I'm sorry, were you close?" I press, even though I know the answer.

"Yes, she was my little girl. I doted on her, more than I probably should, but she was so perfect, our miracle girl. We thought we could never have kids, and then she came along…" He pauses then and moves his piece, his eyes taking on a faraway look.

"I did everything I could to protect her. I sold my soul to the devil for it, and yet it didn't save her. Now I'm stuck with the devil…and he holds all the power." He looks up then. "No one gets free of him, don't you know? Wealthy or slave, we are all just his playthings, and sooner or later he comes to collect what is his."

I blink at him, but he seems to shake it off and nod at the board. I move a piece distractedly and he tuts. "Bad move," he admonishes.

"Do you regret it…selling your soul?" I ask, using his metaphor.

He fingers a rook as he thinks. "No…no, I would do it again because that extra time I had with her made it worth it, but now I must pay the price and I am afraid, Rhea, you are involved in that," he murmurs softly.

I go quiet then, thinking through what he has said as we carry on the game, but I am distracted and he easily beats me. "Don't worry, I will give you another chance to win," he offers.

"Thank you, I would like that." I stand then, knowing they will come for me soon. "Chester?" I call, needing to get out what I wanted before I leave, even if the mood is somber.

"Yes?" he replies, looking up at me.

"Those animals, they are my family, they are innocents. Will you at least see that they are fed?"

He worries on his bottom lip. "I will try."

"Thank you. I fear what I would do if I was to lose them…my family are my entire world. You understand that, and anyone threatening them is merely an obstacle to overcome."

He nods, watching me with sharp eyes. "And I work for that obstacle, so we know where we both stand."

I guess we do. We are both trapped in this game, each move resulting in either death or another day of survival. I turn around and head for the door, with nothing else left to say.

"Goodnight, Rhea," he calls softly, and I turn to see him staring off into space again, his words echoing around me.

Who is the devil…and what did he sell his soul for?

For her? For Marie?

"Goodnight," I say back, turning as the door opens to reveal a grinning Trent.

I would sell my soul to any devil to save my family. I guess, in that respect, we are the same. Rich...slave...we are all at the mercy of our decisions, and my decisions led me here...will they lead me from here as well?

Chapter Twelve

I don't sleep well that night, my mind replaying yesterday's events, consumed by my fear for the animals, *my* animals. People never understand when I say they are like family to us, but I dare them to look into their eyes and say they are 'just' animals. They are freaks, the same as us, and part of that is having a more human-like intelligence. They know more than they should and act in a way you wouldn't expect from a 'normal' animal. I hope Chester will honour his promise and try to keep the animals out of the fights, but the Masters will have figured out by now that they can use the animals against us.

When the guards stalk into the dark room and smack the cell bars with their batons, I am already awake and sitting at the front of the cell, leaning against the iron rods as my mind races.

"Wake up, freaks. It's a special day today!" Trent appears in my line of sight, his face split into a sick grin as his eyes sparkle with dark glee, sauntering towards my cell. Licking his lips, his eyes roam up and down my body, and I have to fight the urge to shudder. I won't let him have the satisfaction of knowing he has this effect on me. "Today is a historic day," he continues, his voice loud for all to hear, but I know his words are directed at me. "Our first female freak will be fighting." The room seems to fall silent as I absorb his words, my mind falling equally as quiet. Taking another step forward so he is almost pressed against the bars, Trent lowers his voice so he's talking just to me. "Ready to show us what you've got, little slave?"

This time, I can't hide the shudder that runs through me, and he laughs as he slaps his hands together in glee. "I've got a bet going on how long you're going to last. I think ten minutes, max." His sneer makes me narrow my eyes and I stand up, leaning against the bars with my arms crossed to show him exactly what I think of him. If that's what he thinks, then I'm going to show him precisely what I'm made of. I'm sure as hell not some meek slave girl, and I'll use their prejudices against them. "Shame, really, to waste a body like yours in the ring. I'm sure I could think of better uses for it…"

"Trent! Stop fucking around, we don't have time for messing with the slaves," the other guard shouts from the opposite side of the room, causing Trent to let out a growl of frustration. He pushes away from my cage and stalks over to the other guard. "After the attack on the city last night, they want to make an example of the slaves. They are sure there is some rebellion scum in here." The words are whispered, but I catch them. Attack? This rebellion must have been behind it, and they seem to think that some of the rebellion are in here. Storing the information away for later, I look around to see if anyone else hears it and I see Xavier looking directly at me, nodding once.

Letting out a deep breath, I lean against the bars, my body slumping now that Trent has gone. That relief doesn't last long, though, as I registered what he said. I'm fighting today. No. No, no, no. I can't fight, I have no training, I'm going to be killed instantly, and even if by some chance I win, can I really kill someone? My thoughts race and I have to grip on to the bars to keep me upright as panic threatens to overtake me. I'm aware of someone moving beside me, but thankfully no one touches me.

"Don't let them see you like this." I hear a voice, but I can't quite register who it is. "Snap out of it, Rhea!" The harsh words pull me out of my panicked state, my eyebrows pulling together in a frown as I turn my gaze on the owner of the voice.

Xavier is standing the other side of the bars I'm leaning against, his hands clutching the rods on either side of me, his knuckles white with the force of his grip. My awareness starts to come back and I'm conscious of Nixon calling my name from the cell behind me, but I keep my gaze on Xavier in front of me.

The sound of the cells being opened on the other side of the room reaches us, and I eventually take a step back from Xavier, turning to face a worried-looking Nixon as we wait for our cells to open. A shout rings out around the room and I frown, moving to the front of the cell to see what's going on, but I can't see anything. Whatever's happening is on the side of the area I can't see. The noises get louder and more shouts ring out, more guards flood into the space, all heading towards the back. My stomach twists in knots, since the other guys are over in that part of the room.

Trent strides to our side of the room, his fury evident as he looks around at us in disgust while the sound of slamming cell doors fills the space. "Thanks to some of your fellow freaks, your mealtime privileges have been revoked." Groaning fills the room, but no one sounds surprised, obviously this has happened before. "Save your fighting for the arena! Remember that you only eat because we *say* you can." His eyes land on me before flicking to Xavier, his expression darkening before he stalks off.

My stomach growls in protest at the thought of receiving no food, especially since we didn't eat last night. My thoughts once again flash to the fact I'm going to be fighting today. Exhaustion runs through me, my limbs feeling weak as I raise my hands to rub my face. How am I supposed to fight like this? The only bonus is that whoever I fight will be feeling just as weak as me. My thoughts run in circles and I push myself to my feet, circling the small cell. What will the guys do if I die? It would kill them, especially Nixon.

"Don't start thinking like that." A dark presence appears at my shoulder and I know it's Xavier without having to look.

Continuing my circuit of the cell like a caged animal, I keep my eyes on my path. "What do you mean?"

"You're already thinking like you're going to lose." The anger in his voice has me stopping, and a frown pulls at my brow as I glance over at him. "Think like that and you will lose." I've seen Xavier angry before, it seems to be his default setting, but there is something different about his anger this time.

"How am I supposed to win? What if they pit me against one of my guys?" The hopelessness of the situation hits me. "I'm not a warrior like you!"

"You don't want to be like me. Stay true to you, otherwise, they will turn you into a mindless killing machine like me." His self-loathing is clear to hear, and it makes me frown. Although I don't really know him, he's like us, and it makes me want to comfort him.

"You're not like that." There is a confidence in my voice that makes my comment into a statement, and I find that I believe every word of it. He may be harsh, brutal, and deadly, but I bet he thinks of every person he has been forced to kill. A mindless killing machine wouldn't do that, they would revel in the death. Xavier doesn't. He pretends that it doesn't affect him, but it does, I can see it.

My words obviously disturb him, as a strange expression crosses over his face. Pushing away from the cage, he snorts and shakes his head. "You don't even know me."

His comment makes me smile as he turns his back. "I don't need to know the details. I know enough."

I DON'T KNOW how long we wait in the cells until the fight. Without the morning meal to break up the time, it's difficult to tell how many hours have passed, not to mention my nerves are getting the better of me. I try to think about it like it's just another show and start going through my warmups in the small space. Eventually, Trent and the other guards come in and start unlocking cells, leading the others into a line, and bringing them out into the arena one by one.

Looking around me in shock, I realise that it's just me and Xavier left in the room. Why have we been left until last? Is Xavier going to be my opponent? My stomach drops. Can I fight him?

Feeling my gaze, he turns and looks at me. A coldness I've not seen before settles into him and I shudder. Yes, if I had to, I would fight him, but I don't hold out any hope of winning against him.

"They won't put us together to fight. Not today." I barely recognise his voice as he turns away from me.

"How do you know?" I croak, and I curse myself for sounding so weak. Balling my fists, I stand up straighter, determined to go out there looking strong.

"I'm one of their best fighters. You're a new, shiny toy for them, they won't kill you off just yet." The matter-of-fact way he says it makes me go cold, like I'm just a thing, an *object* for them to do with as they please. I've been treated like this my whole life, but it stokes the fury that has been steadily burning within me.

"I'm not a toy. I'm Rhea the fucking Immortal, and I will show them what happens when you mess with the freaks."

Something that looks like respect flashes in his eyes, but it soon disappears as Trent stalks towards my cage.

"It's time for the big show," he says mockingly, as he unlocks the door to my cell, his arm grabbing mine roughly as he escorts me to the large doors that lead out to the arena. I wonder for a second why they have left Xavier behind, but I quickly forget as I walk out of the shadows and into the ring surrounding the pit in the center of the arena. I can hear my name being called out by my guys and I try to spot them in the cages lining the wall, but my eyes are still trying to adjust to the light.

A loud beat that I can feel more than hear sounds through the arena, pulsing in time with the frantic thudding of my heart, and I realise it's the pounding of people's feet.

"Gentlemen! We have a treat for you today! There will be several fights, and our first ever female freak will be fighting today, Rhea the Immortal," someone announces loudly, and there's a raucous cheer that goes up at his words, along with some laughs as he broadcasts my name. Someone releases the shackles around my wrists, and I feel my powers return as a shove on the small of my back has me staggering forwards, but I manage to catch myself so I don't go sprawling down the steps into the pit. That fire starts to burn in me again, and I grab on to it. If I'm going to get through this, a bit of anger will only help me.

There is movement on the other side of the arena, and I brace myself for my opponent. Although Xavier said they wouldn't put us together, I can't help but worry that they will anyway. Could I hurt Xavier? If my life depended on it?

A guard steps out of the shaded area and starts walking down the steps, holding up his arms as the arena cheers at the appearance of my opponent. "Her opponent is one of our very own guards, Charlie! Give him a big applause as he puts our newest freak through her paces."

Letting out a relieved sigh, I start to examine the guard. I don't have to fight anyone I know—at least, not today.

"The rules are a little different for this fight," the loud voice proclaims, and I try to focus on what he's saying. There are rules? "The fight is to the death, the freak can use her powers however she likes, weapons in this match are only allowed by guards."

Voices from the cells behind me call out in protest, yelling foul play, but I know it's useless. None of this is fair, and I'm not surprised they are changing the rules to suit them. I try to remember what Xavier said, they won't want to kill me off yet. Snorting, I shake my head, looks like he was wrong.

Walking down the steps and into the pit, I keep my shoulders back and my head held high. The midday sun is beating down on me, warming my skin as I go to meet my opponent. Keeping my focus on the man before me, I fade out all other sounds that could be a distraction, leaving only the thud of my heart and the tread of my bare feet against the ground. The difference between when they paraded me around the arena before and now is obvious. Before, when I was presented for everyone to see, I was dressed in bright clothing. Right now, I'm wearing the dirty, simple, oversized shift and loose trousers that swing around my legs as I walk. I look like a child playing dress up in her father's clothing. My mind flicks back to the conversation I overheard between the guards in the cellblock. Are the changes because of the attack they were talking about? Are we all being punished as a result? No food, multiple fights, no shoes, or a chance to change into anything more suitable for fighting, and I've never fought before, but in the previous fights I watched, the freaks were allowed weapons.

Reaching the pit, I walk out towards my opponent, standing on the X that marks my starting position. The stones on the floor are biting into my feet, but I ignore them, keeping my focus on the guard before me. From the previous matches I've watched, there is always a signal before the fight starts, so shifting my weight from foot to foot, I wait for the signal.

When the guard suddenly shouts out and runs towards me, swinging his sword, I jump back instinctively, only saved by my fast reflexes.

What the hell? Did he start before the signal? I think to myself. Glancing up at the Masters and seeing their smug faces, I realise that this has been done on purpose. Movement to the side of the Masters has me pausing, my eyes flicking to the man standing just to the right of the others. Shock hits me in the gut like a physical force.

Alcide. Why is he sitting in the Masters' box? I didn't see him in the cells this morning, and as I stare up at him, I see he looks clean and is in new clothing I don't recognise. He meets my gaze and I'm shocked at the blank expression I see there.

A change in the air around me is the only warning I have of the guard's next attack, and I manage to dodge him at the last moment. Putting aside my confusion and pain at seeing him with our captors, I focus on my opponent. Getting upset will only get me killed and I'm not prepared for that to happen today.

They want entertainment? Then it's time to put on a show.

As the guard turns to attack me again, I throw myself forward into a cartwheel, easily moving out of his way and avoiding his strike. I continue to do this for a few minutes, barely winded, but I can see the guard is struggling to keep up, his heavy armour weighing him down. The crowd is getting restless, their thirst for blood not being met.

My distraction of looking up at the crowd costs me valuable seconds as my opponent surges towards me. I spin at the last moment, but his sword catches my shoulder, cutting a long line from the top of my arm down to my elbow. Hissing in pain, I back away, surprised that my powers didn't protect me, but then again, it was too fast for me to protect myself. My body starts to tingle as it works on knitting my skin back together while I wearily watch the guard.

I still don't want to reveal too much of my powers, but using healing always weakens me, and the lack of food and being under this burning sun is draining me. I need to end this quickly.

The next time the guard charges me, I twist out of his way, kicking out a leg and tripping him in the process, calling for the vines to grow up out of the ground and hold him down. They obey and he screams out as they cover him, pinning him to the pit, but the effort this takes is exhausting. Here in the dusty arena there isn't much plant life, and I have to dig down deep into the ground to find potential aid. I can't just create vines and plants, I can only encourage their growth, and having them buried so deep down makes it much more difficult.

Kneeling down on the chest of the thrashing guard, I see his eyes are wide with fear. He's scared of me and that shocks me more than anything.

"Sorry," I apologise softly, before I produce a knife in my hand. His expression turns to horror as he opens his mouth to plead with me. Before he can speak, I bash the pommel of the knife into his head, wincing as his skull bounces off the hard ground, but it has the effect I need it to as the guard passes out.

Standing up, I back away from the unconscious guard and look up at the Masters.

"The fight is to the death," the loud voice declares again, but I refuse to move, staring up into the eyes of the Masters. I doubt I will get away with it for long, but I won't kill, not today. I'm not sure how long we have this silent standoff, but the crowd starts to get restless. One of the Masters waves his hand and the doors to the pit open, then five armoured guards march in with their swords drawn.

"The fight is to the death." The rules are spoken again, and one of the guards stalks forward to my injured opponent. I think they are going to take him away, caring for one of their own, and give me another opponent to fight. Except, I'm not sure that I have it in me to fight another challenger.

However, I was wrong. Kneeling, the guard removes the injured guard's helmet, and without a flicker of emotion on his face, brings the knife to my opponent's throat and slashes it in one quick strike.

Horrified, I take a step back as the blood quickly pools around us, disgust and fear running through me.

"The winner is, Rhea the Immortal."

Chapter Thirteen

Later on, when we are pushed back down to our cells, I debate showering. My skin is filthy from sleeping on the floor and being up in the arena, a thin layer of dirt and grime cover it, and I am starting to smell. Tonight, we aren't locked up right away, and everyone else heads straight for food, so I lean into Nixon, thinking this is the perfect time.

"I need to shower, could you maybe stand in the entryway?" I request quietly, not wanting to give anyone a shot at me, and my cheeks heat at the idea of strangers seeing me naked. I'm comfortable in my skin now, probably from all the time with my men and the lack of modesty they have, but it doesn't mean I want to flaunt it in front of these men. I'm not a fool, it doesn't matter if they find me attractive or not, they have been locked down here for a long time without a woman. Add in adrenaline and a need to fight, and I look like the perfect prize, so I am taking no chances.

I glance up at Nixon, almost begging with my eyes, but he frowns, staring across at the showers. "There are two open doorways," he points out in a rumble, and I whine, realising my mistake.

Shit. He's right.

I sag a little, knowing I won't be showering tonight.

"I'll take the other one," comes Xavier's voice from behind us.

I spin and eye him. "Why?"

He shrugs. "Don't look a gift horse in the mouth. I won't look, if that's what you are worried about. I'll turn my back and block the entrance, and if you use one of the showers closest to a door, they shouldn't be able to see in."

"Done." Nixon nods and I trust his judgement. Not for the first time, it does make me wonder, though, what he said or did to win my fierce giant's trust. But if there is one thing I know for sure, it's to trust Nixon's judgement, plus Xavier has never hurt me. In fact, he has helped me, saved my life, when he didn't have to. Maybe it's time I started trusting him too, a strange thought since I trust no one outside of my family, but we are in a whole new world right now and friends might mean the difference between living and dying.

Nixon twines my fingers with his and I lead him over to the showers. I pick the one closest to the door like Xavier said, and watch as he locks eyes with me from the other doorway. Something passes between us before he turns, crosses his arms, and blocks the doorway completely with his back to me. Nixon does the same in the entrance closest to me and I sigh in relief. I can't wait to be clean.

I shuck out of my clothes quickly, folding the garments knowing I will have to re-wear them. I am also going to have to wash them in here at some point and try and dry them so that they aren't as…nasty, but for now, they will do. Stepping closer to the cracked, tiled partition, I pull the silver handle to the side and water sprays instantly from the head built into the wall higher up.

It hits my skin cold and makes me jump. Shivering, I cross my arms over my chest, but force myself to duck under and slick back my hair. Slowly, the water begins to heat up to the point where I can relax and start cleaning my skin.

There's no soap, but I don't care, not when I see the colour of the water hitting the drain between my feet. I'm just happy to get rid of the grime and dried sweat feeling. I daren't stay in here too long, so I scrub my hair as best as I can to get any sand or dirt out, and then linger just for a moment longer, letting the water hit my sore muscles.

"Yo, big guy, let me see our Firecracker," comes Jessie's voice from behind Nixon and I grin, turning to see him leaning down to peek between Nixon's parted thighs. He winks at me and waves before straightening.

"Alcide know you're here? What happened to the plan?" Nixon inquires.

"Don't know, haven't seen him, and guess what? I don't care. Come on, I want to see Rhea, I miss her," he whines, and my heart thumps. I miss him too.

"Nix," I call softly.

He looks at me over his shoulder, his eyes softening, and he nods. He lets Jessie squeeze past then goes back to blocking the door. Jessie grins at me and opens his arms. I rush into his embrace, slipping across the floor. He picks me up and spins me around, making me laugh before he lets me slide down his body.

He cups my face, his eyes sparkling and his smile sad. "I missed you," he whispers.

"I missed you too," I reply, leaning into his touch and pressing my body against his. I think this is the longest I have been without their touch, and my body is starved for it, craving each rough stroke of Blain's pleasure pain touch, Jessie's soft, worshipful gaze, and Rex's firm, sweet love. I can't help it, I know I shouldn't, we have a plan to stick to, and even though the other fighters are eating, they could finish at any moment and come exploring, but I lean up, place my hands on his firm chest, and press my lips to his.

He groans, his chest rising and falling faster against my palms. I can feel his heart racing, matching mine. "Rhea," he whispers raggedly against my lips.

Draping my body against his, trusting him to hold me up, I lick the seam of his lips before nibbling on the plump bottom one. Stroking my hands up his chest and around his neck, I clasp them there, holding him to me as I kiss him. I need him to show me that he is right here with me, that everything is still the same between us. That he and his body miss me as much as I miss him.

He groans and then seems to snap, kissing me back. I can taste his desperation as he sweeps his tongue into my mouth, tangling it with mine before teasing me. His kiss is like him, flirty and playful, and I'm soon gasping into his mouth. My body is on fire and he hasn't even touched me. My legs are shaking, my nipples are pebbled and hard against his chest, and my center is slick with my desire for him.

Keeping his mouth locked with mine, he walks me backwards until my back hits the cold tile, then he hoists me up against it. Gripping his hair in my hands, I wrap my legs around his waist, the water hitting us from the side, not that either of us care.

Releasing his curly locks, I trace my hands down his shoulders, tugging at his shirt. He pulls his torso away, still pinning my lower half to the wall as he rips his shirt over his head and then swoops back to kiss me. Moaning into his mouth, I scrape my nails down his sculpted back, feeling the pull of his muscles before he shudders against me. He pulls away slightly, his eyes wide and filled with hunger, his plump lips red and parted as he breathes fast.

"Firecracker," he rasps, lust coating the word, making me rub against him.

"I need you," I whisper.

He closes his eyes as if in pain and leans farther into me, his bare, slick chest rubbing against my breasts. "Are you sure?"

Grabbing his shoulders again, I dig my nails in and force his eyes to mine. "Inside me," I demand, and he grins, his eyes twinkling.

"As you wish, Firecracker." He kisses me again, sweeping his tongue in and tangling with mine. Whatever was holding him back is now setting him free. His hand comes between our bodies, cupping my breast and making me gasp. He pulls away from my lips, kissing down my shoulder and chest, sucking my nipple into his mouth.

My head falls back into the wall, my eyes closing as I grab his hair and hold him to me. He twists and flicks my nipple, moving his mouth from one to the other until I'm biting my lip, trying to stay quiet as I rub myself against his hard length pressed between my thighs. Rocking against him, I coat his cock with my cream. He catches his teeth on my nipple and my eyes fly wide, my whole body shivering in need. My gaze drifts up of its own accord and clashes with Xavier's. He doesn't look away or even pretend he isn't watching us, and I don't seem to care.

I push my breast farther into Jessie's mouth, rocking harder against his cock as pleasure ripples through me, building up, seeming to pull from my very toes. Xavier's dark eyes stay locked on mine, his jaw grinding as his gaze drops to my body, taking it all in before he meets my eyes again, and the hunger there, coupled with Jessie's mouth, throws me over the edge.

I nearly scream, but Jessie reaches up and covers my mouth with his lips, swallowing my whimpers as I shake against the wall, my pussy clenching on nothing. My eyes close, breaking mine and Xavier's stare, and when the shock of my orgasm passes, I open them only to see him with his back to me like nothing happened. But the tight muscles on his frame remind me he watched, and he liked it. Jessie moves back again, letting me suck in uneven breaths as he smirks at me.

"Didn't even touch your sweet little pussy, Firecracker," he murmurs softly, before trailing his hand down my stomach and cupping my center. I groan and rock into his hand, still needy as he strokes my pussy. He winds me back up again until I'm rubbing against his palm, hitting my clit on it again and again, and just when I'm about to explode, he pulls his hand away, making me whine while he laughs.

"Jessie," I hiss, "will you—" My words cut off and my eyes roll into the back of my head as he lines up and slams into me. He doesn't give me time to stretch around his long length before he is pulling out and pushing back in, forcing my pussy to accept him.

He kisses me again, silencing my moans I didn't even realise were escaping my lips as he picks up speed, fucking me hard and fast. His cock hits that spot inside me that none of the others ever seem to reach. Biting at his lips, I lift my hips to try and meet his thrusts. Kicking my feet against his ass, I urge him on.

He groans into my mouth, his movements stuttering before he lets go and slams into me again and again. The bite of pain makes me wild as I scratch my nails down his back. My pussy clenches on his cock, and he taps my clit with his fingers, making me come again.

I scream into his mouth and he howls into mine, slamming into me again before stilling and emptying his come inside me. Pulling my mouth away, I suck in air, trying to calm my breathing as my body turns weak. The only reason I stay upright is because of Jessie, but then his legs seem to give out as well and he stumbles, trying to right himself, but he skids on the wet floor.

We slip from the slick tiles and fall to the floor. He twists mid-air so he is beneath me, and he grunts as he hits the floor with me sprawled on top of him, still trying to catch my breath. Lifting my head, I meet his eyes and we both burst into laughter.

Shower sex is harder than it looks, but it was amazing.

He pushes some wet, tangled hair away from my face and cups my cheek, looking up at me with serious eyes. "I love you, Firecracker. No matter what is happening, or where we are, I always will. We will get out of this and be a family again, and then I can spoil you and show you the world like I've always wanted to. Me and you, Rhea, we are going to grow old together," he whispers, and Nixon clears his throat, making us both smile even as I stroke Jessie's face. "Okay, all of us will," he corrects, and I blink back the tears in my eyes.

"I can't wait," I whisper, my voice cracking. "I love you too," I reply, before dropping a soft kiss on his lips.

Another throat clears and we both look up. "Better hurry up, love birds, people are starting to head this way," Xavier calls, and I curse as I jump up.

Jessie follows and I slip, but he catches me. He helps me back into my clothes and throws his wet shirt over his shoulder before smirking at me. "We should shower together all the time, Firecracker."

I giggle and nod. "We should."

"Time to go," Xavier snaps, and I sigh, kissing Jessie again. He winks and slips past Nixon, and I wring out my hair before plaiting it, and then nodding at Nixon who has turned to see me.

"Okay, let's go." I look over my shoulder then, meeting Xavier's eyes. "Thank you," I murmur, not mentioning him watching and me enjoying it, because guilt is coursing through me. I should have been concentrating on Jessie, not making eyes at a man I barely know.

We leave the bathroom together and head to the eating area where people are starting to get up. I wave at Rex and Blain, who are sitting with a grinning Jessie. I search for Alcide, but don't spot him anywhere. I look back to Blain with a frown, and he shakes his head and mouths, "Not here."

What does that mean?

Is he still with the Masters?

Swallowing back my worries, I sit at our table as Nixon places our bowls of food in front of us. This time, Xavier sits with us. He's at the end of the bench, but still with our group. Others notice, throwing him narrow-eyed, calculating looks, but he ignores them as he scarfs down his food.

Trent stomps towards our table then with an evil grin on his face, and I know whatever he has to say isn't going to be good. He scans us all, pausing on me, his eyes lighting up. "Slave, you are fighting tomorrow!" he calls, and all of my men get to their feet, but I stop them with a shake of my head. "Fighting tandem, with Immortal," he finishes, and my eyes widen before swinging to Xavier's.

His eyes clash with mine, both of us wondering why. Has he ever fought in tandem before? I think not, so what has changed...what are the Masters planning, and what does it have to do with Xavier and me?

I guess I won't know until tomorrow...

Chapter Fourteen

That night, once we are back in the cells, the guards come and collect Xavier and me for training. We don't speak as we are led up the tunnel and onto the fighting sand. Guards mill around, not bothering to watch us, and there are no Masters in sight.

"You have two hours to practice, don't ruin her too much, Immortal, we need to watch her lose tomorrow," Trent sneers, as he unlocks our shackles and then strides over to the other guards. He joins in with their conversation, leaving Xavier and me alone in the sand. He turns to face me, obviously as happy as I am about having to fight together. I'm not a fighter, have never even tried, and he has. He's won every fight, and now he has to deal with having an inexperienced partner.

"Okay, what can you do?" he asks, propping his hands on his hips. "I saw what you showed them, but I need to know if that's the extent of it or if you hid some?"

"I hid some. I've tested my powers, but they still seem to be growing..." I debate what I should tell him, worrying my bottom lip, and he steps closer, lowering his head and his voice.

"You have to learn to trust me. I need you to survive so I do, we have no choice but to work together. I saw you fight, you are stubborn as hell and a survivor, you keep getting back up no matter how many times you get knocked down. We can use that, but you have to be determined to survive, you have to want to live," he rasps, his dark eyes locked on me. I wish I could ask Alcide what I can tell him, but I have to make this decision without my ringmaster and his plans.

"I can't really die. I adapt to everything thrown at me. Fire, water, ice…" I trail off as his eyes widen. "I can be hit with a knife, stabbed, shot, whatever you want, and I can change quickly. I did fly once or twice, but that takes a lot of effort. I can also channel some speed and strength." I don't tell him that I can channel it from my men, but it might come in handy here.

"Good, we can use that." He nods.

"What do you know about tandem fighting?" I inquire.

He sighs. "Not a lot. They tried it before, but my partner died in the second fight. We will be chained together with only some slack to manoeuvre, facing whoever they deem a good fight, and we must fight them jointly. Let's work on getting in sync, since you will have to move when I move. We need to protect each other's back, and just fight like fucking hell and hope we survive, and Rhea, I plan on surviving, so you better give it everything you have," he demands, his face fierce and eyes harsh yet comforting. He wills me to fight, he orders it, and I find myself straightening and nodding. I will do whatever it takes, and from the scars on his body, I know he will do the same.

"Good. First, we will stand back to back, and I want you to move when I do. Feel the tightening of my muscles and follow that movement through. Any hesitation will get us killed, so we will do it again and again until we are in sync. When I duck, you duck, when I lunge, you lunge." I almost blush at the thought of being pushed up against him and feeling all of his body, and his eyes narrow on me as if he can read my thoughts. "Lose the modesty and embarrassment. By the time this is through, you will know my body better than yours. We don't have time to be shy, we have two hours to learn each other better than anyone else."

I swallow at his words, but I know he's right. If I want to survive, I need to do as he says and trust his judgement. After all, he's the better fighter and I need to live—for my men, for my family—so if it means losing the shyness that was hammered into me, I will. I'll become the extension of his body, I will fight with him and win.

We jump straight into it, conscious of the time limit we have to get prepared for the fight. He works me hard, not relenting. He's more stubborn and demanding than even Alcide, pushing my body to its limit and demanding more. I can see why he has survived so long. He does not give up, ever. Not even when he's covered in sweat and his muscles are obviously aching. He keeps going, fighting harder and faster like the pain is only making him wilder. His moves are smooth and refined, precise, and deadly. He's a weapon, he wields death like a dance brandishes a show, and I am entranced by it. By the way he moves, the pull of his muscles, the snarl he wears.

"Again," he snaps, pulling me out of my thoughts and my ogling. I blush slightly at being caught and he narrows his eyes, so I rush to place my back against his, not wanting him to lecture me again on being 'prudish.' He's a lot taller than me, so my head only reaches the middle of his back, with our legs and asses pushed together, and no air between us. I had been really slow the first couple of times, and even now I still lag behind his moves and sometimes go the wrong way, reading his body signals incorrectly, but I'm trying.

"Concentrate," he orders, his voice as sharp as a whip, forcing my body to vibrate with tension. "Stay relaxed, listen to my body, and just react. You have to be fast, smooth, and deadly. You can fucking do it, now move!"

Clearing my mind, I focus only on him, letting everything else but the feel of his hot, solid body pressed against mine disappear. I ignore the gazes of the guards, their jokes and laughter, the feeling of the sand chafing against my skin, my stomach rumbling in hunger, and my hands shaking from exhaustion. I ignore it all like he instructs. I close my eyes like he told me to, letting go of sight, my focus only on sound and sensation. Eventually, I need to be able to do this with my eyes open, but for now we are trying with my eyes closed to see if that helps. The darkness only heightens my awareness of his body, and I find myself licking my lips before getting angry at myself.

Focus, Rhea.

I feel his body tense right before he starts to move, so I lean with him to the left, and when I don't feel air hit my back, I know I moved the correct way. He ducks right and I duck with him, only half a second behind him. We go back to standing before I feel him move away, so I move with him, my feet dancing backwards over the sand. I put my trust in him leading me, keeping my eyes closed and only stopping when he does.

"Good, you're getting better. This time we are going to move faster like we are ducking weapons," he orders, before he moves. I don't have time to think anymore, I just focus on his body and move with him again and again, getting faster and faster until we stop, both of us panting.

"Open your eyes," he murmurs, and I feel him move in front of me.

I blink them open to see him looking down at me, his lips tilting up ever so slightly. "You're getting better, now I'm going to come at you with some weapons. I want you to focus on dancing away and blocking. I will do most of the heavy lifting and killing, your job is to stay alive and protect my back. Okay?"

I nod then, blowing out a breath and standing on the balls of my feet. He kicks my legs farther open and I gasp. "Stance wider, create a triangle, less likely to be knocked over."

I do as I'm told and he grabs my hips, twisting them, and this time I don't tense up at his touch. He's right. My body is getting used to him and his rough handling. I know he's doing it to teach me, but it doesn't stop the hot flush that's racing through my body from his fingers against my skin—I ignore that. "Move when you see where the weapon is landing, never before. Always keep your eyes open and on it, never close them or look away," he instructs, and then steps back. The place he grabbed me goes cold from the loss of his touch, but I push that away and focus as he pretends to have a sword and comes at me in excessively slow movements.

"Change your skin if you can't duck, but try to use your powers as little as possible."

"Why?" I question with a frown.

"You don't want them to know what you can do, they will use it against you. Only use it if you have to," he replies. Still moving, he pretends to swipe across my stomach and I hop back, avoiding it, and he nods in approval.

He feigns again and again, and when I start to move how he instructs, he tries different weapons, giving me tips on each one and how to avoid it, and then we fight for real. He grabs two swords, tossing one to me that I catch mid-air. At least some of my agility from training for the circus is coming in handy. We move around the arena, parrying blows, and then he instructs me to come at him, going on the defensive.

Before I know it, the two hours are up. I feel more prepared, but still nowhere ready to fight at his side tomorrow. "Time's up!" Trent calls from where he was watching on the side.

Xavier strides towards me. "Remember what we practiced, back to back as soon as we are in the arena, be prepared for them to die, Rhea, because it's them or us, and no matter how good a person they might be, I will always pick us."

Then he marches away, waiting at the gate. I follow after him, stepping up next to his side, his words ringing through my head. Is this what I have become now? Killing others to survive? Can I live with that stain on my soul?

As soon as I see my men leaning out of their cells, searching the tunnel for me, I know the answer—yes, yes I can. For them.

THAT NIGHT, I don't sleep well. I toss and turn and eventually give up, leaning back against the wall and just staring aimlessly into the dark. Fear for tomorrow runs through me. I don't want to let Xavier down and I don't want to kill people, but we don't get what we want. All I can do is fight my best and trust that surviving is the right thing to do.

"Can't sleep?" Xavier mumbles next to me, and I jump at the sound of his voice. It's low, but loud enough to be heard over the snores of the other slaves.

"No, you?" I ask, turning to peer into his cell. I can just about make him out in the dark. He's leaning back against the cell wall like me, with his head on the stone, one knee drawn up and his arm lying over it casually, the other stretched out into the cell.

"I never do the night before a fight, not for long at least, running through the odds and my best chances of winning. Yet the night after a fight, even when they used to lock me in here covered in an innocent's blood, I sleep like a baby. Guess that makes me the soulless fuck they always wanted."

"It doesn't, it just makes you strong. You've seen the worst they have to throw at you and come out of it alive every time," I reply, our whispers quiet and just for us.

"Alive, but at what cost?" This time his words are so soft I barely hear him.

"You're alive, that's all that matters."

"Is it? Sometimes being alive isn't enough, sometimes you have to think of the cost and whether facing death is really that bad compared to losing parts of what makes you human. Rhea, if they had thrown me in there with you, made us fight, I would have killed you without hesitation, I would have done it," he snaps, his hand wrapping around the bar between us, hatred for himself coating his tone.

"I know," I murmur, reaching out and cupping his hand where it rests. He jumps at my touch but doesn't pull away. "I know that, but it doesn't make me hate you or pity you. It makes me respect you and fear you a little bit." I smile at the end and he laughs humourlessly. "I wish I was that strong. They need me to be, but sometimes I still feel like the slave girl from Cinders with nothing to offer other than being a hole to fuck like they always told me. It's just for a moment, and then I remember what I am, who I am now thanks to my family, and that scares me even more. What if they take that away from me? I would do whatever it takes to keep them safe and alive, even at any cost to myself...but I've only just started to find who I am...what will be left of me after this? Or will there be nothing left at all?" I admit, slamming my mouth shut, wincing at oversharing. I don't know why I told him all that, apart from the fact that it's dark and he's sharing his soul with me and I feel the need to do the same.

"Whatever is left, whether it is scarred, broken, or empty, is still enough. Because you saw hell and survived the fires and still came out, you will come out stronger than before. They are evil, sadistic bastards, but they do know how to strengthen a person and push them to the edge. Some fold under that pressure, others flourish. You, Rhea, will flourish. I can see it in you, that fire, that determination. Whatever is left, you will have that, and you will have your men. I've seen them with you, they will never leave you." He sighs then. "I wish I had people who would fight for me like that, you are lucky."

"I know," I whisper back, unsure what to say.

He must realise that, because he squeezes my hand before pulling it out from under mine. "Get some sleep, you will need your strength tomorrow."

And just like in training, my body obeys his commands, slipping into the yawning mouth of sleep.

"WAKE UP, slaves! Chow time! Fight starts in an hour and a half!" comes a yell and the sound of the others rising, yawning, and complaining at the early hour.

I blink my eyes open to see Nixon staring at me. I smile at him and blow him a kiss, which he catches and presses to his heart, making me melt. I get up and stretch, seeing Xavier waiting in the middle of his cell, ready to go like always. Does this man ever rest?

When our cells clank open, Nix and I head to the toilets. He guards the stall while I go, and I watch his back as he goes. I'm slowly losing my modesty, and standing at his back as he pees doesn't bother me anymore like it would have before we were captured. Afterwards, we head to eat, where Xavier sits with us again. Alcide isn't with Rex, Jessie, and Blain, so I frown. Blain notices and stands up, ignoring everyone as he comes and sits next to me, placing his hand on my thigh under the table.

"He was in his cell last night, Harpy, told us he is getting in with the Masters and to trust him," he murmurs, his voice right next to my ear. He drops a small kiss there before going back to eating one handed, not moving his palm from my thigh. Jessie and Rex stand at the same time and join us, and even though I am worried about the fight to come, I can't help the wide smile curling at my lips. I've missed them, having them all around me feels better, and when Jessie starts teasing Nixon, I can even imagine we are at home.

The time passes too quickly though, and when the guards call for us to line up, I remain sitting at the table, not wanting to leave, but Xavier catches my gaze and nods, so I stand. Blain ignores everyone and kisses me hard, right there in the middle of everyone.

"You stay alive, Harpy, you hear me? Only I get to try and kill you," he teases, and I grin up at him as Jessie pushes him out of the way and smiles at me, his eyes twinkling.

He dips me for a kiss with a flourish, and I laugh as he brings me back up. He turns serious, pushing away my hair and rubbing my lips. "Come back to us, always."

Then, Nixon picks him up and moves him, taking his place. He simply stares into my eyes before dropping a lingering kiss on my forehead. Rex is waiting at his side and I turn to him. He smiles at me before stepping forward and wrapping me in his arms, giving me his signature hug.

"I have faith in you, Wildcat, you can do anything," he whispers, kissing my hair before letting go.

"It's not a fucking lovefest! Get lined up or you all get thirty whips!" Trent calls, and we all hurry into the lines, not wanting to be punished, but their faith and love in me has me standing taller, ready to face the fight that lies ahead.

Xavier is right, whatever it takes.

Xavier and I are held back, while all the other slaves are marched into the sand and paraded around before being locked away. Only after the Masters are in their box, with Alcide at their side, and the crowd starts chanting, are we announced.

I bounce on my toes, feeling nervous energy winding inside me. "Remember what we did," he mumbles, locking on his weapons, and I nod.

He made me wear some armour, including a leather chest piece, gauntlets, and thigh protectors, as well as using a sword and a spike so I can stab people without them getting too close. I don't really know how to use them, but I guess I'll just stick them with the pointy end.

The crowd quietens as one of the Masters stands up and waves his hand, his announcement ringing through the arena. "We have a very special fight today. Not only do you get to see our reigning champion spill blood, but he has been partnered up! That's right! Today is the tandem fight!"

He lets them cheer as he smirks before waving again and letting them settle down. "Meet, the Immortals!"

I raise my eyebrows at the name, but then we are being pushed into the sand so I clear my face as much as I can, trying not to let them see how terrified I am. Xavier ignores it all, striding into the middle of the arena and standing there with his legs parted and his arms crossed. He doesn't play the crowd, choosing to ignore them, even when they start to chant his name. He looks back at me with narrowed eyes, so I hurry over the sand and stand at his side, copying his pose.

The guards come across the pit holding a chain. Our shackles are removed and our powers freed before they place a shackle linked to the chain on my right hand and his left. It's long but not too long, leaving only enough room to manoeuvre like he said, but not enough where we can fight across the arena. They want us close.

Once the chain is in place, all the guards leave the sand and we are alone, the chants getting louder. A cranking sound has us turning to see the gate opening again, and our opponents are revealed. Shit.

I glance at the Masters with a glare. They want us to die or they are trying to bring out our powers, because standing at the edge of the sand are over fifteen men in soldier's gear. Including full armour, spears, swords, and other weapons I couldn't even name. Theirs are shiny and new, where ours are blood soaked and rusted.

The gong sounds and they waste no time. Instantly, Xavier yanks me with the chain since I was just gawking. I spin and place my back to his, holding out my spike like he showed me. The guards spread out across the sand, circling us and boxing us in. Three guards face me.

They share a look and step forward. I don't react, remaining relaxed like Xavier told me to, focusing on his movements, and splitting my concentration between that and their slow approach.

I feel the bunching of his muscles a second before he moves, and I go with him as he fights the guards he is facing. It pulls me farther away from mine, and when he ducks, I duck, a spear flying overhead and imbedding in the eye socket of a shocked guard. He reaches towards it, screaming as blood runs down his face, but I'm too busy twisting and lunging with Xavier. A guard lunges at me and I stumble back into Xavier, and I hear him grunt. *Shit, focus, Rhea.*

I thrust my spear at him, but it bounces harmlessly off his chest plate. He grabs it before I can react and twists, yanking it out of my arms and tossing it to the sand behind him. I hear the crowd gasp, but I don't look away. I can still feel Xavier moving so I know he's still alive and fighting. I grab my sword, drawing it and holding it like Xavier told me to as the two guards laugh. The one on the left moves first, and I block his swing with my sword, the metal clashing and glinting in the sun. The one on the right darts in, but I see him out of the corner of my eye and let my skin change so the blade snaps in two against my body. He gapes at it, and I use his distraction to thrust forward, blocking the blow with my hand, the blade bouncing from my now hardened, marble like skin and stab at the guard.

I didn't expect it to work, but he must not have seen it coming, because I slice across his throat. His eyes widen, and his mouth opens and closes as blood spurts over my face. I wipe it away quickly, watching as he falls back clutching the wound, but when the other guard really starts to move, I ignore the shock of my first kill. I can deal with it later, now I need to fight. He grabs my sword, cutting his own hands on it, and yanks it away from me, turning it to chop me. He now has two swords and I have none, but just then Xavier lunges so I move back with him, giving me some breathing room from the guard. Xavier spins so I go with him, moving across the sand. He wraps his chain around his fist, smashing it into a guard's face before wrapping it around his neck and choking him. I drag my gaze back to my guard who is swinging his swords and grinning at me. He is loving this, playing cat and mouse, and he thinks he has me. He thinks I'm weak.

Anger pours through me at that, my skin tightening as my power rises. I remember Xavier's warning, but I have no other weapons and I can't drag him away from his fight. I need to kill this man. I've never really tried to hurt someone with them, so I don't know my full capabilities, but I draw on Rex's speed, and with it comes a quiet confidence and Nixon's strength. Darting forward, this time Xavier moving with me, I knock away both swords, hitting them with my stone arms and throwing them across the sand. Before he can draw another weapon, I reach for his throat and pull. Claws glint in the light, and when I pull back, his throat comes with me, my hand covered in blood. I toss it away and watch as he falls.

Two down, only thirteen to go. Xavier moves left and I am faced with two dead bodies and a bleeding guard who's getting back to his feet. He rushes me, yelling as he goes, and I dodge and duck his rage-filled swings, dragging Xavier down with me. His sword aims for my face and I block it with my arm before reaching out and kicking at his stomach. He falls back, gasping, and holding his arm across it as he struggles to breathe, so I grab the discarded spear on the ground and toss it. It hits him in the chest, sinking through a gap in his armour, and he falls to his knees, gaping down at it. We move again, dancing across the sand as Xavier fights and I start to hold my own, moving on instinct and trusting my body like he told me to. It's not as smooth or as quick as Xavier, but it is good enough to stay alive.

I take down another guard by tripping him with our chain and then snapping his neck. I don't question where this blood lust has come from, because I know Nixon's strength and Rex's speed is coursing through me. Xavier takes down two more, leaving only five guards left. They line up and face us, so Xavier pulls me to his side, our chain loose between us.

He looks down at it and then at me and I nod, understanding what he means. We step away from each other slowly, drawing the chain taut and when he yells, I run forward. He does the same, the chain cutting through their line. One manages to duck in time, while the others fall to the floor, and I grab a sword, stabbing one in the heart closest to my feet before racing back to Xavier's side in time to see him heave an axe at a man. It cuts through his head, tossing his body to the ground. The other three get to their feet, and one of them steps on the chain curling on the floor like a snake, dragging me forward. Xavier digs his feet in, not moving and I grunt, trying to do the same, but the guard picks up the chain and tugs me forward.

The other two rush Xavier so he can't help me, and with each tug, the guard's grin grows. He thinks he has me. With nothing else left, my power flows through me like it is being controlled from outside my body or guided by the fear feeding my heart. I watch in shock as vines shoot up from the ground, wrap around his ankles, and yank him backwards. He lets go of the chain, yelping as he falls on his back, the vines pinning him there, and I jump on him, hitting him with my fists again and again, letting my fear and anger out in a yell as I rain down punch after punch.

My ears are ringing, and my eyes are narrowed on the man's face, the beat of my heart the only sound I hear until slowly, the noise of the crowd starts to fade in again. They're clapping and chanting and the man's gurgles reach my ears. I freeze on top of him, sitting back in shock to see his face smashed in and barely recognisable as his chest rattles, a wet sounding noise coming from it.

I feel the air shift next to me and strike out without thinking, but something catches my fist mid-air, and I swing my head to see a panting Xavier. He is covered in grime, blood, and sweat, his dark eyes locked on mine. He glances down at the man and then back at me.

"End it, give him some peace, it was your kill," he states, releasing my fist and stepping back.

I look at the guard, nearly recoiling from the mess I made of him. Rex's speed and Nixon's strength leave me, making me slump slightly and shake in exhaustion and fear, but even so, I reach for the dagger the man was holding but forgot about after my attack. I palm it, my hand shaking as I raise it above him.

I can't do this, I can't. My mind shies away. In the rush of battle, I didn't have time to think about what I was doing, but now I do and the bloodthirsty chants of the crowd are only making bile crawl up my throat. Is this what they really want? Death at any cost?

"Do it, it's the nicest way, or he is going to choke on the blood in his lungs. The Masters won't care, they will leave him here as an example of their failure. It will take hours and it will be excruciatingly painful. You are giving him a mercy."

I stare down at the guard's face, his one blue eye blinking up at me, tears welling there. "Kill—me," he gasps, blood bubbling when he talks.

"Kill him! Kill him!" the crowd chants, and I shake my head and that blue eye shuts for a moment before reopening.

"Please," he wheezes, begging me to end his suffering.

"Mercy," Xavier whispers next to me.

I raise the knife, holding it over his chest, and he begs me with that one blue eye. I can't take it anymore. I don't close my eyes, I stare into his as I sink the dagger through his skin. I watch the light die there, I force myself to. I will suffer his death with him, I don't deserve to look away.

Letting go of the knife, my hand shaking badly, I lean to the side and dry heave. A hand wraps around my hair, the pain stopping me from splashing my breakfast on the sand. "Don't let them see you weak," Xavier demands, ordering me again, and I let myself obey, the pain pulling me back as I climb to my feet and stumble away from the guard. Looking up at the screaming crowd, I let my eyes wander over their masses. They are chanting, screaming, and stomping. Their fists are in the air, their excitement washing over the sand. It makes me feel sick again, watching how they praise me for ending a life. It's so careless and disrespectful. A man just died and they are hailing me.

It's wrong, so fucking wrong, but I can't ignore the relief that rushes through me at surviving this battle. Xavier grabs my hand and I look down at his blood-covered fist, noting mine is also covered in fresh, red blood. When he lifts it in the air, the crowd goes wild, chanting our fighting name, and we both turn to glare at the Masters' box.

I meet Alcide's eyes to see him smiling slightly, but it disappears as quickly as it came, like it was never there, and he turns away to talk to a man waiting there.

We won this fight...so why is my heart hurting and my chest tight?

Chapter Fifteen

It's a blur after the fights. Somewhere, deep down, I know this is shock setting in, but the numbness that accompanies it washes away my pain, so I let it engulf me. I blink, looking around, wondering when and how I got to my cell. Not that it matters.

"Rhea," Nix calls, and when I turn my head as if in slow motion, I see his worried expression swimming in my vision as he leans through the bars to try and reach me. How long has he been calling my name?

Some of the numbness recedes, and I realise I can still feel the blood coating my body. It itches as it dries, and before I know it, I'm scrubbing at it with my hands, tears gathering in my eyes.

"Look at me! Now!" comes a yell, and I freeze, swinging my eyes over to Xavier to see him glaring at me. "Stop it. You can wash it away, you are only taking the top layer of your skin off." His command runs through my body and I stop scrubbing instantly, stumbling back and sagging down the wall. Tears race down my cheeks unchecked, and I can't seem to bring myself to dash them away or care that I look weak.

I'm cracking, breaking in two, my mind hiding from the horrors I just pulled in the arena. I'm becoming what they wanted. I bet they are celebrating right now, while I feel sick to my very core and so cold, my own body is turning on me. My chest grows tight, squeezing down on my organs. My breathing wheezes out as my vision swims.

"It's a panic attack, Rhea, breathe with me. In and out, slowly, in and out, concentrate on your breathing," Nixon calls to my left, and I let his strong voice settle me slightly as I do as I'm told.

It seems to take an eternity until I can breathe normally again, and when I can, I curl into a ball on my sleeping mat and close my eyes, my body giving way to exhaustion and my eyes closing as I give in to the awaiting comfort and nothingness. Everything is sucked away from me.

Let it take my pain away for a while.

"Sleep," Nixon commands.

"We will watch over you," Xavier adds. "It will get better."

When I wake up, my eyes are crusted together and I feel disgusting, like a layer of grime and blood covers my skin, and I want to touch it again, but I don't. Lying on my side, I let the sound of Nixon's and Xavier's voices soothe me as I just let my body relax. I feel like I slept for ages, but when I look up, I realise it only must have been an hour or so. I guess my body needed it.

Nixon is stroking my hair as he speaks to Xavier, and I lean into the touch, but their conversation cuts off, both of them staring at me. "You okay?" he asks, and I nod, curling into his warm hand.

"Sorry," I whisper, and he narrows his eyes on me.

"Never be sorry for being a good person, for having feelings and reacting the way you did. What you did in the ring, you did to survive, but it doesn't mean you should become numb to the effects of killing."

His words reassure me and I close my eyes, just focusing on his touch until I hear the guards yelling. "Chow time, slaves!"

The cells start to open so I clamber to my feet. I don't think I will be able to eat with this knot in my stomach, but I can at least wash off the remains of the fight and see my other men. Nixon waits for me outside my cell and I fall into formation, hidden behind his tall, wide back as Xavier protects us from behind. I keep my gaze downcast, not wanting the others to see the puffiness of my eyes from crying as we head into the bathroom.

Nixon stops me at the door with a look, and I nod and wait there as he kicks some men out before he sweeps back to me and lets me in. I head straight for the showers, stripping as I go, uncaring who sees me anymore. My whole focus is narrowed to getting the blood off me. I flick on the showers and scrub at my skin, not feeling the temperature of the water and not caring. It's only when I see the blood washing down the drain between my bare feet when I break down fully. Falling to my knees, I start to sob, unable to help it.

I killed them. I killed those men. They could have families, they could have children, they could have been made to fight like us and I took their life away. Arms wrap around me, more than one set as they hold me together. Letting me break as they pick up the pieces and glue me back together with their love, and when I am finally all cried out, I lift my head to see a grim-faced Blain, a sad-looking Jessie, and a distraught Rex, yet they all smile at me when I look.

"Thanks," I croak, and Blain leans closer, wiping my eyes gently, and it does soothe the ache from crying.

"Let's finish getting you washed. Rex will clean your clothes and get them dried. Jessie, go get us some food before it all disappears. We won't be long," Blain orders, taking charge. I simply let them, not having enough energy to care, and I know they are just wanting to look after me, so I let them. I need it right now, I need their comfort.

Jessie kisses my cheek before hopping up and racing away. Rex cups my face and lays a soft kiss on my lips before getting to his feet, leaving just Blain and me. He hauls me to my feet gently and turns me to face his chest, his hands going to my hair. He works through the knots and tangles there, meticulously taking his time until he can wash it, and then he baths my body, making sure to get rid of all the evidence of today.

I let him, just leaning against his strength, and when he flicks off the shower, I shiver from the cold, finally noticing it. He rips off his shirt, drying me with it before pulling me to the middle of the room, where him and Rex dress me. Rex kneels at my feet and I lean my hand on his shoulder as he picks up my foot and places it in my trousers before lifting the other, laying gentle kisses on my ankles as he goes. He pulls them up and smooths them over my hips before kissing my belly. Blain pulls my top over my head and rights it before wringing out my hair and twisting it onto my head so it is out of my face.

When they are done, I feel more human. "Thank you," I whisper.

"Don't get all sappy on me, Harpy," Blain jokes, and I crack a smile at him. Relief flits through his eyes at that. "You can thank me with a kiss though, gotta say I missed this mouth." He winks and I know he is just trying to distract me and it works. He kisses me hard for a moment before Rex nudges him out of the way.

"You handsy prick, I missed her mouth too," Rex states before kissing me softly, brushing butterfly pecks on my lips before pulling back and wiggling his eyebrows at me, making me giggle.

Their shoulders relax a fraction, and it's only then I realise how worried they were about me, so I make the effort. I reach across and grab both of their hands and squeeze. "Let's eat."

Blain leads the way as Nix and Xavier fall behind us, my hands still held in Rex's and Blain's as we head into the eating area. Jessie is at our table with all the trays there, so I head over and plop into a spot, picking up the spoon and just playing with the gruel, but when Xavier glares from me to the food, I take a mouthful and swallow as if to say, see? His lips curl up a fraction before it disappears, and I force myself to eat. The others do the same, but they are quieter, madness hanging in the air and worry in their eyes.

"I'm fine, I promise," I finally say, and they nod, believing me, and once I say it, it's true. I do think I lost a part of myself today in the arena, and I will always have to live with their deaths, but I survived it and I can survive this.

Sometimes you need to break in order to put yourself back together again, stronger and sturdier than before. There might be some cracks along the surface, but it will only highlight the battles you have won.

Once we have finished eating, I let my gaze wander around the slaves, and it catches on Jacob. He nods at me and then stands, purposely passing me as he goes to take his tray back. "We won't let it stand, we will fight back," he whispers.

What does he mean?

I turn to ask him, but he is gone. I spin back to the others to see if they heard him, but they are lost in their food. Fight back? Like…like a rebellion of sorts? Where does that leave me?

I'm no fighter, but I won't lie down and die, so if joining a rebellion is what it takes, then sign me up. It's time to put a stop to this and save my family before there is nothing left of us to save.

Chapter Sixteen

I don't get time to corner Jacob before we are led back to our cells again, informed there won't be any fighting today. I wait on my mat, hoping Chester will come and get me. I need information about Alcide and he's the only one I can get it from.

I wait for hours in the same spot and just as I start to give up hope, Tobias heads my way and unlocks my cell.

"You have a visitor," is all he says, and I get to my feet, throwing Nixon a smile on the way to let him know I'm okay. I feel his and Xavier's eyes burning a hole into my back as I am led past the cells and to our usual meeting room at the back. He is waiting with the chess board set up when Tobias shuts the door behind me, and I slip into my seat and wait.

It feels like so long ago since I was first brought in here. I thought the worst then, but now? Now I feel in charge. Chester needs me and that works to my advantage. I don't speak straight away, I lull him into a sense of security. Instead, I make my move and watch as he considers the board before making his. He sits back, finally raising his eyes and looking me over.

"Are you okay?" he inquires, making me jump at the suddenness of his question.

"Would it matter if I wasn't?" I counter bitterly, but seeing him flinch makes me sigh. Truthfully, I'm not okay, but I need to keep Chester on my side and make him think I'm playing his game. "I'm not, but I will be. It wasn't easy killing that man and I know it will haunt me."

"You gave him a mercy. They would have left him there in the heat to bake to death or bleed out," he informs me sadly, watching me. "You won't forget his face, you will see it every night in your dreams, but you will come to terms with it, everyone always does."

"Like you? Did you come to terms with losing her?" I ask out of the blue, and he drops his gaze again.

"No, I guess I haven't. When you lose someone you love, there is no healing from that. All you can do is keep moving, the pain a constant reminder until one day, you start to remember the good and the beginning, not just the bad and the way it ended."

"You miss her," I whisper, softening.

"Every minute of every day. I still turn to share things with her or tell her of the sights I have seen before I remember she isn't there. It's just a split second, but in that second I feel whole again until it comes crashing down around me," he admits.

I move my chess piece and then cover his hand on the board. "I'm sorry that you lost her. How did it happen?" I query, pushing for details. He looks at my hand and I slowly withdraw it, and he blinks before seeming to shake it off.

"I shouldn't—" He cuts off, staring at me.

"Just like I shouldn't be sitting here playing, but I am. Like you said, I'm safe in here. So are your secrets, who would I tell? Entertain me, distract me from my own morality issues for a while. Please," I add, begging slightly, and I do mean it. I need to focus on something else, and with his pain and compassion, Chester just might be that. When I understand him, I can control him.

"I guess you're right, there is no harm in telling you." He sits back then, crossing his legs as he looks at me. "You might not believe me, Rhea, but she was like you."

"Like me?" I repeat with a frown.

"A freak, her mother wasn't, we don't know how it happened. It was just her, it didn't even start at birth, so we had no idea until it was too late. She was growing so quickly and so were her powers. They manifested and we instructed her to hide them, to protect her, since we knew what kind of people we lived with, and the games here had just started, but like anything...hiding doesn't work. That control broke, and when it did...there was no putting it back. She was out shopping with a friend, she saw someone get hurt. She just wanted to save them, Rhea, that's all she ever wanted, to help people." His eyes mist then. "She could seal wounds and heal people, and without thought she healed that man, only for him to turn around and turn her over to the guards. When the others found out, I was punished for lying to them, for withholding information. They used her to remind me of their control. They threw her in the ring." He looks right into my eyes. "She wasn't like you, she couldn't survive it, she couldn't even protect herself. Didn't even try. She saw the brutality and the horror, and she became a shell. She sat there and died before my eyes. It was my punishment, to watch her be killed for entertainment, of course, not before they had their fun —" He chokes off then, sucking in a deep breath.

"It was a lesson I will never forget, Rhea. They control everyone and everything. No one escapes them, ever. I fell into line, I became the perfect puppet. Did everything and anything they wanted to protect the rest of my family, but my wife, she couldn't forgive me or live with the guilt. She killed herself. My son is all I have left, and they know it. They brought him into this, made him like them. I see it every day, the way he's changing. He doesn't know what they did to his sister or maybe he doesn't care, I don't know anymore. I'm alone, Rhea, I had everything a man could want and then it was taken from me just like that."

I find tears in my own eyes, not for him, but for that poor girl. She was tortured and killed simply for wanting to help someone, for being born the way she was. This world is wrong when the very body you were born into is used against you. They couldn't fight this anymore than they could fight nature, yet we are punished for being who we truly are. None of it should matter.

Not the colour of skin, sexuality, or the powers we are born with...yet it does. It's time that changed.

"I'm so sorry, I don't even know what to say," I murmur, watching him as he falls apart. He wipes his eyes and clears his throat, looking away, his eyes seeing into the distance.

"You see now, don't you? Why you will never be free? Why I can't help you?" His eyes focus on me again and I nod. I do. He can't help us, not physically, but he will without even realising it.

We carry on the game in silence until I break it. "Can I ask you something?"

He inclines his head.

"My friend, Alcide...is he okay?"

He glances up at me, ignoring the board, obviously trying to see through my expression. "He's safe, if that is what you mean."

"I haven't seen him," I remark, still trying to dig for information. After seeing him in the Masters' box and hearing the other guys' comments, I don't know what to feel. He's our ringmaster, our family, he wouldn't leave us. He has to be playing an angle, using his charm...but what for? To get us free? Why couldn't he tell us that?

"I believe he is assisting the Masters with some matters, nothing for you to worry about. He is becoming quite invaluable to them," he says distractedly, moving his next piece. "Checkmate." He grins up at me.

I swallow, nodding with a fake smile. "Good move," I praise, but my heart is racing and my mind whirling...invaluable to them?

It begs the question, how well do I really know Alcide?

I WAS ESCORTED BACK to my cell after that and locked back in by Tobias. As he was turning to leave, I caught his hand on the bars. "Tobias?" I whisper.

He looks around before narrowing his eyes on me. "Sorry, I just wanted to know if my animals were okay." When I don't think he's going to answer, I grip his hand desperately. "Please, I just want to know, they are my family," I murmur brokenly. It's killing me that I can't be there to protect them.

He sighs, his gaze darting around again before he lowers his head slightly. "They are okay, they can't make them fight so they are just in holding, but that won't last forever. If they can't use them, they will kill them. I'm sorry," he offers and walks away, leaving me staring after him. I won't let that happen. I don't have long. I need to do something. But what? How do I get us free?

Sighing, I slump against the back wall, my head leaning against the stone as I think through our options. The main issue is the shackles we have. If we could get rid of them, we could overwhelm the guards. Then I remember the other day, and how I managed a trickle of power even through the shackles. Sitting upright, I turn so my back is to the cell bars and I am facing the wall, shielding what I'm trying.

I see Nixon watching me, and Xavier turns his head and stares as well, but I focus on my power. Holding my hands out in front of me, the light of the torches only just reaching where I'm huddled, I gaze at the brassy shackles before closing my eyes and reaching deep within myself, searching for that spark of power.

It seems to elude me, like smoke trickling through my hands. As soon as I think I have it, it drifts away again, blocked from me by the power of the shackles. I wonder how they made them. How do they keep my powers from me? I need to remember to ask Chester. As if he can hear my thoughts, Xavier's voice comes from the cell next to mine.

"It won't work, the men have tried everything. Breaking them, burning them, snapping them. They are indestructible, and even when your hands are cut off, they stay on your skin, I've seen it happen," he rumbles.

I turn my head to see him and frown. "What else do you know about them?"

He eyes me again and I let him. If he thought I had given up on trying to escape then he is a fool. I will never accept these bars and cells. I will be free no matter what it takes. He nods like he can see my determination. "Just what I have pieced together over the years," he starts, then looks around when we hear boots. When they fade, he slides closer and lowers his voice so even I can barely hear him.

I scoot closer, his breath wafting over my face and his dark eyes locked on mine, making me shiver before I focus on his words. "It isn't magic or shielding, it's a power," he continues, and for some reason my eyes keep dropping to his plump lips. He goes quiet so I drag my gaze back up and it clashes with his. We both freeze, just staring into each other's eyes before I look away.

"A power?" I prompt, my voice rougher than I intended.

"Yes," he rasps, his voice deep like rocks crashing together, and if I didn't know better, I swear I see his lips curl up as he glances down at my own. "A freak, one with nullifying powers, was found. He could drain anyone else's powers away, make them nothing but a dud, a norm. They found a way to harness that, a tailor or crafter in the city. The only freak they allow to be free so he can work for them."

"How do you know this?" I ask, curious.

"Secrets, Rhea, people's lips are loose after they get what they want. They trade in flesh down here. I had no choice, so I made the most of it," is all he says, and I see the anger vibrating his body. "So you can't break them."

"What about not trying to break them off but to work around them?" I mumble, closing my eyes and focusing again, blocking it all out.

I did it before, my emotions were heightened, maybe that's what I need. So I recall it all, all my fear, anger. I picture Nixon fighting, my animals being hurt. Recall the terror when I was dragged from my cage. I feel it moving under my skin, but I don't open my eyes, not wanting to break that connection. I add more and more, every slight against us, letting the emotions rush through me until I hear a sharp breath, then I blink open my eyes, staring at my hands. I grin, noting they have changed to stone like the wall I face.

Xavier seems to perk up then, watching me intently. "Impossible," he whispers.

"Nothing is impossible if you try hard enough and come from the right angle. You said this is a power, a nullifying power, but a power nonetheless. Every power has a weakness and a way around it. I just need to find that."

I close my eyes again, pushing through that barrier. It seems emotions heightened my power, which I already knew, but if they are strong enough, I can bypass the nullifying effects of the shackles. They have to be strong though, I can't fake them, and it is draining as I gather all the bad memories and things that have happened in my life and push them through my body, dragging my power from it. When I open my eyes again, the stone has traced all the way up my arms and I'm exhausted.

Letting out a shaky breath, I turn and lean against the wall, gathering my strength. "I'll keep trying, there has to be a way," I whisper, and Nixon reaches through the bars and strokes my hair, making me close my eyes in bliss.

I must fall asleep, because when I wake up, my neck is aching from leaning against the wall in an awkward position. The cells are dark and snores sound through the air, so I sigh and lay down on my bed, curling around Nixon's hand he still has through the bars, and close my eyes again.

"Wake the fuck up, slaves! Chow time!" comes a yell, which jerks me from a deep sleep. Sitting upright, I forget where I am for a second until Trent bangs his baton on my cell, making me jump and he laughs and walks away. Rubbing my eyes, I stretch as I stand up, sharing a soft look with Nixon as our cells are opened and we head to the bathrooms, falling into our routines.

I pee quickly and then so does Nixon. I spot Xavier already in the shower and my eyes catch on his peachy arse before I drag my gaze away and stare at the floor. What is wrong with me? As soon as Nixon is done, I rush from the bathrooms to escape a naked Xavier and head to our table where Jessie, Blain, and Rex are waiting.

They already have our bowls and cups there, so I slump down between Jessie and Rex, leaning my head on Rex's shoulder. He kisses my forehead as Jessie twines our fingers under the table while he eats. "Anyone seen Alcide?" I ask.

"Nope," Blain says around a yawn, and Rex sighs against me.

"I'm sure he's okay, Wildcat," he whispers, and I nod and perk up, forcing myself to eat. I'm still lethargic, whether from the fight or all the emotions and pushing yesterday, I don't know.

Once we are done eating, we all sit around, our muscles tense, knowing they will soon announce who is fighting today. It seems we wait with bated breath, and a bad feeling balls in the bottom of my stomach until Trent stands up in front of us.

"Fighting today—Pretzel boy, Ray, and Hatchet," he calls, and my eyes swing to Jessie, fear roaring to life as I grip his hand tighter.

He sits up straighter, grinning at me. "Don't look so worried, Firecracker, I'll kick their ass and be back in time for wet shower cuddles." He wiggles his eyebrows at me and I crack a smile, but my heart isn't in it. It's clenching in my chest at the thought of him getting hurt.

Unlike Blain and Rex, Jessie isn't a fighter. He's powerful in his own way and he only seems to be getting stronger, but these other fighters are brutal and bloodthirsty, they seem to thrive on hurting others. His teasing, flexible body, and showmanship won't help him here. "Promise me you'll fight with everything in you? Don't hold back," I beg, searching his eyes.

He leans closer, pressing a soft kiss to my forehead making me close my eyes for a moment. "I will fight hard, anything to get back to you. Trust me, Firecracker, nothing will keep us apart. We have a whole life ahead of us, you'll see," he whispers, dropping a kiss on my lips before getting to his feet.

We get up as well and watch as he grabs some weapons and straps on his armour, all the while ignoring the other two fighters. Is this a punishment? Because of the way Xavier and I finished our fight? It feels like one.

We are told to line up and we do, my eyes on Jessie the whole time. He blows me a kiss and I'm forced to turn away as we are marched onto the sand. We are led out, no parade today, and just locked into our cages to watch the fight. The stands are already filled with excited fans, the promise of bloodshed hanging in the air, making me nervous. I spot Alcide in the Masters' box again and narrow my eyes on him, but he won't meet mine.

Turning away, I face the pit, waiting for them to announce the fighters. Once they do, I glance back at Alcide to see him frozen. He didn't know. That settles me a bit. His eyes run over the cages and catch on me, a promise written there before he moves over to the Masters and starts talking.

I don't spare him another glance as I hear the cranking of the gate again, emitting the fighters into the pit. I turn and watch, my eyes locked on Jessie as he strides confidently into the middle and bows, playing to the crowd, always a showman.

The words of the Masters fade away as I focus on the man I love. When the gong sounds, I gasp and press myself to the bars, watching the two fighters surround Jessie who does not look in the least bit bothered. The two men are large, scarred, and wield swords with a precision that shows practice.

They swing them in arcs as they circle Jessie, who stands with a smile on his face, waiting for them to move. When they charge him, he just isn't there anymore, moving between them and facing his opponents with a smirk as they spin and glare at him. The crowd hollers, egging them on as they swing and aim for Jessie who avoids each hit, bending and twisting into incredible positions. Jessie doesn't even bother to try and fight back, just dances and twirls around them like they are on stage and he's in the spotlight. The crowd eats it up, loving it and screaming his name.

He taunts the other fighters, moving around them quickly and laughing as they start to get annoyed. Their anger only makes them more lethal, and I want to scream at him to take it seriously, but I don't want to distract him. Is this what he felt like, waiting for me, watching me?

He doesn't manage to move fast enough and one of the swings connects, cutting his arm. I cover my mouth to swallow my scream as blood drops to the sand below. His grin slips for a moment, but he dances away again, ignoring his arm which has to be going numb. The cut is deep, still weeping blood, and the sight of it against his skin has tears filling my eyes.

Come on, Jessie, keep moving, fight back.

Like he was waiting for me to think that, he swings his sword and meets their attacks, dancing backwards and forwards in the sand as they strike from both sides. He's fast, but it's clear he isn't as practiced as the other two, and soon three more cuts join the first.

He rolls between one's legs and puts some space between them, breathing heavy now, his arm holding the sword dipping slightly. Sweat beads on his forehead and his other arm hangs uselessly at his side.

My fingers turn white on the bars, and I taste blood in my mouth from biting my own tongue. Fear winds through my heart as they come after him again, one feigns right, but moves left, and goes for Jesse's neck. In slow motion, I see the sword coming for his neck and all I can do is gape.

My eyes widen in horror when I see a sword protruding through his chest. His eyes widen in terror and meet mine as I shake my head.

No, no, this can't be happening.

Everything else fades as the sword is pulled from his back and the two fighters step away. I realise someone is screaming—oh wait, that's me. He looks down at the wound, which is bleeding profusely, before he raises his wide gaze back to me, his mouth opening and closing, regret forming in those eyes usually filled with happiness.

He falls to his knees and power flows from me, shaking the arena. The crowd screams in fear, but I ignore them. My family is shouting and screaming, fighting to get to him as he falls to his side in the sand, his eyes wide and unseeing as he begins to go pale. The shaking of the ground carries on and guards rush about, but I don't move my gaze from Jessie's unmoving form as his blood soaks into the sands.

A baton smacks my cage and catches me in the temple. "Fuck, you were just supposed to shut her up!" someone yells, as I slump to the bottom of the cage, my fingers reaching through the bars towards Jessie.

No, he can't be—

He can't leave me…

He promised. It's the last thought I have before darkness claims me, swallowing my screams of terror and grief, and welcoming me like an old friend.

CIRCUS

My head pounds, as if matching the thumping of my heart, or the tread of hurried footsteps rushing through darkened passages. My eyes feel heavy and want to close, but I force them open to see where I am. It's cold down here, like I'm underground, and I want to rub at the goosebumps that cover my arms, but my limbs feel like they are laden with lead. I get the sense I'm moving as stones dig into my skin, a tightness against my ankles that makes me want to kick out.

Where am I? What's happened? I think to myself, a pained groan filling the passageway, echoing around me.

"You shouldn't have hit her so hard," a gruff male voice scolds, his disapproval easy to hear in his voice. I don't think he's talking to me, which means there is someone else down here with me.

"She was going fucking crazy!" Indignation follows and the voice brings a memory with it. I know that voice, but I'm struggling to put a name to it. Twisting my head, I try to work out where the voices are coming from, my throbbing head making it more difficult than it should have been.

"Well, if you've fucking broken her, you can take the blame. I'm not fucking getting punished because of your need to hurt the freaks," the first voice replies, and I get the impression he doesn't like the other person. Trent, that's who the second person is, the one that hit me over the head.

All of a sudden, the events of the last hour smashed into me like a brick wall. The fight. Jessie. The expression on his face as the sword sliced through him. No. This isn't happening. Twisting, I try to push up into a sitting position, but I'm too weak and my legs won't move. Forcing my eyes open again, I stare down and see the reason why. Trent and another guard are dragging me down the tunnel towards our cells, each one tightly gripping my ankles. No wonder my back is stinging like it's been scored with sandpaper, I'm lucky I haven't hit my head again.

With a cry, I twist once more, this time so hard I manage to turn myself over, the guards cursing as they lose their hold on my ankles. I try to scrabble upright, but my limbs fail me, the pounding of my head making my vision foggy and the world move under me. Rough hands grab at my shoulders and arms as they haul me up to my feet, the world spinning as I try to steady myself, but I'm being dragged away again.

No, I need to get to Jessie. I need to see him, my joker who always makes me feel better. Images of his shocked face flash through my mind and I let out a cry of frustration and grief. Pushing my heels into the ground, I try to stop myself, I need to get back to the arena. If he really is dead, I need to see him. Cursing, the guards start pulling me again, my futile attempts at stopping them useless.

"Stop struggling, bitch," the first guard demands, his grasp on my shoulders tightening as they drag me into the room, where the door to my cage is open, waiting for me.

"I need to see him." My voice comes out as a croak, broken. A small part of me is screaming, telling me to hold my ground, to shout and lash out, anything to try and get to him, but a feeling of hopelessness washes through me.

We are going to die here.

"Shut the fuck up, slave," Trent sneers, his grip turning painful on my arm as he pulls me closer towards him, and a sick excitement fills his eyes as I flinch at his proximity. Jerking my arm, I try to put some distance between us, but this only seems to please him and he steps in close, a grin filling his face. "Go on, keep struggling, you'll only make this worse for yourself."

The other guard stays silent at my other side, but I can feel him stiffen at Trent's whispered words. Reaching my cell, I stagger in as a shove between my shoulder blades sends me forward, and I have to put my arms out to stop myself from colliding with the wall at the back. The sound of the metal door slamming shut rings in my ears, and I spin around to see the guards talking to each other in low tones.

"It's fine, I'll wait down here… make sure she doesn't cause any trouble." Catching the end of Trent's words, I shudder, realising he's trying to get me alone, and I have no illusions as to what he's planning to do with that time.

Snorting, the other guard frowns at him, crossing his arms, and I get the impression Trent is scared of him. "I'm not fucking stupid, Trent. You know she's off limits." His deep voice makes Trent scowl, but he takes a step back as he moves away, shooting me an angry glare, as if this whole thing is my fault.

"For now." His voice is quiet, but I hear it loud and clear.

Stepping toward Trent, the other guard gives his shoulder a small shove towards the passage that leads to the arena. "Will you fucking go? I want to see the end of the fight before we have to move the rest of the slaves back."

Backing away, Trent leaves the room, but I don't miss the expression on his face before he goes.

Looking around, I see that I'm completely alone. The cells around me are open and empty. Stepping away from the wall, I walk to the front of the cage, gripping on to the rods that trap me. I have not been this alone for a long time, since before the guys found me. Closing my eyes, I press my face against the bars, savouring the cold bite of the metal against my skin. My head still feels like it's spinning from where I was hit, but now the loneliness and hopelessness starts to seep in. When I have the guys around me, I feel hopeful. As long as we are together, we can get through this, but right now, I find that difficult to believe.

Images flash through my mind again and I hear someone cry out in pain, the sound echoing around the empty room until I realise it's me. I can't do this, not without Jessie. They are going to keep killing us one by one, and I'm not sure I can keep watching it happen.

No.

I can't think like that. Jessie is dead and part of me died with him, but the other guys need me, just as I need them. I can't give up, I need to be strong for them. I've made it through this much, and for them, I can keep going.

I'm not sure how long I stand there clutching the cell bars, but noise fills the room as the other slaves are marched back into their cells. I stay there like a statue, watching as each of my guys are led back in, seeing the grief and anger in their eyes. All of them are back, except for Jessie, his empty cell mocking me as I was lead past it earlier.

Nixon is the last to be led in, and bruises mar his body that weren't there before, his face tight with worry, but once Nixon is locked in the cell next to mine, I let go of the bars and take a step away, retreating to the back of the cell.

"Rhea." Nixon's voice is rough, like he's been shouting, but that doesn't sound like something my gentle giant would do. Leaning against the wall behind me, I slide to the ground and stare out the front of the cell, pulling all of my emotions in close, holding them to my chest.

"Why isn't she responding?" Xavier appears in my peripheral vision as he grips the bars separating us. His voice sounds concerned, although I don't know why, he's been here long enough to know our fate.

"I don't know," Nixon rumbles, as he presses against the bars, his arm reaching out to me. "Rhea? Talk to me, baby." The pain in his voice breaks through my haze and I shuffle over so I can press myself against his arm.

I hear the two of them talking quietly as a numbness starts to settle over me, protecting me from the horrors of today.

I eventually fall into a deep sleep, my dreams full of the sounds of applause and clapping, along with an image that will haunt me forever —me standing in the center of the arena, covered in blood with blades in my hands, and the bodies of the guys littered around me as I am crowned champion.

I'M WAITING at the iron bars when they come for us the next morning. I am drained and cold and oh so numb. Somewhere deep inside, I realise this is wrong, I realise I'm not handling it after my initial breakdown, but this numbness doesn't hurt as much as my emotions. My broken heart cuts me deeply, the shards travelling through my blood and ripping apart my body from the inside...it feels like my world has been taken away. That I won't ever feel happy again, my breath won't catch...no, the numbness is better. It masks the pain, it allows me to function as I lose myself in my mind...in my memories of him.

Nixon is waiting next to me in his cell, his worried eyes locked on me. He tried to help me all night, but how can he? Jessie is gone…no, I can't even think his name or I will spiral again. Instead, I focus on the tiny details, the feel of the rough bars under my skin, the flecks of dust floating in the air. The odour of the cells and unwashed bodies. I go through my senses, calming myself once again, only stepping back when Tobias comes to unlock my cell. He winces when he sees me and I step out after him, concentrating on placing one foot in front of the other. I don't bother eating or going to the bathroom, I wait near the gate. Time passes oddly, like I am floating outside of my body, and when I blink the rest of the slaves are lined up waiting with me...all eyes on me. I don't meet them. I don't want their pity, glee, or anything else.

We are led into the arena, and before I know it, I'm pulled away from the line. Blinking, I look down at the hand digging into the tanned flesh of my arm. I can see the tight hold, it's almost cutting through my skin, but I can't feel it. Glancing up, I meet Trent's eyes as he drags me over to the racks and starts throwing weapons at me. His voice drifts to me as if from a great distance, the malice evident.

"...no tandem today, no, not after yesterday. You are going to suffer and once you lose, I get you. They won't let you die, you are too valuable, but they will make it hurt and so will I. My reward."

Good, I should suffer, I should be in pain.

I couldn't save him.

I push that thought away, burying myself deeper in my mind, pulling the protective layers closer around me and muffling the rest of his conversation. This must displease him, because he back hands me, my head snapping to the side. A burst of pain flashes through my face, which is once again smothered by the numbness, and I move my head back to face him, not the least bit affected. He frowns at what he sees there and Tobias steps up next to him, then they start to argue. I can see their mouths moving, but don't hear a word they are saying.

Maybe I'm finally broken beyond repair, maybe this will be my life without *him*—so cold with flashes of pain. It seems oddly fitting. He was my sunshine, my light in the dark, and now he's gone and I am lost in the shadows once again, with no way out.

Tobias eventually backs away, throwing me a pitying glance before turning his back on me and marching up into the sand above, leaving me with Trent. I wait, unmoving, as he steps towards me, his rancid breath wafting over my face and still I don't move.

"I'm going to fuck every one of your holes tonight, see what that pretty boy was willing to die for," he snarls, and somewhere deep, deep in the dark, a spark ignites from his words. "I'll make you scream his name as I take you again and again, ripping you apart...but he won't ever come. I watched his dead body be tossed to the crows, left to rot and be eaten like the parasite he is." The spark grows stronger, not burning away the dark, but using it like fuel, the fire spreading through my veins as he laughs and grabs me again, dragging me on numb feet to the open gate for the fighting pit.

Sometimes in the dark, we find ourselves. Lost in the shadows, we find a strength we never knew we had...it wraps around me now, echoing with my distant screams, his smile and flashes of my life, calling to me. Pulling me back from the edge, the warmth pushing me to go on. Yes, the darkness can be scary, but it can also be reassuring, where our nightmares and worries become real, or where we pull ourselves out of and build ourselves back up...but we never thank the dark for its tight grip, for being the thing that keeps us going. Instead, we worship the light, we huddle in it...I will embrace the dark instead. I will offer myself to it freely. Let the cocoon carry me away, morph me into something new...something stronger and much less breakable, because the dark will always blot out the light...the dark is eventual. The end and our beginning, and now my future.

I fan the flames of that dark spark, calling to it, asking it to burn my pain away. It responds to my voice, to Trent's horrid words that he spews as we wait, from his grip on my arm, and his wandering hand exploring my ass. I feed it Jessie's dying screams, his pain and his dimming eyes. I offer it all as I am forced into the middle of the sand.

"...Immortal!" I hear the announcement, but I tune it out, the crowd's thunderous roar turning to a muted buzzing as I huddle around that dark flame inside.

Vibrations run up my spread legs, and it's only then that I lift my head and look around, seeing the men surrounding me...fighters, all grim-faced, with excitement running through their eyes. This is my punishment, a fight I have no chance of winning, they want me to suffer, but I won't die...no, like Trent said, they won't allow that, but they forget. They forget I have suffered. I have suffered since the day I was born for simply being a woman.

I have been beaten.

I have been abused.

I have been kidnapped, drugged, and chained.

I have been taken from my home.

I have had my family tortured and killed in front of me.

I have watched my love die.

I have suffered and they forget...those who have suffered have nothing else left to lose. A grin turns up my lips as I salute the Masters and face the fighters, the numbness fading as that fire grows, the flames racing through my body, sealing my cracks and strengthening me.

The gong sounds.

Nobody moves, as all of the fighters wait to see what I will do. I grip the swords tighter and one of them finally makes the first move, his foot sliding in the sand before he rushes me. I duck under his swing, bring up my sword, and gut him, letting him scream as he drops to the ground behind me. I face the others, stilling again. That blaze still races through me...the pain and power almost too much yet not enough to break free.

One man swipes a dagger towards me, but I grab his wrist, twist it around, and plunge the blade into his neck before stopping again, waiting for the next fighter. They hesitate now, knowing I am stronger and faster than they were expecting, so they start to take me seriously.

Another man comes at me, slower this time, swinging his sword. His eyes alight with glee and his lips tipping up as he circles me.

"I watched him die, you know, saw him scream and cry like a fucking child. I'm betting he begged like a cunt in that last moment, I bet it was agony," he taunts, and I stagger back slightly, caught off guard. He sees it and moves closer, his grin growing larger. "What was his name...pretzel...prick...no, no...Jessie, wasn't it?"

His name on this man's vile lips, the way it rolls from his tongue...a man who has no right to use it, is the last drop of darkness the fire needs to turn into a volcano which erupts inside me.

My swords drop to the sand uselessly beside me, a scream leaving my throat. A battle cry, a grief howl, an endless wave of agony that has the fighters nervous as they glance at each other...and with that scream comes my power, rushing back to the surface, surging through my body with a strength I've never felt.

The shackles on my wrists crack but do not fall, no, my power simply explodes through them, like an anchor. It blows out of me like a great storm, each wave a pulse of power. My hair floats around my head in the invisible wind, and my feet lift from the ground until I am dangling in the air with my arms spread out, my head falls back, and my mouth opens in another silent scream. Waves of agony race through me with the force of the power, but I accept it, I welcome it, and when the power leaves me, it uses that to strengthen it.

I hear the screams, I feel the warmth of blood splatter me. Panic fills the air from the fighters and even the crowd, their gasps of shock reaching me, so I open my eyes and gaze around. I'm in the center of the storm...of the hurricane.

Wind rips around me like mini tornadoes. It picks up a fighter and tears him apart. The ground shakes and erupts, vines reaching up and wrapping around another fighter, constricting him until his face turns red as his eyes bulge out of his head and his mouth opens, letting a vine snake down his throat. Rocks move from the ground, tripping the fleeing fighters as they try to escape.

Ice encases a fighter, freezing him to death, and spreads across the sand around him like a giant snowflake. Fire races over the sand, not touching it as it reaches the remaining fighters and creeps up their legs, engulfing them in flames, their screams of agony as they burn to death splitting the air.

Four elements, all coming from me, rip through the training pit and kill all those who stand. My head turns around as if beyond my control, and I meet the wide eyes of Trent where he stands just before the cages. I let everything else but his face go.

I want him to hurt, I want him to die for everything he has put me through. My powers pull back into me, all focused on him, and when he narrows his eyes on me, I smile.

My power shoots out of me like a gun, aiming straight for him. It hits the barrier, the same power which nullifies ours that surrounds the arena, and I watch it crack and shatter just before Trent. My power hits him like a sledgehammer. Ice forms in his eyes and fire burns along his limbs. Vines trap him, keeping him still as the earth moves up, encasing him in a dirty grave as both fire and ice meet in his body, working together to freeze and burn his organs.

He can't fight, he can't even scream, and when his head is covered by dirt, I feel him die. My powers pull back, showing his stiff and dead body, which makes me laugh. The sound eerie and echoing around the theatre.

I gaze around again, noting the death I have yielded...no other fighters are left alive. Like a snap, the power returns to me, weaker and sluggish after all the use.

When I'm drained, I drop to the ground gently, and when my toes touch the sand, I slump, falling to the ground, my head hitting the cushioning sand...just before my eyes close, I see the havoc I've created and a smile graces my lips.

I slip back into my darkness's embrace gratefully.

My body hurts, all of me. My mind is aching, the pounding at the back of it making me groan. My legs are weak and shaky, my arms too heavy to lift. My chest is sore, and I am struggling to catch my breath. Cracking open my eyes, I look around in confusion...what happened?

It hits me then...what I did in the arena. My powers, killing them all. Yet I have no regret, none whatsoever. I only wish I could have killed the Masters as well.

A groan slips past my lips and I try to move, only to find myself restricted. Frowning, I look down. My arms and legs are locked in shackles chained to the wall...but so is my neck. A steel band around it is locking me in place in my cell. I test it but it doesn't budge, and I can't feel my powers, they must be rebuilding after draining them so completely.

I try to turn my head, but pain cuts through my neck, so I stop, bolted in place, just staring at the iron bars of my cell and the dirty floor that leads up to it. My legs are held at a strange angle and my arms are yanked back tight, almost dislocating them, yet I laugh.

All of this is because they fear me.

Chapter Eighteen

They leave me like that for hours as a punishment, and when the others come back to their cells, I see their worried glances. Nixon seems pissed and Xavier...looks proud? I grin at him and he returns it as his cage is slammed shut. I turn my head as much as I can and meet Nixon's eyes.

"Are they going to kill me?" I ask, knowing I will be punished for that display out there.

He moves as close to the bars as he can and lowers his voice. "I don't think so, Alcide is trying to charm them right now...if anything, they enjoyed it. It was a hell of a show, baby, and that's what they want. I'm worried what they will do next time to get that same reaction," he finishes, and I go cold, my smile disappearing.

He's right. They will want me to do it again, and when they realise that it will only happen with immense pain...they will get creative.

"Only time will tell," Xavier adds from my right.

"He's correct, nothing to do but wait, but, baby? What you did?" Nixon murmurs and shakes his head, a smile turning up his lips. "It was incredible. I have never seen power like that, it was like the elements came to your bidding. Your pain brought them, Rhea." He stops then, his eyes going far away. "Before this is through, it won't be the only time." Then he blinks again focusing on me as I swallow hard.

Not the only time?

I can't lose anyone else, I can't. We need to escape and now. I test my shackles. They are cracked and practically useless, but still hanging in place, so it doesn't draw attention. That's good, that will work in my favour. I can't do much until my power recharges, though, so I relax into the wall, blowing out a breath.

"One of you distract me," I request, almost begging.

"How?" Nixon questions, and Xavier snorts, so I turn to see him pressed against the metal rods, staring at me.

"Talk to her," he tells Nixon.

"I'm not good at talking," he mutters, looking disgruntled. My poor giant.

"Fine, I'll start." Xavier huffs, turning away slightly. The cells are filled with chatter, so ours fades in with the rest and no guards come to set me free. I try and get as comfortable as I can. He goes quiet then and I look at him, seeing him struggling for a moment before he seems to come to some sort of decision.

Any time I stop and think, or it goes quiet, Jessie's face flashes in my mind, spearing pain through my already broken heart, so when he starts talking, I find myself grasping on to his words like a lifeline, pulling me from my grief and heartache.

"I was young when I was brought here, but I still remember my before...my family," he begins, his voice dark and pained. He's putting his pain and ghosts on display so I won't fall back into mine. The least I can do is listen, let him know I understand and feel his pain, after all, that is sometimes all you can do.

"We were farmers. I had a little sister named Sascha, she had the same big brown eyes as my mum, she was her double. We weren't rich, we were poor by all accounts, but we were close and we had each other. We stayed out of the drama, and since we lived away from everyone, we were safe...or so we thought." His eyes meet mine then, so filled with pain that I gasp, unable to look away.

"They came late in the night. We heard the horses screaming in the barn, so I went to investigate. When I got there, the doors were blown open and then I heard screams from the house. I ran, I ran so hard I fell over, but it wasn't fast enough. They were there. They broke my little sister's neck when she tried to get to my mum, who they had dragged into the other room. My dad tried to fight them off, and when he did, they shot him in the chest. It was horrible, there was so much blood, he didn't die straight away. When they were finished with my mum, they hung her by the barn outside on the old tree. I had to watch it. They added my dad's body there next." He blinks, bringing himself back. "I don't know why they did it to this day, maybe they thought we were freaks, who knows, but they didn't kill me. No, they took me and threw me down here. Moulding me, forming me into the fighter, the winner they wanted. Their pawn.

"I hate it, I hate them, but I've seen what they are capable of, what they will do, and that was without provocation, so, Rhea, I never tried to escape...then you came in. So fucking filled with fight and life, and I realized I had given up. You talk of freedom, of escape, and for once I'm not filled with dread, but with hope. Hope that this time, with you, we will win. That we can actually be free."

Tears trail down my face. I am horrified by what this man went through. No wonder he was hard and cold when I first met him. He was trying to protect himself, trying to defend against the hurt.

"I was fourteen in my first fight, barely able to hold the sword they put in my hand. I was pitted against a lanky boy, he was experienced. I was meant to die, but I didn't. I found something that day, a spark, a power to live. To keep fighting...I just got lost on the way, fighting the wrong thing."

"I'm so sorry," I tell him softly, the words lame and unable to offer any sense of the remorse and grief I feel for this strong man before me, the man resilient enough to keep fighting every day, even when it seemed hopeless.

He shrugs then, downplaying his pain. "You are lucky. I hated you for it at first. You were protected. They sold me that night and most nights after to the highest paying patron, to do whatever they wanted...well, at least until I killed one who went too far, and they realized they couldn't make me anymore."

"Good, I'm glad you killed them," I snap, enraged for him. Was it not enough they took his family and freedom, that they had to take his body as well? "You are a fighter, Xavier, you can fight anything. We will be free and you are coming with us."

He grins then, a flash of teeth. "Yeah? You want a pet fighter?"

"No, I want you to be part of our family. We are misfits, but together we are so much more. We protect each other and we find our own happiness," I declare, imploring him to accept. It seems important.

"Family," he whispers almost distractedly.

"I know. I wasn't used to it either, but they showed me how much better life is together. Don't you ever get lonely? Don't you ever wish there was someone to lean on?"

He looks back at me, but it's Nixon who answers. "Our family is open to you. We need you as much as you need us," he states sternly, and I know it's another of the big guy's feelings. Xavier, we need him? For what exactly? I don't ask, since Nixon won't know either.

"Do I have to perform?" he inquires, teasing almost.

"No." I try to shrug and wince when the chains dig in. "Do what you want, but come with us?" I ask again.

"Fine, get us out of here, Rhea, and I will follow you anywhere," he concedes, his eyes serious and intense, so intense I have to look away, licking my lips.

Just then, a bang comes, and I look up as the cell door opens and three guards stream in, led by Tobias. "Don't try anything or attack us, or we will be forced to lock you back up," he warns me, and I nod as he steps closer. One of them points a gun at me as the other unlocks the chains and unwinds them from my body until I am free. Then they step away, walking backwards from the cell, and lock it. The two other guards move away, and Tobias spares them a quick glance before looking back at me. "Trent got what he deserved," he tells me, and then steps away, standing at the end of our row and straightening.

"Immortals, you're up tomorrow!" Tobias calls.

Why are they warning us tonight? I frown, it's going to be bad, I know it. Xavier and I share a look.

"We can win," he says and then he nods. "I want to test my powers."

"What?" I question.

"If we are to escape, we need to know our powers, I've never tested them all. I need to know if it was a fluke that I came back or the real deal, either way, they get a show."

"Xavier," I protest, terrified at the idea of losing him, but I won't analyse why.

"Rhea, let me do this. Tomorrow I will die, but I will come back. I need you to be strong," he implores me, his hands wrapped around the bars, his eyes hard and forcing me to be tough.

"Okay, okay." I nod, blowing out a breath.

Tomorrow, tomorrow Xavier will die. I hope he's right, I hope it wasn't a fluke. I can't watch another person I care about die. Our eyes stay locked late into the night, talking without talking, until I finally fall asleep curled up on the back wall.

Tomorrow comes all too soon.

Chapter Nineteen

I go through the morning routine like I'm in a bubble. I'm aware of the others on the outside of that bubble, but I can't hear them. Their voices are muffled as I try to focus on my fight today. I'm cognisant of the anxious stares the guys throw my way as I sit on the bench with my breakfast mostly untouched. I know I should be eating to keep up my strength, but I know I'll just want to throw it up as soon as we start fighting.

Going through the motions, I focus on keeping my mind on the fight ahead and not on the fears swirling around in the back of my head, or the images that kept waking me up in the middle of the night. I know that if I go into the fight thinking the worst is going to happen, it will. But really, that's what's going to happen anyway, right? Xavier is asking me to let him get fatally injured, just to see if his powers really are that of immortality. But what if it doesn't work?

Jessie's face passes through my mind and the loss hits me like a blow to the stomach. I can't lose someone else. I don't know what Xavier is to me, with the lingering feelings of lust and something else I don't want to examine right now, but I meant it when I told him he is part of our family.

As usual, the others are led out of their cells first, all of them throwing me worried glances in the process, but I turn away, not wanting to see their faces.

A sharp rapping against the bars on my cell have me spinning around in surprise, seeing a frowning Blain staring at me. "What's going on?"

"What?" My voice is raspy from lack of use, but I shake my head in confusion.

"Don't fuck with me. Something's going on, and you're going to tell me what it is," he demands, crossing his arms over his chest, and I know I'm not going to get away without giving him an answer. One of the guards shouts over at us, but Blain ignores him with an expectant expression on his face. Taking a deep breath, I close my eyes against the warring emotions that are trying to get a hold of me.

"Xavier is going to test his powers." The words are quiet, barely a whisper, but Blain's frown tells me he heard what I said. I can feel Xavier's eyes on me from the adjoining cell, but he doesn't say anything.

"What do you mean test? I thought his powers were immortality…" Trailing off, I see the moment he realises what I'm talking about and he turns to glare at the fighter.

"He's going to get killed on purpose."

"Shit!" Blain swears, his face morphing into anger as he gestures to me. "You can't do this, man. What if it doesn't work and you die? Do you know what that's going to do to her?"

"I know." Xavier's acceptance causes me to shiver, and I see Blain's eyes narrow on the movement. He opens his mouth to say something, but one of the guards storms in, scanning the room for the missing slave. As soon as he sees him, the guard marches over and points his weapon at Blain's chest.

"Go," the guard orders, but Blain keeps his hard gaze on me.

"Don't get distracted. Do what you need to," he commands, stumbling as the guard tires of waiting and shoves him in the chest to get him moving. Blain bares his teeth at the guard, and I feel a thrill run through me as I see a feral light in his eyes. What are they doing to us? If we don't get out of here soon, we might be more animal than human.

"Rhea," Xavier calls out, dragging my mind from the dangerous, circling thoughts, which are waiting for me to drop my guard so they can crowd my brain. I turn in my cell to face him, my eyes wide as I meet his steady gaze. "It will work. I promise."

Forcing myself to nod, I turn away from him, unable to look at him anymore. I make myself start warming up, the same one I would do if I was getting ready for a show back at the circus. I can feel his eyes boring into me as I stretch, but I refuse to meet his gaze.

After what feels like ages, the rattling of keys echoes around the room, announcing that the guards are returning for us. Walking to the front of the cage, I wait for him to unlock my cell, holding out my wrists for him to lead me away. Giving me a look, he lets out a barking laugh.

"Eager to fight today, huh, freak?" he sneers, as he grabs my wrists before leaning closer, his rank breath making me wrinkle my nose is disgust, but otherwise I don't move away from him as he continues to leer at me. "Learning to enjoy the blood lust?"

I'm used to guys treating me like this, and I know I will get my revenge on him one day, but until then, I just need to get through today. The guard jerks next to me and makes a choking noise, so I spin and raise my eyebrows when I see Xavier has grabbed the man through the bars, and wrapped his hand around the guard's neck. I can't help the sick little smile that crosses my lips as I watch the guard struggle, his face becoming more and more red, his eyes darting around as he begins to panic.

"If you want to live for another day, you will stop talking to her like that." Xavier's voice is low and dangerous, and as the guard tries to nod, I see his mouth opening and closing as he gasps for breath like a fish out of water. Taking this for agreement, Xavier releases the guard who stumbles away, glaring at him with a hatred I know too well.

"Fucking freaks," the guard spits, before grabbing my wrist again and marching me out of the room as three guards enter, their eyes trained on the only cell still occupied. "He's feeling feisty today. Maybe remind him who's in charge here," my guard instructs the others with a smirk. I want to protest, but I know it will only make things worse, so I keep my lips sealed as I'm walked away, the sound of flesh hitting flesh following me out.

I focus on the noises of the crowd as I'm led out into the holding area. The shouts for blood, the banging of feet on the stands, and my pounding heart are all I hear as I wait for Xavier to join me. A chain is clipped to me and I glance up when I hear feet shuffling in the doorway. It's not Xavier making the noise, he never drags his feet, but it signals that the guards who are bringing him are here. Xavier is dragged in, his face bloodied with bruises forming where they weren't before. I want to go up to him, to run my hand over the wounds and shout at the guards, but I don't, it will only make it worse for us if they see how it affects us. Instead, I meet his eyes as he is brought closer. His expression is heated, determined.

The guards pull us towards each other, attaching Xavier to the other end of the chain that will keep us together during the fight. I keep my gaze ahead of me, unable to look at him anymore, not when I consider what could be the outcome of today. What if it all goes wrong? Could I cope with losing Xavier as well as Jessie?

Marched forward by the guards, we are taken to the holding area before they remove our manacles from our wrists. Immediately, I feel the return of my powers as they back away, locking us into the holding area. My whole body is tense, and I can feel Xavier glance over at me, but I refuse to meet his gaze, instead staring at the gate that will lead us into the arena.

"I'll be fine," Xavier mumbles quietly as we wait. We'll be punished if they see us talking, but I don't care. Staring ahead, I feel the tension rippling through my body whereas he seems calm as he rolls his neck and stretches his arms out next to me.

"Don't do it, it's too risky." I feel him still as soon as the words leave my mouth, but I refuse to look at him since I'm not sure what I would do if I did. Would I cry? Would I scream or beg? No, I won't do that, the Masters would take too much satisfaction from actions like that, and form the way that they expect me to act.

"Rhea, I've had enough of not doing anything. We need to know if I'm right about my gift, we can't risk relying on it when we escape and it does not work. What if your other guys got killed because of it?" That thought makes me feel sick, and it must show on my face since he continues, "I thought so. We will know today, one way or another." So I have to sacrifice Xavier to protect my other guys? If you had asked me a month ago if I would sacrifice this battle-scarred fighter to save my men, I probably would have said yes, but now? Now that I know him and am coming to care for him, it's a different story.

"Trust me," he whispers, and I turn to him, meeting those imploring eyes, and nod. What else can I do? He has made up his mind and he is right, trust is all we have now. So I stumble after him as we are forced into the pit. I ignore the announcement, instead staring out into the crowd with a determined look on my face. I won't let them see me weak or broken. They will never get that again.

Our chain slithers between us as we wait, ready for whatever they will throw at us today. When the cranking of the gate comes again, I know the other fighters are here. I suck in a steadying breath, looking at Xavier once more, taking strength from the steel in his eyes. He stands tall, waiting, like the warrior he is. His head is lifted, his eyes sharp and feet already turned to face whatever threat is coming through that gate. I turn with him and my mouth drops open in shock before I can stop it. It's not fighters we are facing today…but animals.

Xavier hisses out a breath, his only reaction as I swallow hard, my eyes dragging across the animals pulling against the chains that hold them. Snarls cover their hideous faces, and their fangs flash as drool drips to the arena below. I love animals, but these...these are nothing but monsters—four of them, bred and trained to kill. I heard rumours from the other fighters. Demons, they call them, only brought out to punish slaves or if they want a death. They only have one thought—to kill. They play with their food, chasing them and wearing them down. Circling and attacking as a pack until it's too late.

They are similar in size to Fluffy, their eyes black and unseeing. They rely on sound, another fact I heard. The chains cut into the rough brown skin at their necks, where there are old scars from previous battles. They have four legs, like a dog, I think they were called, and long, thick, whip-looking tails. Their faces are flat, eyes small and pinched, with a snout bigger than their head housing sharp-looking needle type teeth and fangs. They look deadly, fast, and scary as hell.

True fear runs through me. How are we going to win this?

Xavier steps forward then, blocking me slightly, and I know he is going to die protecting me. I pull my sword. I refuse to let him die without a fight, even if it is the plan. I will fight, keep swinging and battling for as long as I can, protecting his back like a partner does.

"Stay as quiet as you can, keep behind me. They like to sneak up on their prey. Move quickly and get to high ground," he whispers, but even the low timbre of his voice alerts them. They growl now, low and menacing, all their heads turning in our direction.

Nodding, I look around. The only high ground is if I get up the side of the barrier, so that's what I will have to do. I don't know what his plan is, but I trust him, and I know he won't lead me wrong. I widen my stance, lowering myself with my sword held in front of me, and quieten my breathing as much as I can, but I know it won't be enough. The ground is sand, but they will hear us running or moving and the chinking of our chain will give us away…unless.

"Trust me," I whisper, eyeing the demons who are yanking at their chains now, trying to get to us as the announcer prattles on about their breeding and our powers.

Keeping one eye on them, I force my powers from their place. They aren't fully healed yet, but there is enough to draw from. It turns my hand to stone and I yank and pull, the chain creaking in protest until finally…finally it snaps. I almost stumble back from the force, the two ends long and dangling in the sand. He looks back at me with a smirk on his lips and watches as I wrap the chain around my wrist to stop the noise, and then he copies me, both of us turning back to face the demons just in time as the announcer finishes talking.

"Are you ready, my good people, for the battle of the monsters?" he calls, and everyone cheers.

The gong sounds and my heart slams in my ribcage, my feet hesitating, but the chains on the demons don't release straight away, and with each prolonged second, I start to get more and more nervous.

Then as suddenly as the cheers started, they stop, the stadium going deadly silent until we hear the chains snap, releasing the demons.

Screams mixed with cheers go up as they race forward, heading straight towards us, almost pushing at each other to get to us first. Xavier stands strong, not backing down even as I shuffle back a step before I force myself to remain still. They are almost on us, eating the distance quicker than I expected, their heads tilted as they listen for us. When the first one reaches us, Xavier tightens his grip on his sword and races forward, striking at him before jumping and kicking off of the creature's head, flipping over him to face the next one. The one he stabbed stumbles forward, and a gasp leaves my lips upon seeing the gash carved into its face. It hears, its head snapping to face me as its back end goes into the air. Its head is almost on the ground as he growls and prepares to pounce. He's behind Xavier when he grunts and the demon freezes, starting to turn towards him, and I know I have to do something.

"Hey, you! Ugly!" I scream, and then start walking backwards. It concentrates back on me, stepping in my direction until I suddenly turn and sprint away. It lets out a roar and I hear it racing after me as I head straight across the arena towards the barrier.

Almost there.

One more stride...

I can feel it snapping on my heels, ready to pounce, and at the last second, I duck and roll out of the way as it soars over my head and smacks right into the barrier. It shakes its head, struggling to get up, so I hold out my hand, my power leaving me with a scream. A fireball heads straight towards it before it goes up in flames, a squeal escaping its snout as it tries to roll to put out the inferno. It falls back to the ground, crying out in pain as it burns, and when I'm sure it's not going to get back up, I roll to my feet and turn to see where the rest are.

My body is throbbing from the way I am using my powers, forcing it to comply to my will. My powers are primarily to protect me, adapting to defend me against any threat, but I am asking so much more from it, and the last few days are taking their toll on my body. Not that I will let the Masters or the screaming crowd know that, and as I see Xavier fighting against two massive demons, I know I have to help him. He's holding his own, and I know it's part of the plan for him to die in this fight, but that was when we thought we would be fighting humans. This will not be an easy death, not with these starved and feral beasts. They will toy and play with him.

Checking my sword, I start to run towards him at the other side of the arena, but something is bugging me. A shadow falls over me and a sick feeling in my stomach reminds me what I had forgotten. There were four animals in the arena. While I had been fighting with one of them, the other had been stalking me, hunting me down like its prey, and now it has decided to attack.

Spinning at the last moment, I raise my arms above my head to protect my face as it rears up on its hind legs, its sharp, gleaming claws slashing towards me. I feel my skin harden a second before the beast crashes into me, pinning me to the floor. It lunges forward, its teeth aiming for my face and arms, but thankfully it can't penetrate my skin. In the attack, I dropped my blade, and I can see it glinting to my left. Trusting that my powers will protect me, I throw out my hand, but the blade is just out of reach. Letting out a cry of frustration, I try to buck and shift my hips, hoping to throw the beast off me, but it's too heavy. The animal above me is getting frustrated, its attacks getting harder and more violent as it grips my arm in its jaws and drags me across the sand, taking me farther from my blade. I'm going to have to channel one of the guys' powers, but trying to concentrate when I've got a vicious beast trying to tear me apart is hard, especially the longer I'm under it. Fear stirs in my belly, only riling the animal into a frenzy.

"Rhea, fucking concentrate!" Blain shouts, as if he knew exactly what I needed. Focusing on Blain, on my need for a blade, on the need to protect myself, I try to block out the sounds around me, of the fighting and the crowd, concentrating only on his voice. "Fucking fight!"

It might not be an eloquent speech, but it's exactly what I need, and my eyes snap open as a burning in my wrists tells me the blades are appearing there. Baring my teeth at the animal that is continuing to attack me, I lunge up, stabbing the creature in its belly, slicing down and ignoring its cry of pain. I realise my mistake as it begins to fall down on top of me, and push with all my might so as it drops, most of my torso is out of the way, leaving only my legs trapped by its body. The creature yowls and yips in pain as its blood and organs spill across the ground, and even though it tried to kill me, guilt fills me that it has to die this way. Leaning forward, I shove the creature and pull my legs free.

Pushing up onto shaky feet, I stare down at my blood-stained clothes and grimace, but the crowd loves it. I look exactly like the fighter they want. Walking away from the creature, I grab my dropped blade, the daggers I had created disappeared as soon as I used them—some magic I've never understood—but I turn to face the slowly dying creature and decide to put it out of its misery. As I stride over to it and press the knife to its throat, I swear I see something in its eyes that resembles acceptance. Is this what my animals will end up like if we don't get out of here? Determination steadies my hand as I swipe the blade across the animal's throat, and it quickly dies beneath me.

Xavier's shout of pain has me spinning around, my blood turning cold when I see the scene before me. One of the creatures is dead, leaving the largest fighting against him, except Xavier isn't fighting. Sure, he's defending himself, but he's not attacking the creature, and I realise this is it, this is the moment he is going to let himself get killed. As if I'm watching in slow motion, the creature lunges forward and bites into Xavier's left side, causing the big man to cry out as his knees buckle, his body falling to the floor. The creature then continues to attack him, but he's just playing with him—a bite to the arm, to his leg, dragging him across the sand.

Fuck this, I can't watch him die like this. My body tingles and as I glance down at my hands, I see gleaming blades appearing from my skin. Sheathing my sword, I grip the magical blades, examining them quickly. They are light, perfect for throwing. I've been practicing with Blain, my aim isn't perfect like his, but good enough.

Shifting into the stance drilled into me over and over, I switch the blades to one hand and raise my fingers to my mouth, the piercing whistle cutting through the noise of the arena. The crowd falls silent as the beast turns, narrowing its grotesque eyes at me, but I don't give it a chance to move as I throw two blades, one immediately after the other. The first one missed, landing uselessly in the sand before disappearing, but the second imbeds itself into its target, the beast's eye.

Throwing its head back in a pain filled cry, it moves away from Xavier, shaking its head as it tries to dislodge the knife. It collapses, pathetically whining as it crawls away, a trail of blood following it. I had really hoped that throw would kill it. Sighing, I unsheathe my sword and slowly walk towards it. The beast hears me coming and looks up, snarling at my approach. Then it does something I never would've expected. Glancing up at the Masters, it pushes up onto shaking paws and throws itself into the barrier. The smell of burning flesh makes me crinkle my nose as I watch the creature kill itself, my heart bleeding for the creature.

"No!" Xavier cries out, his plan ruined as the crowd bursts into applause and cheers. The announcement overhead declares we are the winners, but I keep my gaze on Xavier. His eyes are locked on me and I know what I need to do. Checking the grip on my sword, I stride over to Xavier and kneel down next to him, ignoring his open wounds and pained, shallow breathing. Looking up at the Masters, I see unhappy expressions. They wanted us to kill all the animals, but we refused, so they didn't get the ending they wanted, as a show for the crowd.

Narrowing my eyes at them, I turn away. I won't let them see my tears. Raising my sword and whispering my apologies, I plunge the blade into Xavier's chest.

AFTER THAT, the crowd went wild. Fighting broke out and I was dragged out of the arena then chucked into my cell. The others were already there and called out to me, but my mind was numb.

What did I do?

Curling up at the back of my cage, I stare at the bars, the sounds of the other slaves blending into the background. The only noise that breaks me out of my trance is when my cell door opens. Sound suddenly hits me and I can hear the guys shouting obscenities at the guards. I try to make out what they are saying as two guards bustle into my cell, dragging something behind them.

"Fucking bitch, I lost money on that fucking fight," one of the guards sneers, dropping something on the ground before the other guard drags him from the cell. It's not until they leave that I realise what it is.

Xavier.

Jumping to my feet, I rush to his side, only to cry out as I see his glazed over eyes. I drop to the floor and press my hand against his arm, checking his pulse. Nothing.

No. This isn't right, this can't be happening.

Leaning forward, I lay my forehead on his chest as I begin to cry, the sobs racking my frame as grief, shame, and despair run through me.

I'm not sure how long I stay like that for, but my body feels stiff and my face itches from my dried tears. Exhaustion falls over me. I'm not sure how long I can keep doing this, I can't keep losing people like this. I run my hand over Xavier's warm arm, wanting to hold on to his hand.

Wait, warm? Pulling back quickly, I stare down and see his grey skin has regained its colour and his chest starts to rise. Tears form in my eyes again, but this time, for an entirely different reason. Looking down at his stomach, I see the horrendous wounds have scabbed over, and when I glance at his face, he's smirking at me.

"I told you, you could trust me."

Chapter Twenty

Today was crazy. I'm drained from the fight and almost losing Xavier. I slump to the ground, but not twenty minutes later, I see torches heading my way and almost groan. I nudge Xavier who sits up. I don't know why they haven't moved him yet, and when Tobias spots him, he frowns, like he had forgotten he was in here with me. They don't seem to be surprised at all that he's alive, considering when they brought him in here he was most definitely dead.

"Come on, slave, there is someone who wants to see you. Xavier, back to your cell," Tobias calls, as he and another guard unlock my cell and gesture me forward. I nod at Xavier as I pass, and he squeezes my hand as he heads back to his own cage on unsteady legs. I'm betting it's Chester, so I go willingly, letting them lead me down the hall and to our usual room.

The door opens and I head in without any fear, except when I look up it's not Chester I see...but a man. A man I have never seen before. He is covered to his feet in a black cloak, his face peeking out of the shadows, and only when the door shuts behind me does he toss it back to reveal himself.

His face is slim with high cheekbones, but not from fashion, more from malnourishment. His eyes are brown and deep, locked on me. His eyebrows slant angrily over his eyes, his lips thin and pursed. An old, white scar dissects them. He's tall, really tall, and skinny.

I step back, hitting the door, my back slamming into it in my rush to get away. "Who are you? What do you want?" I snap, fear coating my tone.

"Not what you are thinking," he tells me, his voice low and rough, like rocks grating against each other. "Though I did tell Chester that when I bought these hours, I hope you don't mind."

Chester? Chester let him buy me?

I don't know why that stings, but it does. I thought we had reached an understanding...a partnership. But no. He sold me, like a whore, like a slave.

I tilt my head back defiantly. "So what do you want?"

"A bit of your time, that is all, Rhea. You see, I represent a group of people. People like yourself. We are everywhere, even down here."

"The rebels?" I whisper, looking at him with fresh eyes, and he nods.

"The rebels, those deemed not worthy to live or have their own freedom. We have been fighting back in every way we could since we formed, but you are here now. What you did in the ring could change everything."

"You want me to fight for you?" I conclude with a frown.

"With us, for us, whatever way you want to put it. We want your help. We're losing, Rhea, and if something doesn't change, us freaks will all be dead soon. We need your help, Rhea," he declares, stepping closer, but not close enough to feel threatening.

"Fine, you want me to fight, I want something in return," I snarl, my mind whirring.

"What is that?" he asks, a smile curling his lips at my answer.

"Freedom. Help get us out of here, all of us, and I'll fight with you. I will join your rebellion." And I will, to save my family, to free us all...I will. Freaks aren't slaves, so maybe it's time we fought back. Taught them we are not be messed with. "You get us free and we have a deal," I demand, my voice unwavering.

We stare each other down until eventually, he laughs, the sound booming around us. "You have yourself a deal, Rhea. Freedom for your help."

He sweeps across the room, passing me, and heads to the door.

"Oh? And Firecracker, stay strong," he whispers as he goes by, and I freeze at the nickname.

Only one man calls me that.

Only my family knows it.

Jessie.

I spin, but the man is gone, and I gawk after him.

How did he know that? Is Jessie...is Jessie alive? No, he can't be. I saw him die! The hope would be worse than watching it happen all over again.

But, what if?

I CAN FEEL it in the air, the change...the hope. I had spread word. The rebellion is coming, we will be free. Despite my own thoughts, I have hope too. Not just hope for freedom...but for Jessie. I replay the moment when I thought he had died...what if I was wrong? What if he didn't.

Firecracker.

I would give anything, fight in any rebellion, and topple any empire to have him back with me. My sweet, sweet love. If he is alive, if he is with the rebels...I will never let him go again. Nothing else matters but family, and I plan on building mine back together again.

Piece by fucking piece if I need to.

I wait in my cell for anything to happen. He didn't say when he would help us, but it makes sense that it wouldn't be straight away. He would need to organise it all, and then get in to get us out. So I wait, patiently.

I sleep that night, but lightly in case I need to be awake at a moment's notice. The next morning, I shower and use the bathroom before heading to join my men at the table where a tray waits for me, Xavier trailing on my heels. Not that anyone down here would dare attack me, not after that show upstairs, no, they all seem scared of me now or at least respect me.

I plop into my seat between Blain and Nixon, and Xavier sits opposite me with Rex…leaving a space between them for Jessie, which breaks my heart. I swallow and look away before I break down again, and it just so happens that I look up and meet Jacob's gaze. He nods at me, stepping up to our table and the gap there.

"Soon," is all he says, and then walks away.

Soon? For the escape? How soon is soon? How does he know? I can't ask him, so I look back at my food and pay attention to eating, ensuring that I don't draw the guards' eyes to me.

I force myself to eat and drink and then the bell rings. "Time to fight! Line up, slaves!" comes the call and we all stand, with Xavier and me sharing a look. It's time.

We line up, but Xavier and I are held back and chained together. He helps me with my armour, his fingers lingering longer than they need to, and we share another look, one filled with unspoken feelings. When he turns away, the moment is broken, and I shake it off, grabbing my sword and readying myself, facing the emptying tunnel. The slaves are led into the sand above to the sounds of cheers and stomping.

I hope the rebellion comes soon…

I don't know how many more fights we will survive.

Chapter Twenty-One

We stride onto the sand, our heads held high and our swords ready, with our chains dangling between us. The crowd goes wild as we stop in the middle, our eyes running across them, dismissing them the same way we dismiss the Masters. They are nothing to us now.

We show no fear.

We bend for no one.

We are the Immortals.

The time ticks by as the crowd still goes wild, chanting our names, screaming them. We wait, still and ready for whatever they are going to throw at us. I hear the crank of the gate again. Day after day, fight after fight, I stand here. When is enough... enough?

I don't turn this time, not yet. I grab my sword and lift it into the air, feeling Xavier copy my movements. I stare down everyone, giving them a message, and only when they start to get uncomfortable do I turn to see what we are fighting today.

Other slaves troop in, all grim-faced, knowing what and who they are facing...two immortals. They know this means their death, but to not fight would mean an even worse fate. They are choosing the lesser evil and I hate that this is all we are.

A lesser evil.

No.

I glance at Xavier, and a look passes between us so I step closer, trying not to move my lips. "I'm not doing it, not again. I'm not killing these men, they do not deserve to die simply for being them. I won't lose my soul just to save my life."

He searches my eyes. "Are you sure?"

"I am, I am not asking you to do this with me. I know what it means, I know the sacrifice I am—"

"I'm with you, always, no more death. We will show them they can't control us any longer. I will follow where you lead, Rhea," he states, his voice strong and sure.

It's decided. No more killing. We are taking a stand. For us, for our souls, for the freaks...for the rebellion.

The other slaves don't know it though, and they share worried glances with sweat covering their pale faces as they shift in the sand. Not attacking, just waiting to defend themselves.

"Fight!" comes a yell, which is taken up by the rest of the crowd until they are chanting it at us. The slaves facing us move in slightly, watching us closely as they do, the guards straightening at their back to force them if need be.

I step towards them, swinging my sword, and they don't step back. "Fight us," I call as loudly as I dare without being heard. "We won't kill you."

They share a look again, and one to the left with an unkempt beard snorts. "Sure, they are just trying to trick us."

"We aren't," I hiss, and then run my eyes over them. "We are done killing our own."

They share nervous looks, but the one with the beard rushes at me with a yell, his sword raised. I hold my hand out to stop Xavier, and I wait for the man to get close before I sweep my leg and send him tumbling, pressing my sword to his throat. "I am not killing you."

He looks past the sword to me, his eyes holding shock. No doubt he saw me kill Xavier and thought if I could turn on my partner, I would kill anyone, but they don't know me. They don't know it was a plan and how much it broke me to watch him die, even though he was reborn.

"Why?" he finally asks, his gaze clashing with mine, the word holding so much despair. Why, why am I helping him? Sparing him? When the world and the people in it have done nothing but betray and abuse him?

"Because we are freaks, we stick together," I answer him and remove my blade. Instead, I hold out my hand to him, letting him decide. His life is in his hands now, like it should have always been.

He glances from it to me, finally coming to a decision. He places his hand in mine, and I help him to his feet and turn and face the others who drop the tips of their swords to the ground, all of their decisions made as well.

"Slaves! Fight," comes an order from the Masters' box. I look at them and grin.

"Make us!" I call back boldly.

I hear some boos, but some of the crowd laughs as well. The Masters look infuriated, and they turn to the guard in their box and whisper something. Not two minutes later, the gate is rising again, and guards are streaming in wearing battle gear. They face us, all angry and ready to die for their orders and Masters. I swing my sword and step forward. Xavier mimics my movements as the slaves suck in a breath, their fear evident.

I stand before them, my sword held out to protect the slaves with Xavier at my side, and stare at the Masters as they give orders to their troops. The slaves in the cages, my family, cheer for me. For us and what we are standing for.

"Fight!" a Master calls, and their guards step forward, banging their shields to their chest. The sound echoes around the arena as they try and herd us, and with less room to fight, they could stay behind those shields and slaughter us. I don't think so. I call my magic again, it comes easier every day, and now it races across my skin, turning me to stone, but I go one step further this time. I let Jessie's magic burst from my palms, fire from one and ice from the other. The fire hits a guard in the face and he screams and falls back, the hole being quickly filled by another guard. The ice hits one in the chest, crawling along his breast plate then up his neck and arms and finally, to his face, where his mouth is open in a silent scream.

He falls backwards too, and this time there is no guard to fill his spot.

I count the rest—fifteen. I look at Xavier and he grins. "Easy," he replies to my silent question. He's right, but I don't want the slaves getting hurt, so I form a blade in my hand, using Blaine's power, and release it. It imbeds in a guard's neck, blood squirting across the one next to him as he, too, falls.

"Now it's easy." I laugh.

"Huh, I bet you can't take out another before they get mad and charge," he teases.

"You're on." I close my eyes this time, my power draining slightly from the use, but I manage to coax it out. I hold my hand out without looking, and when I open my eyes to see, two guards are skewered on wood, which has speared up from the ground. Another is covered in rocks. Eleven to go.

They charge us then, not giving us a chance to rely on my powers anymore. Xavier and I stay close, almost touching with just enough room to fight. I duck under a spear, swiping my sword up to break the wood halfway down. I catch it as it falls, twist it mid-air, and thrust it back at the guard. It impales his eye and he stumbles back, screaming as I turn to the next one. He lunges with his sword and I duck, but not enough. I feel it graze my cheek, fire trailing in the steel's wake as blood wells, but I dart back up, evade his next swing, and hack at his side again and again until he falls. I glance at Xavier to see at least three bodies at his feet and grin, there are only six left now. Two face each of us, while the rest have snuck around to get to the slaves behind us, but they are holding their own, so I turn back to the guards who are going slower this time, analysing me.

Instead of waiting for them to come at me, I run at them. I drop to the ground, skidding on my knees until I am behind them, then I wrap the chain around one's legs and drop him as I cut along the other's back. Grabbing the chain, I encircle it around the first man's neck and choke him with it as I stab at the other. He falls, gushing blood, and I lean back, pulling the chain tighter until the first man stops moving and fighting. Gasping, I stumble to my feet, unwinding the chain as I take in how everyone else is doing.

Xavier is watching me. Everyone is dead around him, and when I meet his eyes, he winks. I look to the slaves to see their chests heaving, but the guards are also dead there too.

We won.

I turn to the Masters, spotting the fury on their faces, even as the crowd cheers, loving the bloodshed.

They will kill us for this...unless. "And that is the story!" I scream, and the crowd hushes, turning to me, as do the Masters. "The story of the underdogs, the Immortals! Can I get a cheer for the Masters and their new creative show?" I know how to work a crowd, so I do it now. A cheer goes up and I grin at the Masters. We, the slaves, know it wasn't a show and so do they, but they can't kill us now. They can punish us for sure, but not too severely, we are the crowd favourite. I have backed them into a corner and they know it.

This is my message to the rebellion, my stand, our stand.

We are escorted from the arena with a troop of guards, and we all hold our heads up high as we are led back to the main eating area downstairs. None of the other slaves are here and the guards make a circle around Xavier and me, while the others are led away to watch. I know they are going to punish us. Can I survive it?

Two guards step forward, one holding a whip. The other stomps across and before Xavier can stop him, he grabs me and grips the back of my shirt, and tosses me forward until I hit the table, my face smacking into the wood. I grab a goblet there and throw it at him, but I am pushed back down. I hear fighting and look across to see them trying to subdue Xavier as I hear the whip uncoil and snake through the air before it snaps across my skin.

I scream before I can help it, my skin on fire as I feel it split. I choke it back, swallowing the blood in my mouth from biting my tongue. I hear it whizzing through the air again before it lays another bone cutting lash against my skin, crossing the other. I feel my blood dripping down my back as I hang onto the table to try and keep myself up, my legs turning weak.

"No!" I hear Xavier yell, and I close my eyes, not wanting them to see me weak. I will take it.

But the next blow never comes. I crack open an eye and turn my head, my mouth dropping open. Xavier is next to me, holding the end of the whip in his hand from where he stopped it in mid-air. Blood drips down his hand from the force of him stopping the lash. He tugs on it, yanking the man holding the other end closer, but the guards move forward again. They use the end of their swords to kick out his legs and he releases the whip.

He grunts as he falls before he gets back to his feet, his eyes darting around as I hear the whip being pulled back, ready for another strike. He dives on top of me, his face curled into my neck, covering me completely.

"Xavier!" I gasp.

I hear a thud, and a grunt leaves his lips as he is pushed against me. Did...did he just take the lash for me?

"I'm okay," he whispers against my skin, but I hear the pain he tries to hide as he jerks against me again, and again. I can't move, can't stop it, and when it's done, he slides down my back to the floor. The guards kick him, laughing as they leave us there. The crowd roars overhead, obviously enjoying another fight. I slip to the floor next to him, my hands hovering over him unsure how to help. His back is a mess, covered in blood and broken skin.

"You idiot," I whisper.

Two slaves come forward then, the ones we saved upstairs who were forced to watch as we were punished. They grab him under his arms and drag him to my cell, lying him down as softly as they can on his side before nodding at me and leaving. I slip in after they leave, wrapping my arms around him so his back doesn't have to touch the floor, and pull him to me until I am looking down at his face, my legs folded beneath us.

I hold Xavier as my fingers slip in the blood and raw meat of his back from the whip. My own flesh stings from the few they managed to land on me before he dove on me and took the lashes meant for my skin. Tears drip down my face as he stares up at me with a smile, even though he must be in agony.

"Don't cry for me, Rhea, we both know I can survive this. I couldn't survive watching you suffer. Just hold me until they heal? Please?" he requests, his voice shakier towards the end, showing me weakness. He is asking me not to leave him, to stay...like I would leave.

This man has stuck by me, protected me, saved me, and taught me to fight. He is family now. He will never be alone again, it's about time he realised that. So I hold him closer, stroking through his hair and start to sing. The song is a rough one that I used to hear the slaves belt out when no one was watching. I start off soft, my voice growing louder, and before I know it, another voice joins mine.

My head jerks up as I look around, spotting the slaves at their bars, watching us. Another voice joins in, then another, all of them adding their strength to mine, the song binding us together, showing us that no matter how hard it gets, we have each other.

Us freaks will never be alone again.

Chapter Twenty-Two

We fall into a weird sort of routine, all of us ready to drop everything at a moment's notice and fight our way out. We don't know how it will come, what the signal will be, but we know we need to be ready. We stick together. Xavier has been accepted among my group, there were no spoken words, but they know he is one of us now. They have seen how he looks at me, at us, and they've noticed something in him that I'm not sure he even knew about—a need to be more, to be better than what they make him.

There is a strange unity in the underground room ever since the fight where we refused to kill them, and then took a punishment that should have killed us, but we never backed down. It's as if the rest of the slaves know something is coming too. The evening where they joined in my song is still fresh in my mind, and I can't help but wonder if there is more to it. If—no —*when* we escape, can I really leave with a clear conscience if the rest of the slaves aren't freed too? What if the others are like Xavier? Becoming killing machines because of the cruel treatment of the Masters. What if they could be more? When they joined in my song, they showed solidarity. I can't leave them behind. When we leave, they leave with us. Jessie is always on my mind, the horror of his death branding my insides. My heart feels fragile and oh so cold without him, the downtime we have giving me nothing but time to think about life together...the life we should have had.

Xavier and I haven't fought in a couple of days, but we've been given time to train together, which makes me think something big is going to happen. The Masters are planning something, something to get us back for our stand. A whipping isn't enough, they are going to want to humiliate us the way we humiliated them. I throw myself into it though, anything to keep me busy, keep me distracted.

It's the end of a long day of training, and I've just washed the sand, sweat, and dirt from my skin before retreating back to my cell. I lean against the bars in my cage that separate me from Nixon as he braids my hair for me, while I hum a circus tune Jessie taught me.

My chest constricts painfully at the thought of him, of my happy-go-lucky Jessie, but I won't let the pain of losing him take away the happy memories. Nixon tries to hum along behind me, but he is so out of tune that he keeps making me laugh and lose my place in the song. My gentle giant is not a singer, but this is so badly out of tune that I am guessing he is doing it on purpose to make me smile.

When I was walked past, I could see Blain watching me with a small smile on his face, but when I looked over at him, his smile disappeared and he glanced away, scowling. My typical, grumpy Blain. I know he hates that his cell is so far away from us, and I suspect he feels jealous of the time I get to spend with Nix. I know Rex is struggling with being away from his animals, especially during the fights, since that's where he draws his powers, but thankfully he hasn't had to fight much. I worry more about his mood. He seems to be sinking within himself, my gentle Rex isn't a fighter, and all of this is starting to take its toll.

Glancing around the room, I sigh, wishing I could see into Alcide's cell to see if he's here. He's so distant now, it feels like he has taken a step away from us. When I told him about the rebellion, he looked frustrated. I had expected many expressions, but not frustration.

The sound of booted feet on the steps has me raising my head, and as I see a guard walking towards my cell, I can't stop the sense of trepidation running through me. Will it be the guy from the rebellion, or Chester? Usually, I wouldn't be worried about going to see Chester, but after the last few days, I'm not so sure. Chester sold me out to be used as a whore, and then we stood up to the Masters in the arena. I've not seen him since then, so I had assumed I was in his bad books and I wouldn't be seeing him for a while. As the guard stops outside my cell, I push to my feet with Nixon and Xavier doing the same in their cells on either side, watching me carefully as I am led towards the meeting room.

Trying to calm my rapid heartbeat, I focus on taking steady breaths. I will deal with whatever waits for me behind this door just like all the other times. The guard is one I don't recognise, and he doesn't talk to me, his face set in a rigid mask. As the doors open, I am shoved over the threshold, and the heavy doors slams shut behind me loudly. The room is dark, and I blink as my eyes try to adjust to the lack of light when the sound of a match being struck tells me I'm not alone in the room. Light fills the room as a lamp is lit and shock fills me when I see who's waiting for me.

"Alcide?" Surprise tinges my tone and I take a tentative step towards him, but his hard expression stops me. His usually neat hair is mussed, and his face is lined with tension as he raises his eyes to meet mine.

"I had to use a lot of favours to arrange this."

Frowning, I take a small step towards him again as dread lines my stomach. "What do you mean?" His eyes track me like that of a predator, like he's hunting me and I'm his next meal. I've always felt reverence towards Alcide, he is our ringmaster, our leader, but I've never been fearful of him, and right now, fear is pulsing through my veins. Not necessarily fear of him, but of what he's become, who the Masters have made him. Is he still the man who I love…or something else?

"What were you playing at, Rhea?" His words are sharp like a whip and I recoil in shock. "You should have just killed the slaves like the Masters wanted you to." Gaping at Alcide, my mouth drops open in shock, did he really just tell me I should have killed innocents?

"Those slaves are just like us, Alcide. I'm done killing for the Masters," I reply bluntly.

He hurries towards me, his eyes flicking around the room like he is fearful someone is watching us, listening to everything we say. "You can't say that," he chides me, his hand landing on my shoulder.

My heart flutters at his touch and I remind myself that this is the Alcide I love, not a stranger. His face changes at the touch, softening, and a hint of a smile appears on his handsome face, but it soon drops and his expression becomes serious again. "They aren't happy with you."

Frustration bubbles up within me and I take a step back, breaking our contact as I throw my hands out to the side. "Why do you care what they think of us?"

"Because I'm trying to keep us all alive!" he shouts back, his face contorting into someone I don't recognise.

Taking a hurried step away, my heart hammers in my chest. What have they done to him to turn him into this person? His expression quickly falls and grief lines his face as he sees my fearful look.

"Rhea…" His voice breaks and my heart aches to go to him, but I stay where I am, watching him warily as he grabs a couple of chairs and gestures for me to take one. "Sit, please. I'll explain everything, I promise." I watch as he sits and waits for me to join him. "Please?" he asks again, and I can hear the panic in his voice, fear that he has pushed us away, that he has gone too far and lost us in the process. The real Alcide is reaching out to me, this is the Alcide that I know and trust. Nodding once, I take the few short steps towards him, sitting opposite him as he pours us both cups of water from a small table laid with a jug and two glasses that I hadn't seen before. Taking a sip, he clears his throat and begins.

"Since we've been here, I've been trying to charm the Masters, to make sure we are given the easier fights, to stop them from selling you or the others. At first, I thought it was working, then they decided that they wanted something from me."

"Did they make you…" I can't say the words, I can't ask if he slept with another woman because the Masters sold him. I feel physically sick, but he quickly shakes his head.

"No, never. There is no one but you," he quickly interjects, a hard edge to his voice. "They would take me away, outside of the arena, and have me use my powers of persuasion to make things go their way. Political parties, meetings with other Masters, things like that," he explains then sighs, rubbing a hand over his tired face. "But then things changed."

"What changed?"

"They figured out that all they had to do was threaten you and I would do anything." His humourless laugh is self-mocking, and I realise he is blaming himself for everything that has happened to us. "After Jessie died…" He trails off, and I know my pain at the loss is mirrored in him, except he feels responsible. "After he died, I was furious and tried to use my powers to make them fight themselves. I knew they would kill me if I so much as raised a spoon against them, but at these parties they let me have full rein of my powers, they under-estimated me." Anger laces his words and his hands are clenched into fists.

"What happened?"

"They realised it was me. I snapped, tried to fight them, and they threw me back in the cells." I remember when he was with us in the cells for a few nights, he had looked haggard, completely unlike my usually put together ringmaster. "I've been having to work to rebuild their faith in me." Shaking his head, a wry smile greets me as he raises his eyes to meet mine. "They don't trust me, but they've realised how much they need me. I can work with that." My heart starts to sink as I see the calculating glimmer in his eyes, and I realise he's retreating from me again. Grabbing his hands, I clutch them tightly in mine, refusing to let go as he frowns at me.

"Alcide, I just want you back with us, the others do too. Do you know how worried we've been?" His expression starts to soften, but I can tell he's going to brush me off, to tell me that he's fine and not to worry. That's not going to cut it with me, not when we've already lost Jessie and I watched Xavier die in my arms. I'm not going to let him push me away again.

"We thought we had lost you," I press, needing him to understand what he was doing to us while he was working his schemes. "You were physically there, but the Alcide we knew had gone. I can't lose you too." My eyes are dry as I speak, I've shed too many tears because of the Masters, but I put all of my feelings into my words. He needs to understand. "We need our ringmaster. Please." My voice breaks as I push up from my chair, circling around until I stand in front of him, placing my hand on his shoulder as I sit in his lap. His arms wrap around me, his eyes solemn as I speak.

"I need my ringmaster."

Something snaps within him as he surges forward and presses his lips to mine, his tongue skirting across my lips, seeking entrance as he continues with his demanding kisses. Gasping into his mouth, I return his kiss, our tongues dancing together as he pulls me closer, his hands tugging at my clothing. Need courses through me, the need to be close to him, to connect with him, the need to feel his skin against mine.

"Take your clothes off," he orders between kisses, and the ringmaster tone that I know and love is back. Pulling away, I climb off his lap, and after a brief glance around to check there is no one else in the room, I pull my shirt off over my head. This is new, this animalistic need. He always held himself back from me. I once doubted that he even wanted me. Where my love with the others turned physical, his was slowly growing and consuming. Different yet the same as the others, but this here? This is what I have been waiting for.

Alcide makes a noise that brings my attention back to him, a primal sound that heats my blood as he watches my every move. Bringing my hands to my waist, I shimmy out of my trousers, making sure to slowly draw them down my legs, the heat of his gaze hot against my skin, leaving goosebumps in his wake like he is actually touching me. As he stands up, I drop the fabric to the ground, completely bare before him. His hands go to the waistband of his trousers, his fingers flicking open the button holding them closed.

My eyes follow those movements, and my mouth goes dry as he reaches up and pulls off his top, his defined chest greeting me before his hands go back to his open slacks. I can see his erection pressing against the fabric, begging to be freed. With the others, I know where we stand, I know what to do...but I feel so lost...so out of control with him. His eyes shutter for a moment like he sees my doubts and his hand freezes, and I know he feels the same, unsure how to bridge this gap and give us what we both want so desperately. If he can't, I will.

Closing the distance between us, I slide my hand past his waistband only to find he's not wearing underwear beneath. My hand encircles his hard length, like steel wrapped in velvet. Fucking hell, that's hot. Glancing up, I meet his heated stare, his eyes trailing over me as a knock sounds on the door. Clutching me close to his body, Alcide lets out a feral growl, his hands moving to grab my butt, lifting me up so I can wrap my legs around his waist.

"We don't have much time," he tells me, and I know he is offering me an out. If I don't want to do this, all I have to do is say so. We would go back to the way we were before, but I don't want that. I don't know if I am going to live through the next day, or if he will. I need this, I need him. I want this more than anything, so when my voice comes out, it is strong and sure.

"I need you."

My words have the desired effect and he presses fierce kisses against my lips, walking through the room with me clinging on to him. The breath is forced out of me as he pushes me against a wall, the cold, rough stone a huge contrast to his hot, soft skin. Shifting his weight, he moves one of his hands and presses it against my center. He groans into my mouth as he feels how wet I am, how ready I am for him. Throwing my head back, I lean into the wall as he slides a finger into me, quickly followed by another, curling them up so they hit that sweet spot inside me. I'm fiercely aware that there are people outside this room, probably listening to us, but I don't care. I've been waiting so long for this, so long to have him. He groans against my lips, fucking me with his fingers as he drops his head and sucks my nipple into his mouth, making me gasp and push closer, wiggling with need.

"Please," I beg, lifting my hips to meet the thrust of his hand, I need more, so much more. I need his cock inside me, filling me, offering me the pleasure only he can. "Please, Ringmaster, fuck me," I whisper, and his eyes flare as he kisses me hard, his fingers speeding up, building my release until suddenly, they are gone. I cry out and he swallows it, so I let my frustration out on his lips, sucking and biting him in punishment as he smirks against me.

He shifts me and I feel the head of his cock pressing against my entrance, followed by the glorious sensation of being stretched, being filled to my limit as he presses inside me. I moan, my walls clenching around him as he pushes into the hilt. We pause for a moment as he lets me adjust to the feeling of him filling me, bringing one of his hands up to my breast, and guiding my nipple into his mouth again. Desire floods my veins as his tongue flicks the buds, moving from one to the other as I lean against the wall, my legs clinging on to him. He bites down gently on my nipple and I get impatient, rocking my hips to get some friction, some relief from the feeling building up inside me. I'm sick of his teasing, of all this pent-up need. I need him to fuck me, hard.

A moan escapes his lips as he pulls away from my breast, giving me a stern look, and I know he is dying to punish me for being so impatient, but we don't have time. Rocking my hips again, I break his control and he pulls back, almost completely, before plunging completely inside. Biting my lip, I can only hold on as he pounds into me, our sounds of pleasure echoing around the room. It's rough and primal, but it's what we need.

I can feel the orgasm building, I'm close, and as I look at Alcide, I know he is too. We stare into each other's eyes, my hands gripping his shoulders, my nails digging in...probably leaving a mark. I like that, I want my marks on his body. For everyone to know he is mine just as much as I am his. He grunts, the sound so raw that I cry out, arching into him, my nails scoring my pleasure down his back as he forces me higher and higher, my eyes still unable to leave his. To leave the dominance I see there.

"Come for me, Rhea," he orders, and it's all I need to push me over the edge. The orgasm is blinding, and I feel the moment Alcide joins me, his cry of pleasure loud in the empty room, his cock pulsing as he spills his come inside me, fills me with it until it starts to drip down my thighs. Panting, I open my eyes, which I hadn't realised I'd closed, and press my forehead against his. He leans into me, breathing heavily as he holds us both up. His eyes search mine as a soft smile curls his lips and I know he's back.

My ringmaster is home.

I know we don't have long until we will be dragged back into our cells, but I soak in this moment, unsure when, or if, we might get the chance to be with each other again. It was our first time, and so fucking perfect like the man himself.

He shakes his head, letting out a laugh as his hand comes up, shaking as he strokes my cheek. "I don't know how you do it," he whispers.

"Do what?" I ask, my voice still breathless.

"Tame me," he offers, his words making me clench around his already hardening cock, but I know we don't have time for anything else. I wish we did, I wish I could explore his body and he mine, that we could spent all night in each other's arms.

"I love you." His words are quiet and breathy as he clings to me. The sound of the door opening behind us makes him stiffen, but he doesn't drop me. Instead, he covers me so that the person behind him can't see any of my body—my protective, jealous male. Lifting my hands, I cup his face, making sure his attention is on me as I speak.

"I love you, too."

Chapter Twenty-Three

"Wake up, slaves!" comes a yell from outside my cell, jerking me awake. My whole body is sore after the fights and Alcide's tryst last night. I felt like I was floating, but now I am crashing back down to reality. Afterwards, I had been escorted back to my cell where I fell into a deep sleep. Groaning, I pull myself to my feet using the bars and peer at the guards, who are banging on the metal to wake up the other fighters. "Fight starts in an hour, get your asses up! Chow time!"

"Fight?" I whisper to Nixon, who is standing at my bars, watching me with a frown etched onto his face.

"First we've heard, come on, you need to eat," he grumbles.

I nod, and when my cell is opened, I meet him outside. Xavier trails behind us as we head to the tables. I flop down between them, perking up with a grin when I spot Alcide here today. He holds his head high as he joins us, a twinkling in his eyes that wasn't there yesterday. He winks at me.

"Morning, *cariño*." His accented voice washes over me and I can't help but recall our time from last night. My pussy clenches in memory, which is embarrassing since we are in public and I am pressed between my other men...

"Morning," I greet with a smile that is split by a yawn as a tray bangs down in front of me. Blain drops a kiss on my forehead as Rex squeezes my shoulder, both of them sitting on the other side of Alcide.

Without any further words, we start to eat, aware of the clock counting down.

The room is filled with tension as all the fighters share looks, wondering who will be against whom today, speculating what the Masters have planned now. I lower my face and ask Alcide, "Who do you think is fighting?" He shakes his head with a frown.

"I don't know, this wasn't planned though," is all he offers, and I don't know if that comforts me or unsettles me more.

Once I'm finished eating, I lean into the person on my left, thinking it's Nixon as I lay my head on his shoulder, but when the body freezes against me, my eyes fly wide as I look up to see Xavier staring down at me. Shit.

I go to lift my head up and scoot away, my cheeks burning, but he softens against me. "Lean on me, it's okay," he encourages, pressing his arm to my back to help support me. Licking my lips nervously, I stay where I am, my eyes meeting Alcide's across the table to see that he has a strange smile on his face as he watches us.

"Whatever happens today, we stay together," he instructs, his eyes flicking between us, and I can't help but notice that Xavier is included in that.

"No shit, boss man, glad you are finally back on the team," Blain mutters.

"I agree." Rex bobs his head, still eating and half asleep.

"Do not let each other out of your sight, something is coming," Nixon adds ominously. We all look to him to see him blinking and shaking his head before he carries on eating like nothing happened.

"Something's coming?" I repeat, I wonder what…

"Chow time is up, animals, to your feet!" comes an order from a guard as they stream into our midst. We are obviously not moving fast enough for them, because they start yanking people up and pushing them towards the tunnel entrance where more are waiting.

Xavier stays behind me, while Nixon is in front, as my other guys spread around us. They are never far, close enough that I can reach out and touch them, making sure to heed Nixon's warning as we march along the hard earth towards the racks of weapons. I peek around

Nixon, frowning when I realise that no one has been given weapons yet. Shit, is it going to be us fighting again?

When Xavier and I reach the rack, they pass our weapons over… only it's not just us. Alcide, Rex, Blain, and Nixon all get weapons too…but no armour. What are the Masters planning? Are we going to be fighting together? Is this their punishment, their way to finally break us and control us?

Worry surges through me, waking me up fully as my body jitters anxiously, our feet crunching against the ground as we walk slowly forward, the guards leading us to the sand above. The gate hinges squeak loudly against the silence, the only other sounds coming from the whispering of the other slaves and the pounding of my heart.

The sun is blinding, and I have to cover my eyes as we step out into the arena. A shove causes me to stumble into Nixon as we are pushed from behind. My family is being forced farther into the arena as the other fighters are led to their cages and locked up.

The Masters' box is full today and I can't help glancing at them as we all move closer together, trying to predict what they are going to do. The crowd is fuller than ever, seats so busy people are actually standing, cramming to get close to the edge to see us. I can almost taste their excitement on the air…they know what is going to happen.

This has been announced.

I look over at Alcide to see the same conclusion and fear reflected back in his eyes. Is this where we die? Where our family, our circus finally ends? If it is, at least we're together. I have a passing moment of regret that I couldn't free our animals, but it's gone as soon as a hush falls over the crowd and the Masters stand, their hands raised to silence everyone.

Like the amassed people, we turn our eyes expectantly to them to see what fate they are offering us today. Death or life, they hold it all in their hands, and I am acutely aware of just how powerless I am right now to protect my family.

How foolish I was, thinking I could win this game. That I could manipulate them, use them, turn it on their heads and escape. I should have learned with Jessie's death, but I didn't, and now it's going to cost the ultimate price.

My eyes flicker to Chester, only to see him watching me also, and something passes over his face, almost too quick to see. Was it regret? Anger? Or simply acceptance? He told me once it was easier to be led than to have to feel, I guess for him that is true.

Me? I would rather feel it all, the pain, the love, the anger...everything if it means I get to hold these people close. That I get to actually *live* my life. Just another way we are different.

"Ladies and gentlemen, we have a true treat for you today!" one of the Masters begins, the crowd letting out whistles and excited yells. "A month ago, we captured those you see in the pit, the *circus*, a place where they boasted about their differences. Freaks, the lot of them." The voice is full of disgust and contempt, making my heart sink as a bad feeling settles over me. "Taking our money and eating our food as they openly mocked us! No longer! Today, we bring them to you as slaves, their final act, if you will! Their finale!"

Cheers go up once again as my suspicions are confirmed.

"Today, we will turn the circus on each other, family on family...lovers against lovers. Who will come out victorious?" he yells, further amping up the crowd.

A surge of white-hot anger races through me, but I push it away for now, we need to be smart. We need…a fucking miracle at this point. If we refuse to fight, we die at their guards' hands. If we fight, we die at each other's hands.

There is no way out, maybe there never was. Is this what all slaves feel, this impending doom, the crashing of reality, before they die?

Only, I won't die a slave. They can kill me here, kill us all, but we will die the way we lived—together and free.

"Slaves! You have your orders, you will fight each other. The one who survives will win their freedom! The rest will sadly be lost to the sands!"

The crowd starts stomping now, ready to see us die for their entertainment.

"Ready? Fight!" a Master screams, as they all sit back into their seats.

We look at each other, lost on what to do, until Alcide steps forward. He cups my face, blocking out everyone but him. The crowd, the cheering, even the angry cries of the other slaves fall away until all I see is him, my ringmaster. My lover.

"*Cariño*, you have to win, no, listen to me for once." He stops my protests before they can even begin, his intense eyes locked on mine. "We are going to die no matter what, you have to win. Gain your freedom and get as far away from here as you can, start a new life. Be happy. I'm sorry I got you into this, all of you into this. My pride was my downfall, I won't have it be yours as well."

I shake my head, tears filling my eyes and making him swim in front of me. "Alcide," I whisper, but he covers my lips with his, kissing me so soundly, so fully, that he wipes away the memory of anything and anyone else just for a moment. All I can feel, all I can taste, is him, but it's over too soon as he pulls back, smiling at me sadly.

"I was a fool to wait so long. I was scared, Rhea. Scared of how completely I love you, how much you consume me. I need you to know how much I regret not holding you close every day and night, never letting you go. I wish we had one more day, one more night, just one more minute together...even one more show. I wish I could see you sparkle under the stage lights again, charming the audience the same way you charmed me." His hand comes up to rest over my racing heart. "We will be in here, always. You can never lose us, not really. I will be waiting for you in the next life, where we can have our happy ending." He steps back then, even as I try to cling to him, and Blain takes his spot.

"Harpy," he starts, his voice cracking. He swallows, stands up taller, and his cocky look comes over him, his protection. "Win, you have to." Then he grabs me, his arms wrapping around me tightly, like he might never let me go. He kisses me too, sweeping his tongue inside my mouth and tangling it with mine before pulling away. He presses his forehead against mine, his dark eyes filling my vision. "I love you, Harpy, even when you're a pain in the ass, I can't think of anyone else

I would gladly die for…so I need you to live. For me." He covers my lips when I go to protest, smirking at me in the way only Blain can, but I see emotions swirling in his eyes, too many for him to hide. "Otherwise, I'll come back and haunt you, you hear me?"

"I hear you," I mumble against his palm.

He nods and steps back as Rex moves to fill his spot. His eyes are downcast, his face pale. He licks his lips and it's me who steps forward now, rushing into his comforting embrace. Rex, my softie, the man who brought me to my family. "I love you," I tell him.

He sighs, wrapping his arms around me. "And I you, Wildcat, more than you can ever know. When you love something so fully, so completely, it can never truly disappear." But then he does, he steps back, and I am turned to face Nixon.

He stares down at me, saying nothing, as his hand rises and strokes my face, his eyes tracing my features as if trying to memorise them. "Love you."

I sob then, unable to help myself as he, too, steps back. I look to Xavier to see him shaking in anger as he paces. "There has to be a way," he snaps, looking at me helplessly. "You have to survive, this wasn't the plan!"

He rages, screams, but none of it does any good.

"Fight, or we will make you!" comes the order from the Masters.

I wrap my arms around myself, watching my men as they stand in a line facing Alcide, who is standing tall with his shoulders thrown back, but his eyes are tight and his hands are shaking slightly.

"We performed, lived, and loved as one. Today, we die as that," he declares loudly. "For her! For our future! You will never stop the freaks!" he yells, then turns back to his men, they all nod at him, closing their eyes, ready to meet their fate…

No! He can't!

I leap, throwing myself in front of them. If we die, we do it together. There is no life without them, there is no me without them. They want me to survive, to go on, but how can I when they would be gone?

"No!" I scream, just as a loud bang comes from outside. We all turn slowly, frowning when a plume of smoke goes up beyond the colosseum. "What the…" I whisper, confused.

Another boom has me jumping, and I whirl to see the gate that leads to the slaves' cages exploding outwards as splintered wood rains everywhere. It's dark for a moment and I squint into the smoke, trying to see into it. Then, there is a scream, a collective cry of outrage, and from that darkness flows men…and women…

All holding weapons, all with the slave symbol. The mark of freaks.

Of the rebellion.

They rush onto the sand as guards jump down, their weapons clashing. The two forces, the enemies, come together. I can hear the Masters shouting orders, and the cries of fear from the audience as they try to escape the bloodshed and death…the war occurring before them. Once they craved it, now they fear it—how the tables have turned.

"Rhea!" comes a yell, and I turn, my hand already rising as Xavier throws me a sword. I grab it, holding it in front of me as the rest of my men close in on either side, their own weapons gleaming in the sunlight. But the fighting moves around us like water around a rock as screams of pain fill the air. The scent of death and blood is so strong I crinkle my nose.

"Here!" comes a yell. I turn again, my head swivelling to keep what is happening in my view to protect my family. Is this what the man meant? Was this their plan? But who are the good guys here? Guards are crying out for mercy, trying to escape the never-ending horde of freaks, some who aren't using weapons now but their powers.

One burns alive.

One is ripped to pieces.

It's a massacre.

"Rhea!" The shout catches my attention, and I spot the hooded man at the gate to the slave tunnel, holding out a sword covered in blood. "Here!"

A guard stumbles towards him, his arms binding his stomach as blood and guts spill between his fingers. He falls to the floor before the man who, without hesitation, slices his neck with his sword.

Is this really what the world has come to?

Death and bloodshed brought us to this world, the bombs killing everyone and everything. It feels like we are reverting to old ways, is...is killing the only way to solve anything? I don't know, but sometimes you have to trust that the universe has a plan.

Something grabs my free hand and I turn, swing my sword, just stopping it centimetres from Xavier's face. "Come on!" He has to yell to be heard over the sounds of the fight. He yanks me after him, carving his way towards the tunnel. I look behind me to see my family close by.

Once we reach the tunnel entrance, I stare into the darkness of the hood the mysterious man wears. "Remember your promise. Outside the gate, you will find the freedom you requested. Go, now. It won't be long before reinforcements for the Masters arrive."

I nod, unable to do much else as I am yanked down the tunnel by Xavier, leaving the sounds of fighting above as we race on quick feet down the passageway. We burst out into the slave quarters. It is empty, silent almost. Dust rains down from above from the amount of people in the pit, while bangs and cries reach us as if from far away. The sound of running footsteps echoes around the room and I spin just as someone comes into view.

"Jessie?" My words are soft, unbelieving. Has all the fighting finally made me go mad? Or have I died? Is this the afterlife and I've been reunited with him? When I heard my nickname on that rebel's lips, I convinced myself I was hearing things I wanted to, that he couldn't possibly be alive...but now, here he is. Standing before me.

His signature grin spreads across his face at my surprise before he breaks out into a run, colliding with me.

"Hey, Firecracker." His voice is muffled by my hair as he nuzzles against me, my arms holding onto him tightly as if he will disappear if I let go. An awkward cough and shuffling feet remind me of the others, and I realise this is *real*.

"H-How are you alive?" I stutter, my body shaking, whether from the adrenaline of fighting or seeing Jessie alive in front of me, I don't know. The others gather around us, their questions echoing in the dusty air, all of them wanting to be close to the brother they thought they had lost.

"The rebellion, they saved me—" He begins, but a loud bang fills the arena above us, causing the room to shake.

Xavier steps forward and grabs my shoulder, steering me towards the exit. "We don't have time for this." I nod in agreement, but my eyes keep falling on Jessie as we run.

"The animals!" I gasp, my heart in my throat as I think about the other part of my family we nearly left behind.

"No time!" Xavier shouts, but I tug free and turn to see Rex and Blain already gone.

"Where are they?" I scream, starting to run back up the tunnel, but Nixon catches me around my waist and yanks me back. Hammering my fists against his chest, I struggle against him. "Let me go! We can't leave them!"

Just then, a growl sounds, making me freeze as Rex appears, followed by Blain rushing towards us. Fluffy bounds in front of them when he sees me, his face lighting up. Tiny is behind them with Sid weaving through their legs. Bubbles/Rumple is wrapped around Rex's arm, holding on.

"Go, you idiots!" Blain screams, and Nixon lets me go, pushing me ahead.

I race to the other stairs, hearing the sound of boots heading down the tunnel entrance, undoubtedly looking for any survivors. Friend or foe, we don't know.

I leap up the steps two at a time as the gate comes into view, the exit lighting our route ahead as we climb. My breathing saws from my chest, my lungs tight and legs aching, but I still push on. I smash into the gate and yank desperately on the metal, fearing we will be too late. Nixon grabs me, moves me to the side, and kicks at it, slamming it open with the force. I run outside and collide with a boy waiting there.

A familiar boy, and I realise it's the one I fed when I first came here, when we first arrived. He shows me his tattoo, and now I know what it means. It was meant as a mark of slavery, of ownership, but the rebels turned it into a rally cry.

"Come with me!"

My eyes widen as he turns, ready to lead us away, but a grinning guard pops around the corner, shoving his sword through the little boy's stomach before yanking it back. "Not so quick, rebel scum," he spits, and swings at me.

I scream and fling my out hand, my powers reacting to my fear and anger, causing a wave of power to push into the guard, making him fly backwards. Knives quickly imbed into his chest as Blain uses his powers. Knowing we are safe from the guard, I rush to the child's side just as he starts to fall. I hold him, cradling him in my arms, his hands clutching at his bleeding stomach. His face is pale, but his eyes, his eyes haunt me. They are so accepting. There is no fear, nothing.

"Go, Gregor's," he whispers, blood filling his mouth.

"Not without you," I tell him, and swing him higher. "Jessie, lead the way."

He nods at me, staring at the kid for a moment before shaking his head and starting to run, we follow after him. Nixon offers to take the child, but I refuse, heaving him higher and grunting with the effort as he clings to me, trusting me with a childlike innocence I didn't know he still possessed.

When we are far enough away from the fighting, I start to slow. "Stop," the kid begs, so I do, slipping into an alley as the others follow us.

"Rhea!" Blain hisses, peeking around the corner, jumping back when guards race past. "We have to go now!"

I slide down the wall, still holding the child, and look into his eyes as he smiles up at me. His lips are covered in blood, as are his teeth, and his body is weak now. "Freaks will rise, we are the future, Rhea, and they are the past," he whispers, his frail voice small but filled with conviction, even as blood bubbles from his mouth. Tears track down my face as regret and denial fills me.

"Stay with me, okay?" I plead.

His hand comes up, so small yet possessing such strength as he grips mine, his blood coating my fingers. "You were foretold, Rhea the Immortal, we died for you, now live for us."

"No," I gasp, as his hand drops away, hitting his chest. His eyes turn glassy as his chest stops rising and falling. I look up then. "He's dead," I whisper to my men, my family, gathered around me.

"They killed him," I state numbly.

"We have to go!" Jessie insists, crouching in front of me, his eyes imploring me to listen. "I'm sorry, I'm so sorry, but we have to go. He knew the risks, we all did. It was worth it, but now, Firecracker, we have to go. The fight is just beginning, the rebels won't stand idly by anymore. The city will be the battleground, the arena, with you as their leader."

ABOUT ERIN O'KANE

Erin lives in the UK with her cat and works full time as an independent author. Now a *USA Today* bestselling author, she began writing in 2018 when she published her first book, *Hunted by Shadows*. She specialises in writing fantasy and reverse harem paranormal romance.

Previously to writing, she worked as an intensive care nurse. Despite having to now use a wheelchair, she doesn't let it stop her and loves to travel the world.

She met K.A Knight in 2018 when they became partners in crime and began writing together. In 2019, she became co-authors with Loxley Savage, writing fantasy reverse harem.

She's Disney obsessed, loves to read, craft and snack, and is always planning her next story.

Make sure to follow her on her social media pages for updates on what she's currently working on:

Facebook group: https://www.facebook.com/groups/ErinOKanesShadowRealm

Facebook author Page: https://www.facebook.com/ErinOKaneAuthor

Newsletter: http://eepurl.com/gJhSd9

Instagram: https://www.instagram.com/erin.okane.author

ABOUT K.A. KNIGHT

K.A Knight is an USA Today bestselling indie author trying to get all of the stories and characters out of her head, writing the monsters that you love to hate. She loves reading and devours every book she can get her hands on, and she also has a worrying caffeine addiction.

She leads her double life in a sleepy English town, where she spends her days writing like a crazy person.

Read more at K.A Knight's website or join her Facebook Reader Group.
Sign up for exclusive content and my newsletter here
http://eepurl.com/drLLoj

OTHER BOOKS BY ERIN O'KANE

The Shadowborn Series:

Hunted by Shadows

Lost in Shadow

Embraced by Shadows

The Shadowborn series- the boxset

Born From Shadows Series:

Demons do it Better

The War and Deceit Series:

Fires of Hatred

Fires of Treason

Fires of Ruin

Fires of War

Fires of the Fae:

A Lady of Embers

A Spark of Promise

A Legacy of Hope and Ash

The Cursed Women Universe:: Venom and Stone

Betrayal and Curses

Fractured Wings

Bloodlines series:

Midnight Magic

Midnight Trials

Midnight Deception

Midnight Conviction

Midnight Ascension

The Complete Bloodlines Series – omnibus

The Brides of Darkness – interconnected standalones

A Kingdom of Broken Bonds

A City of Embers and Brimstone – coming soon

Standalones:

Second Chance

Love Bites

CO-WRITES

By Erin O'Kane and K.A Knight

Her Freaks Series:

Circus Save Me

Taming the Ringmaster

Walking the Tightrope

The Wild Boys:

The Wild Interview

The Wild Tour

The Wild Finale

The Wild Boys Series- The boxset

Standalones:

Hero Complex

Dark Temptations

By Erin O'Kane and Loxley Savage

Wicked Waves duet:

Twisted Tides

Tides that Bind

OTHER BOOKS BY K.A. KNIGHT

CONTEMPORARY

LEGENDS AND LOVE *CONTEMPORARY RH*

Revolt

Rebel

Riot - coming soon..

PRETTY LIARS *CONTEMPORARY RH*

Unstoppable

Unbreakable

PINE VALLEY COLLEGE *CONTEMPORARY*

Racing Hearts

DEN OF VIPERS UNIVERSE STANDALONES

Scarlett Limerence *CONTEMPORARY*

Nadia's Salvation *CONTEMPORARY*

Alena's Revenge *CONTEMPORARY*

Den of Vipers *CONTEMPORARY RH*

Gangsters and Guns (Co-Write with Loxley Savage) *CONTEMPORARY RH*

FORBIDDEN READS *(STANDALONES)*

Daddy's Angel *CONTEMPORARY*

Stepbrothers' Darling *CONTEMPORARY RH*

STANDALONES

The Standby *CONTEMPORARY*

Diver's Heart *CONTEMPORARY RH*

DYSTOPIAN

THEIR CHAMPION SERIES *Dystopian RH*

The Wasteland

The Summit

The Cities

The Nations

Their Champion Coloring Book

Their Champion - the omnibus

The Forgotten

The Lost

The Damned

Their Champion Companion - the omnibus

PARANORMAL

THE LOST COVEN SERIES *PNR RH*

Aurora's Coven

Aurora's Betrayal

HER MONSTERS SERIES *PNR RH*

Rage

Hate

Book 3 - *coming soon..*

COURTS AND KINGS *PNR RH*

Court of Nightmares

Court of Death

Court of Beasts

Court of Heathens - coming soon..

THE FALLEN GODS SERIES *PNR*

Pretty Painful

Pretty Bloody

Pretty Stormy

Pretty Wild

Pretty Hot

Pretty Faces

Pretty Spelled

Fallen Gods - the omnibus 1

Fallen Gods - the omnibus 2

FORGOTTEN CITY *PNR*

Monstrous Lies

Monstrous Truths

Monstrous Ends

SCIENCE FICTION

DAWNBREAKER SERIES *SCI FI RH*

Voyage to Ayama

Dreaming of Ayama

STANDALONES

Crown of Stars *SCI FI RH*

SHARED WORLD PROJECTS

Blade of Iris - Mafia Wars *CONTEMPORARY RH*

CO-WRITES

CO-AUTHOR PROJECTS - *Erin O'Kane*

HER FREAKS SERIES *PNR Dystopian RH*

Circus Save Me

Taming The Ringmaster

Walking the Tightrope

Her Freaks Series - the omnibus

STANDALONES

The Hero Complex *PNR RH*

Dark Temptations *Collection of Short Stories, ft. One Night Only & Circus Saves Christmas*

THE WILD BOYS SERIES *CONTEMPORARY RH*

The Wild Interview

The Wild Tour

The Wild Finale

The Wild Boys - the omnibus

CO-AUTHOR PROJECTS - *Ivy Fox*

Deadly Love Series *CONTEMPORARY*

Deadly Affair

Deadly Match

Deadly Encounter

CO-AUTHOR PROJECTS - *Kendra Moreno*

STANDALONES

Stolen Trophy *CONTEMPORARY RH*

Fractured Shadows *PNR RH*

Shadowed Heart

Burn Me *PNR*

Cirque Obscurum *PNR RH*

CO-AUTHOR PROJECTS - *Loxley Savage*

THE FORSAKEN SERIES *SCI FI RH*

Capturing Carmen

Stealing Shiloh

Harboring Harlow

STANDALONES

Gangsters and Guns *CONTEMPORARY*, IN DEN OF VIPERS' UNIVERSE

OTHER CO-WRITES

Shipwreck Souls *(with Kendra Moreno & Poppy Woods)*

The Horror Emporium *(with Kendra Moreno & Poppy Woods)*

AUDIOBOOKS

The Wasteland

The Summit

The Cities

The Nations - *coming soon*

Rage

Hate

Den of Vipers *(From Podium Audio)*

Gangsters and Guns *(From Podium Audio)*

Daddy's Angel *(From Podium Audio)*

Stepbrothers' Darling *(From Podium Audio)*

Blade of Iris *(From Podium Audio)*

Deadly Affair *(From Podium Audio)*

Deadly Match *(From Podium Audio)*

Deadly Encounter *(From Podium Audio)*

Stolen Trophy *(From Podium Audio)*

Crown of Stars *(From Podium Audio)*

Monstrous Lies *(From Podium Audio)*

Monstrous Truth *(From Podium Audio)*

Monstrous Ends *(From Podium Audio)*

Court of Nightmares *(From Podium Audio)*

Court of Death *(From Podium Audio)*

Unstoppable *(From Podium Audio)*

Unbreakable *(From Podium Audio)*

Fractured Shadows *(From Podium Audio)*

Shadowed Heart *(From Podium Audio)*

Revolt *(From Podium Audio)*

Rebel *(From Podium Audio) - coming soon*

FIND AN ERROR?

Please email this information to thenuttyformatter1@gmail.com:

- *the author name*
- *title of the book*
- *screenshot of the error*
- *suggested correction*

www.ingramcontent.com/pod-product-compliance
Lightning Source LLC
Chambersburg PA
CBHW051113300726
48981CB00001B/112